Secrets

Other Books by Lesléa Newman

Fiction

A Letter to Harvey Milk
Good Enough to Eat
Heather Has Two Mommies (children)

Poetry

Love Me Like you Mean It
Just Looking for My Shoes
Bubbe Meisehs by Shayneh Maidelehs:
An Anthology of Poetry by Jewish Granddaughters About Our Grandmothers (edited by Lesléa Newman)

Secrets

Short Stories
by
Lesléa Newman

New Victoria Publishers, Inc.
Norwich, Vermont

ISBN 0-9-34678- 24-3

Part I of *The Dating Game* appeared in *Common Lives/Lesbian Lives* and the entire story in *Lesbian Love Stories*, Crossing Press, 1989. *Right off the Bat* first appeared in *Sojourner,* and *Speaking for Ourselves*, Crossing Press, 1990.

Cover Design Ginger Brown

Library of Congress Cataloguing-in-Publication Data

Newman, Lesléa.
    Secrets : short stories/ by Lesléa Newman
        p. cm.
    ISBN 0934678-24-3: $8.95
    1. Lesbian--Fiction.   I. Title.
    PS3564.E91628S4   1990
    813' .54--dc20

                               90-313003
                                   CIP

Acknowledgements

Oh the girls, the girls, what would I do without the girls? All of them, especially Arachne Rachel, Janet Feld, Prudy Smith, Marilyn Silberglied-Stewart, Anne Perkins, and Felice Rhiannon. I'd like to thank Claudia Lamperti of New Victoria Publishers for having faith in my work and for pushing me to write these stories. Thanks to Sue Tyler for the picture (only one roll this time!) and to Mary Vazquez for always being there.

For Arachne Rachel, my very best friend

Most of us are aware of the power of words both spoken and written, but what about the power of words not spoken or written— the power of secrets? What happens when we keep secrets from each other? What happens when we keep secrets from ourselves? What happens when we choose to share these secrets? What happens when we discover a secret about someone else? About ourselves?

I wrote this book to answer these questions, and in doing so, I discovered some secrets of my own. Perhaps in reading these stories you will discover secrets, too.

— Lesléa Newman, January, 1990

Contents

One Night in the Middle of My Lover's Arms

Staring through the semi-darkness at Carol's thigh, I wondered, does anyone else ever do this? My head was resting on her belly, and I was touching her cunt the way she likes best (middle finger deep inside, thumb going back and forth on her clit). She was breathing deeply, moaning occasionally, and damned if I wasn't thinking about Nancy, my ex-lover.

Now don't get me wrong, it's not that I'm a horrible person, you understand. I love Carol, I really do. It's just that Nancy and I were together for almost two years, and I was really used to her. When we made love she would really carry on—groaning and screaming and calling out my name even. And Carol, well Carol's kind of quiet. When we first got together, which was, I don't know, maybe about four months ago, I couldn't even tell if she liked what I was doing or not, she kept so still. But that's just the way she is—quiet—not only when we're making love, but other times too, like when we're eating dinner or going for a walk in the woods. Sometimes it bothers me because I never know what she's thinking, and I'm always worried that she's bored with me or something. But most of the time I kind of like it. It's what drew me to Carol in the first place—she's the strong silent type, and me, well me, ask anyone, I'm a regular motormouth.

Maybe that's why Nancy and I never made it. God, that woman talks even more than I do, if such a thing is humanly possible. She loves to spout theory and she loves to argue. Not about stupid things, like whose turn it is to clean the bathroom or anything, though we did fight about things like that too. Mostly she likes to debate about politics. Why, the first night I brought her home, she went on and on about Nicaragua and the Contras and the Sandinistas for so long that I finally kissed her just to shut her up. Now don't get me wrong, I think the revolution in Nicaragua is important, I really do, but I was beginning to feel like I was listening to National Public Radio or something, instead of getting involved with a woman. There is a time and a place for everything, you know.

Like now is not the time to be thinking about Nancy, I remind my-self, turning to look at Carol. Her eyes are closed and her head is turned to one side, but when I reach up and touch her breast she opens her eyes and smiles at me. God, Carol is beautiful, especially right now. Did you ever notice how a woman's face changes when she's making love? Maybe it's the candlelight, or maybe it's the horizontal position, but whatever it is, the way Carol's looking at me right now is just about the most beautiful sight in the world.

I reach up and touch Carol's face. She kisses my fingers and closes her eyes again. I know she's getting ready to come, the way her breathing is speeding up, so I pay attention to what I'm doing. This making love stuff is pretty tricky, you know. Carol says I'm the best lover she's ever had, but frankly, my dear, just between you and me and the lamppost, sometimes I'm not really sure what I'm doing down there. I guess I'm doing okay though, because Carol's letting out a groan and thrashing around now, and her cunt is going in and out, in and out, drawing my finger deeper and deeper inside her.

After a minute she pulls me up in her arms, so my head is on the pillow next to hers and she's looking right at me with those eyes of hers again. That look—I wish I could describe it to you. Carol's eyes are blue and round and soft, like the rest of her (round and soft, that is, not blue) and so full of caring it almost hurts and it takes practically everything I have not to look away.

Nancy never looked at me like that. Oh God, here I go, thinking about Nancy again. Well, I suppose it's only natural. Or maybe I'm just really fucked up, I don't know. Anyway, Nancy's eyes are also blue, but narrower and cold. Ice cold blue, like the sky on a below zero winter day, when the chill cuts through to your bones and the snot freezes up in your nose.

"What are you thinking about?" Carol asks me, her two eyes staring first at my right eye and then my left.

"Oh nothing much, this and that." I stroke her long black hair away from her face (Carol's got this terrific long black hair, butch that she is, that reaches almost to her ass). "Mostly about how beautiful you are." She smiles then, and the lie seems worth it. I mean it wasn't a lie exactly (if you doubt me, just go back half a page), but it wasn't the whole truth either. But there's no need to tell Carol I was thinking about Nancy, is there? It would only hurt her and she doesn't need that.

Carol kisses my forehead and hugs me tightly. This girl's got real upper body strength—there's a bar across her kitchen doorway for chin-ups and she never goes in or out of the kitchen without doing at least five or six. "Do you want me to touch you again?" she asks.

"No, just hold me," I answer, and I snuggle down between her breasts and sigh as if I've just died and gone to heaven. Carol's the only woman I've ever been with whose breasts are bigger than mine and they drive me absolutely wild. Sometimes she even lets me suck on her nipple before I fall asleep, like a little kid.

"Are you going to sleep okay?" Carol asks, tracing the shape of my cheek with her finger.

"I'll try," I answer. Sleeping is not something I do well. Usually I manage to get in four or five hours, but the first night I slept with Carol, I didn't sleep at all. She finally went to sleep after we'd each come about forty-seven times (well, three each to be exact), and I just lay there watching her sleep and fantasizing about living with her someday in a big old farmhouse with an old brown dog and a black-and-white cat and some chickens, maybe a horse even. (I know I was getting carried away and it was only the first night and everything, but there wasn't anything else to do, and besides I'd rather think about that than the stuff I usually think about which I'll get to later). So the next morning when Carol woke up and caught me staring at her, she asked me how long I'd been awake and I'd had to tell her the truth—all night long.

"Why didn't you wake me up?" she'd asked.

"You looked like you needed your beauty sleep," I'd answered. "I mean, you looked so beautiful sleeping," I'd quickly corrected myself. I tend to mess my words up a little when I'm tired. Then Carol asked me why I couldn't sleep, and I went into my whole rap about how I'd gotten raped when I was sixteen and then I'd been really promiscuous after that because I felt like such a piece of shit and I got into all kinds of trouble picking up men in various places I'd really prefer not to go into right now. And the strange thing is, I never even remembered this stuff before I'd started sleeping with women.

My therapist says that's when I started feeling safe enough to start remembering, but it's pretty weird. I mean, there I'd be practically snoring next to some guy who probably did God only knows what to me while I slept, and now here I am with a gentle, soft, trustworthy woman, and I lie awake all night, on guard like a goddamn watchdog or something. I mean, I try going to sleep, I really do. I shut my eyes and snuggle down in my lover-at-the-time's breasts (usually I am the holdee, rather than the holder) but just as I'm about to drop off, something in me jerks me awake and I lie there in the dark, suspicious as all hell, next to a person who wouldn't harm me for anything in the world.

So there I was on the first morning of the first night Carol and I had made love, and while I should have been telling her how happy I was to be with her and how beautiful she looked in the morning with the sun just coming in and splashing across her face, there I was going on and on about my sordid past. But Carol was really good—she just listened and held me and even cried a tear or two, which is more than I can say for myself. I'm the keep-a-stiff-upper-lip type. Carol wanted to know what she could do to help me sleep, and short of living my life over for me, I really couldn't think of anything.

Nancy used to sing me to sleep sometimes, but somehow I knew Carol wasn't exactly the singing type, and anyway, asking your new lover to do the same thing your old lover used to do is just asking for trouble. I've never told Carol this, but sometimes when I can't sleep I still imagine Nancy's voice in my ear, singing me a little song. She used to sing me *Tender Shepherd* from *Peter Pan* sometimes, or *Rock-a-bye Baby* only she'd change the ending so that when the bough breaks the cradle wouldn't fall and smash up the baby. It's a kind of weird song to sing to little kids when you think about it.

Anyway, I do go off on strange tangents, don't I? Nancy used to call me the Queen of Non-sequitors and I'd had to look up non-sequitors the first time she said it. So now Carol and I are in our traditional go-to-sleep positions. She's lying flat and holding me in her arms, though she should be curled up on her side with a pillow between her knees because she has a bad back (oh the things we do for love), and I'm all snuggled up with my head on her breast. Soon Carol's arms relax and her breathing deepens. Then we roll over so she's spooning me from behind, and there I am alone in the darkness with nothing in front of me but a blank wall and the entire night, or what's left of it anyway. I think it's probably close to one o'clock by now. We got into bed around eleven-thirty and I figure we messed around for a good hour and a half.

So it's time for the late show or Roberta's home movies, as I call it. (I'm Roberta by the way). I pick something to think about and follow the show that unfolds in my mind. Tonight's film stars Nancy, since I've been thinking about her for a couple of hours already. Good old Goat. I sure do miss her, but I sure as hell wouldn't want to be lovers with her again. Why, you might wonder, do I call my ex-beloved Goat? Well, you see, first I shortened Nancy to Nance, which soon became Nan, which then lengthened into Nanny and then Nanny-Goat, which shrank back down to Goat. She called me Bert (as in Bert and Ernie, though short for Roberta) and then Bertie, which sounded more like Birdie, then became Little Bird, and soon after became Sparrow.

So there we were, Goat and Sparrow. I swore up and down and sideways to Nancy that I'd never tell anyone, and I haven't yet. I used to think I'd slip and call her Goat in public, but I never did, and there's no danger of that now because Nancy won't speak to me because I have another lover. She literally crosses the street when she sees me coming, and whenever she's invited to a party or something, she always asks, "Will Roberta be there?" as if sitting in the same room with me is worse than catching the plague.

Carol's moving her mouth around now, like she's chomping on something. I hope she's not having a bad dream, and I hope I'm not keeping her up with all this mental activity. Sometimes Nancy used to wake up in the middle of the night and say, "Sparrow, your brain is bothering me." Really. We were that tuned in to each other.

I guess I really can't blame her for being so pissed off at me. I barely waited a week before I jumped in the sack with Carol. Well, that's not true exactly. Things were on the rocks with Nancy, and I had officially broken up with her, though we were still living together. (Try that for laughs sometime—I mean how broken up can you be when you're still sharing a bathroom and buying groceries together?) Anyway, I'd met Carol at this party and we'd gone out to dinner a few times. I was straight with Carol (not straight-straight, you know what I mean—honest), so she knew the score. I also knew, and she did too, that we were positively wild for each other. I did restrain myself though, and didn't touch the woman until Nancy moved out (I do have some scruples you know), but whenever I came home from having dinner with Carol, I'd have this big shit-eating grin on my face (ugh, what a disgusting expression). And I knew I had to tell Nancy. I mean, anyone could tell something was going on, the way we gazed at each other over the guacamole (oh, those eyes of hers) and anyone could tell Nancy. You know how these small dyke communities operate.

So I did. As gently as I could. But things got nasty, as you can imagine. Out of the frying pan, into the fire. God, that break-up (or bust-up as my friends called it) was awful. I hope I never have to go through that again. I've had enough break-ups to last me the rest of my life.

I really hadn't planned on getting involved with anyone so soon, but you know, these things just happen. Okay, okay, these things don't "just happen"—I made a choice. Christ, you feminists don't let up for a minute. I had planned on cooling out for a while, and trying to figure out what went wrong between me and Nancy and me and everyone else I've ever been with. Not that there have been all that many women; I mean, I haven't set any world records or anything— five women. Five women in the last five years, give or take one or two one-night stands. That's not so bad.

Want to hear about them? Oh good, I knew you would. I mean what else is there to do while we're passing the time?

So here's the line-up. There's Nancy, whom you've already met, leaning back against the wall with her arms folded across her chest, wearing a T-shirt that says BREAK THE CHAINS. Next to her is Isabel, wearing a denim skirt and a pink blouse (the only femme I ever went out with). Michael is standing next to Isabel, eyeing her with a mixture of lust and suspicion. Then there's Barbara, straddling her motorcycle, and last but not least, Judy, smoking a Marlboro. A motley crew if I ever saw one.

Of course they'd never really be in the same room all together like that, except in the movie theater of my mind. The only thing they have in common is that they all put their fingers inside my cunt at one time or another. God, what a weird common denominator. And the fact that they all left me. Oh, there I go lying to myself again, for if the truth be known, I'm the one who left them. Every damn one of them.

Why, you ask. All of them were and are wonderful women, I suppose. There are the obvious reasons, or the reasons I gave them and myself. Barbara was leaving for California in a year, so why get involved, just to break my heart? Judy chain smoked, and we fought about that all the time—I wouldn't let her smoke in my house, so she never wanted to come over, and I never wanted to go to her house—it was like walking into an ashtray. Isabel was just coming out—I was her first lover. Boy, I'll never do that again. She didn't want to call herself a lesbian. "Why do you have to label yourself?"she asked. "It's so narrow." Michael was a stone butch which was really boring, though I did manage to flip her once. She was into non-monogamy besides. Nancy had this really fantastic temper which went off once a week as regular as clockwork. She'd slam doors, smash plates, call me names. I just couldn't handle it. I know what you're thinking, nobody's perfect, and I know that's true. I think the truth is that all of these women really loved me, and that scared the hell out of me. Really. I just couldn't deal with it at all.

It's easy to blame it on the rape. The rape, the rape—I thought by now I'd be finished with the rape. After four years of therapy, for God's sake, you'd think I'd be able to get over it. ("There you go beating yourself up again," I hear my therapist saying. God, for forty bucks an hour, you'd think she'd at least help me get to sleep.) I really didn't want to get into the rape here, but I guess it's unavoidable. I mean we are talking about sex, right? Though rape is not about sex, it's about violence. It took me a long time to figure that one out. Well, not figure it out exactly, but to believe it.

You see, I feel really ashamed about the whole thing. I know it wasn't my fault; at least part of me knows it—part of me still blames

myself. But still. You see, I did dress in a certain way, when I was sixteen. You know, sexy—short skirts, heels, make-up, the whole bit. I
know it's hard to believe when you look at me now, with my buzz cut
and all (we are a strange pair, me and Carol—a butch with long hair
and a buzz-cutted femme), but that's the way I was. My parents
thought I was so-o-o cute, my father especially. He called me his little
doll. "There's my little doll," he'd say when I'd come down the stairs.
"Isn't she a little doll?" he'd ask no one in particular. I mean there
was no one else in the room anyway. And then he'd tell me to come
give him a kiss, and it didn't seem like I had much choice in the matter. Sometimes he'd even sit me on his lap, and I could feel his thing
getting hard underneath my ass, and I just couldn't move.

Where was my mother while all this was happening? Good question, dear reader, you're really on the ball (don't mind me—I tend to
get sarcastic when I'm feeling a lot of pain). My dear mother was at
work (she's a part-time bookkeeper), or at a PTA meeting, or getting
her hair done, or drinking coffee next door with Mrs. Lamsky. For
some reason, I don't remember my mother being home a lot. Especially when my father was around. I don't blame her really. I didn't
want to be around him either.

Though that's not exactly true. I really hate to admit this part. You
see, I did like the attention he gave me. I didn't get it from my mother, so I got it from him. I didn't know until years later that it was *in-
appropriate* (my favorite therapy term). I just thought that was the
way things are: my mother paid more attention to my brother and
my father paid more attention to me. Until the rape, that is. Then
everything changed.

Wow, I'm really getting into it tonight. Wonder what time it is. I
turn over and lean up on my elbows, looking over Carol's shoulder at
the clock—three thirty-six. She has one of these digital clocks that
shine red numbers out into the night. Sigh. Another four hours to go
at least. Me and my home movies. Lots of times I wish I could shut
off the projector but I just can't find the on/off switch. Carol says I
can put the lamp on and read if I want to, the light wouldn't bother
her (this girl sleeps like there's no tomorrow), but I'm too tired to
read, even though I can't sleep. Though I wish I could distract myself
from my own mind.

Carol turns over and I spoon into her, resting my cheek against her warm back. This, dear reader, is how I used to sleep with my father. I hope that doesn't shock you (it shocked me the first time I remembered it). My mother slept in the guest room a lot, and I had nightmares as a child. So my father would lie down next to me to help me sleep (this is when I was maybe six or seven). I don't think he tried anything funny then, but I'm not sure.

I'm not sure about anything anymore, except one thing—that I wouldn't wish the experience of rape on anyone, not even my worst enemy, because it makes you feel like shit, worse than the lowliest goddamn awful old dog that ever lived.

So I wouldn't blame you if you stopped reading right about now, because who really wants to read about rape? Not me. Because it happened to me, you understand, and I'm real—flesh, blood, eyes, nose, ass, cunt—a real person, not someone in a book or movie. You think these things don't happen to real people, but they do. And we survive through it, and we live to tell the story because unfortunately the story has to be told, if we are going to heal from it and get through it and beyond it to whatever comes next. And I do want to get beyond it, you know, I really do. For God's sake, I'm thirty-four years old and all I want out of life is to sleep peacefully in the arms of my lover. Is that too much to ask?

Now you get to see how I stall around for time. Anything to avoid the pain, though the avoiding is painful enough in itself. I used to drink some so I wouldn't feel things, but I stopped that years ago after I blacked out twice because that really scared me, that not being able to remember what I'd done the night before. But that's another story. This is the story about the rape.

So like I said, I was sixteen (I almost said sixteen and asking for it, but I restrained myself). It was summer, and I was a camp counselor. Me and this guy Ralph (I will not change the names to protect the guilty) had taken some kids on an overnight hike up in the mountains, and one of the kids had spilled water all over her sleeping bag. She refused to sleep in it so I gave her mine, and good old Ralph offered to share his sleeping bag with me.

Stupid, right? Well I just didn't think. I mean it never occurred to me that he would try anything funny. And then when he did (this is the part I'm most ashamed of) I thought it meant that he loved me. I mean that's what I was taught, right, that sex equals love. What did I know, I was only sixteen, just a babe. I didn't even call it rape for a long time. I just lay still, pretending it wasn't happening. (Where did I learn that, I wonder. Why didn't I jump up and scream and yell, *what the hell are you doing?*)

Anyway after that night everything changed. I acted differently toward Ralph. I felt really shy and I felt like now he had this kind of power over me, like I belonged to him and I had to do what he wanted. I was always on my guard when he was around.

So are you surprised? Did you think I was going to tell you a real horror story, with guns, knives and seven men all over me? No, it was a *gentle* rape, if such a thing is possible. In a way I wish it had been more blatantly violent, so I could claim it for what it was, rather than carry around this vague feeling that something was wrong. Because Ralph acted differently towards me too after that. The bastard ignored me, acted like I didn't exist, like I wasn't worth the time of day. And I couldn't understand why. I mean he had done it to me and everything, didn't that mean that he loved me? Weren't we supposed to get married now or something? I tried flirting with him, I tried wearing shorter shorts and sexier halter tops, I left him little notes, I tried everything. When none of it worked, I tried flirting with the other counselors to make him jealous. That didn't work either, but it sure got me in a lot of trouble. I slept with five out of the eight counselors during that summer. It hurts to say it but it's true. My therapist insists it's not my fault—that I didn't know any better, that starting with my father I learned I only existed to please men, and that I had a lot of unlearning to do. Sure, it's easy for her to say, she wasn't the slut of Silver Lake Camp, the summer of sixty-nine.

Oh God, I'm crying now. I hope Carol doesn't wake up. Well, I guess I wish she would wake up, except that then I'll have to tell her why I'm crying and then she'll be really grossed out and then I know she'll leave me. Carol's never been abused—she doesn't really understand how deep the hurt goes, how long it takes to heal. I'm just beginning to understand it myself. Maybe she'd understand better if I talked to her more, but I'm scared she'll think I'm too fucked up to have a relationship with. I mean, already I ask her all these dumb questions like do you love me, are you sure, do you want to stay with me a long time, et cetera, et cetera. She's really good and patient with me and answers all my questions no matter how stupid they are, but then I don't believe her and I think she's just saying what she thinks I want to hear, but she doesn't really mean it. You see, she can't win. Really what I think is that she's just biding her time with me, waiting for someone better to come along. What do I mean by better? Oh you know, someone smarter, someone more sure of herself, someone prettier, someone who could sleep at night, someone who didn't need so much damn attention.

"There, there, Roberta, it's all right. It's all right, baby." I'm whispering this to myself and stroking my own cheek. I wish Carol would call me baby or honey or something, but she's not the type, so I just say it to myself, but that only makes me cry harder. Carol rolls over and takes me in her arms. "What's the matter, did you have a bad dream?" she asks, and even though she doesn't call me darling or sweetheart or anything, I can tell by the tone of her voice that she does really care.

Oh, don't care about me, I think, it only makes things worse, and then I start to cry even harder. Great big gulping sobs now and for a minute I worry about Carol's downstairs neighbors, but then I decide to let that go. What am I crying about, you may wonder, along with Carol. Oh God, what am I not crying about? I'm crying for that six year old girl who couldn't sleep at night and that fourteen year old girl sitting on her father's lap. I'm crying for that sixteen year old girl who lost her innocence in a sleeping bag she thought was safe, and for the teenager who tried to find love in all the wrong places. I'm crying for Michael and Isabel and Barbara and Judy who all tried to love me even though I was too afraid. I'm crying for Nancy and me and all the mean things we said to each other that were too true to take back. I'm crying for my dog that died when I was twelve and my cat that died when I was twenty, and all the puppies and kittens I can't rescue from the animal shelters that are going to be put to sleep forever. I'm crying for all the little children in the world who don't have enough food to eat and all the little girls who will be raped by someone they trust and there's not a damned thing I can do about it. And I'm crying for me and Carol because I want this thing between us to work and I don't know if it can because I don't know, even after all this time, if I can really trust anyone. And most of all I'm crying because I'm tired—tired of being up all night, tired of running from town to town and woman to woman, tired of being tired.

When I got involved with Carol, I made up my mind that I would be willing to stay with her for at least five years. Short of physical violence, I decided it was important for me to stay, no matter what, because I was so tired of the face on my pillow changing every couple of months, like a goddamn TV set switching channels or something. Even after two years, I felt like I was just getting to know Nancy. Of course it's up to Carol too, and you never really can know what's gonna happen, and all. I mean, I haven't even told her about my five year plan yet but time will tell, I guess.

I'm really worn out now, and I wipe my nose on the sheet. Immediately I whisper, "Sorry." (Carol's really fussy about her things). I look up into Carol's eyes, and they're like two tiny blue mirrors. I see myself reflected in them looking so incredibly sad that I start crying all over again.

Carol strokes my back up and down and waits until I'm quiet again. "Do you want to talk about it?" she asks. I shake my head no. I don't want to talk about it. I don't want to talk at all. I want. . . I want. . . I don't know what I want. I want someone else to figure it out for a change.

Carol sits up, fluffs up her pillow and leans back against it. "I'm not going to sleep until you do," she says, gathering me up in her arms. I look up at her in surprise. Carol's an eight hour a night girl all the way. "But Carol, you know I'll be up all night. You need your sleep."

"I need you to feel safe with me. This has gone on long enough," she says. She runs her hands gently over my eyes. "Rest now. Close your eyes and rest. You're safe here. You're safe with me. I'm going to stay up all night and not let anyone hurt you." My own personal bodyguard? I try to protest, but Carol shushes me. How can I tell her I'm not afraid of anything more than the demons and ghosts inside me? And that it's not that I don't trust her, I don't trust anyone. Carol's the most trustworthy person I've ever met—real sweet and gentle—a roll-over butch if I've ever met one, but it's hard to trust that she's not secretly laughing at me and secretly planning to leave me.

Is she really going to stay up the rest of the night? For me? I sneak a glance up at her. "Hello," she says cheerfully, ruffling my hair. "Nobody here but us chickens. Four-thirty-three," she says, "and all is well." I sigh and shut my eyes again, burrowing into Carol's breast. I remember the first night I slept with her when I buried my face inside her cleavage and I thought I had died and gone straight to heaven.

I take Carol's right breast into my mouth and suck at it gently. I feel my breathing deepening and my hold on Carol relaxing (I've got one of her legs clamped between my thighs and my arm is circling her waist). I'm drifting off now, despite myself (all this crying wears a girl out) and Carol's nipple slips out of my mouth. I'm half asleep when suddenly I feel cold all over, freezing cold, and my body jerks in little spasms. I sit up, terrified, and Carol leans forward to hold me. "It's all right, Roberta, you're safe here. You're safe with me. I'm right here with you."

"I'm cold," I say, and Carol pulls the blanket up over my shoulder. We lay back down again, and every once in a while I say, "Are you sleeping?" and she answers, "No." Then I ask her if she's bored and she says, "No, I'm taking care of you. It's not boring at all."

Then I want to ask her if it's going to get boring soon, and how long she thinks she'll be able to stand being with me, but thank God I refrain from dumping all this self-hating shit out on her, for once in my life. Instead, I take a deep breath and say, "Carol, can I tell you some things?"

"Sure, if you'd like," she says, "I'm all ears." No, I want to say, looking up at her, you're eyes and lips and breasts and everything else too. But it's not the time for fooling around, I tell myself. I want her to know—to know who I am. So I tell her everything, (I mean we've both given up on the idea of sleep by now anyway) everything I've been thinking about since we made love hours ago—everything about Nancy and my other ex-lovers, my father, the rape, the other men, in short, everything. And you know what? Carol didn't leave me. She said, at the end of my long-winded sob-filled soliloquy that she loved me even more, because she knew me.

What does one do with such a girl as this? How did I, of all people, wind up in the arms of such a wonderful woman? Do I deserve this? ("You certainly do," my therapist said the next Thursday, at ten a.m.). Carol wasn't even mad that I'd been thinking about Nancy when we'd been doing it. (At least that's what she said—do I believe her? Partly). She wasn't even disgusted with my sordid past, though she did say she wasn't exactly looking forward to the day she'd have to meet my father. She wasn't even mad that I was keeping her up all night (though of course I didn't believe that either). Maybe, just maybe, we'll be able to stay together for a while. When I told her about my five year plan, she got really worried. "What's going to happen after that?" she asked. "Are you going to leave me the day you turn thirty-nine?" God, I hope not. "I don't ever want to leave you," I say, staring into those deep blue eyes.

And then, the strangest thing happens. I feel my eyelids start to droop. I do everything I can, but my eyes just won't stay open. Every now and then I force them to, and I look up at Carol to make sure she's still there. And she is all right, looking at me with those eyes of hers that melt me right down to my bones. I stare at her eyes until I just can't anymore and I finally fall asleep and dream that I'm floating peacefully on my back in a sea of blue water the exact color of Carol's eyes, and instead of the sun, my own face is shining down on me, warmer and brighter than any star, moon, or promise.

Not That Easy

It was the first sunny day after a week of solid rain. Judy took that to be a good sign, for it was April 24th—her and Annie's one year and three month anniversary. They celebrated every month, and sometimes Judy thought it was a little silly—surely after the first year they'd cut it down to every six months or so. But Annie insisted; lesbians don't get enough holidays, she said, and Judy certainly couldn't argue with that.

Last month they had fought on their anniversary because Judy had wanted to go to her friend Pat's birthday party. "I'll be home by eight. It's just a dinner," Judy had said, "and then we can celebrate."

"I thought you'd want to have dinner with me on our ann-i-ver-sary," Annie had said, drawing the word out slowly, in case Judy had forgotten what it meant. So Judy had given in and apologized to Pat, saying something important had come up, but knowing she wasn't fooling her. Anyone who had two eyes in their head could see that she and Annie weren't doing too well these days. Judy had pouted all through dinner, wishing she was at Pat's party, and Annie could tell, and had acted all hurt. "I can't believe you'd rather be at a party than have a romantic dinner with me on our anniversary," she'd said. They hadn't even exchanged presents, or made love.

This month is going to be different, Judy vowed, even though she didn't feel really different. She felt trapped. Am I going to have to spend the twenty-fourth of every month with Annie for the rest of my life, no matter what else is going on, she wondered.

Judy pulled into the driveway, took a bag of groceries out of the back seat and balanced it on her hip. Even though she had mixed feelings, she had stopped at the store and bought food for a special dinner for Annie. For us, she reminded herself as she unlocked the door and walked into the house. At least she won't be able to say I didn't make an effort. I hope she's not in one of her moods, Judy thought, heaving the groceries onto the table. As she did so, her keys slid from her fingers onto the floor. She bent down to retrieve them and noticed a streak of mud on the blue linoleum.

"Oh shit, Annie, I just mopped the floor yesterday. Can't you take your shoes off by the door? I've asked you a hundred times, especially with all this rain we've been having."

Annie came into the kitchen and tossed some flowers that were wrapped onto the table. "Happy anniversary," she said, her voice heavy with sarcasm. "God, you haven't been in the house for two seconds, and already you're bitching. If I wanted to hear complaints I would have stayed at work, or better yet, called my mother."

Annie folded her arms. Actually she wished she had stayed at work. Her co-workers at the print shop had ordered beer and pizza to celebrate a big job they'd just finished and Annie had almost called Judy, but she knew she'd catch hell— especially after last month when she wouldn't let Judy go to Pat's party. Now she wished she had let her go. But...oh well. Annie had wolfed down a piece of pizza, skipped the beer and stopped for flowers on the way home. At least I'm making an effort, Annie thought, watching Judy wipe the floor with a paper towel. But if she's gonna whine all night, I'd rather forget the whole thing and just watch TV.

Judy threw out the paper towel and sighed at the sight of Annie standing stiffly in the middle of the kitchen with her arms folded across her chest. "Honey, let's not start, okay?" Judy put her hands on Annie's shoulders. "I'll put the food away and start dinner, and you can tell me about your day. Please?"

Annie hesitated, then unfolded her arms. "Okay." She gave Judy a quick hug and a kiss on the cheek. Judy hugged her back and started emptying the bag of groceries onto the table. "Here," she said, handing Annie a hunk of Parmesan cheese to put away.

"Judy, why the hell did you buy this? We have some grated Parmesan cheese already." Annie yanked open the refrigerator door and took a green container off the top shelf. "See? Why don't you make a list so you don't buy things we already have? I'm not made of money, you know."

Judy, her back to Annie, continued taking food out of the bag. "It wasn't that expensive, Annie—it was on sale. And anyway, that Kraft stuff tastes like shit. And," Judy's lip began to tremble, "I wanted to make something special for our anniversary. Let's not fight tonight. Please?" Judy hated the pleading note that had crept into her voice. It seemed to be there a lot lately. "Look, I'm sorry I got down on you about the floor. You know how compulsive about housework I am. I'll try to be less rigid, okay?"

Annie came over to the table with the fresh Parmesan cheese in one hand and the Kraft in the other. "I'm sorry too," she said softly, putting the cheese down and picking up the flowers. "Here Judy, don't cry. C'mon now. Happy anniversary. I mean it. I love you."

"You do?" Judy wiped a tear from the corner of her eye and took the flowers.

"Of course I do."

Well why don't you act like it then, Judy thought, unwrapping the flowers—two irises. "Annie, they're beautiful." Judy hoped Annie wouldn't hear the disappointment in her voice. Annie always gave her two irises—two was Annie's lucky number, and irises were her favorite flower. Just once I wish she'd do something different. Roses maybe, or even daisies, Judy thought as she filled a vase with water. It's like she's buying them for herself, not for me.

Annie watched Judy cautiously. Hopefully the storm had passed and the evening could be salvaged. They'd been bickering a lot lately, almost every night, and their fights were so predictable. It was almost like they were reading the same TV script over and over, and even though both of them were aware of it—they'd even talked about it— neither one of them could stop it.

"I got you something too." Judy reached into the grocery bag. "Shut your eyes." Annie closed her eyes and held out her palm. Judy handed her a small brown bag.

"What's this?" Annie opened the bag and sniffed. "Strawberries?"

"The first of the season. Aren't they gorgeous? I picked out the fifteen best—one for each month. Happy anniversary."

"Thanks." Annie put the bag down and gave Judy a hug, trying to act pleased. Strawberries weren't so special, even if it was only April. What happened to edible massage oil and bikini underwear with red hearts all over them, Annie thought. After a year and three months, already it's strawberries?

Judy kissed Annie on the cheek. "I'll make dinner, okay? I think there's some leftover spaghetti sauce that's still good." She opened the refrigerator and moved some things around on the top shelf.

"I'm not really hungry," Annie said, watching her.

"But Annie, it's our anniversary and I'm making you a special dinner." Judy had opened a yogurt container to investigate the spaghetti sauce inside it, and now paused mid-sniff.

"You call leftovers special?"

"It's just the sauce that's leftover, silly. I bought fresh Parmesan cheese and strawberries, remember?"

"I'm not hungry," Annie repeated, shoving her hands in her pockets and leaning her butt against the stove. "I had a piece of pizza around four."

"That's not enough dinner," Judy said, taking the wooden cutting board off a nail in the wall. "You gotta eat more than that." Judy began cutting a head of lettuce into strips and tossing them into a bowl. I'm just going to pretend everything's normal, Judy thought, pulling apart a bunch of sprouts. She'll calm down. I hope. Judy sprinkled the sprouts into the salad bowl. I'm acting just like my mother, she thought, taking a blue rubber band off a bunch of scallions and putting it around the knob of the kitchen door. No matter what happened, dinner was on the table at six sharp. Even if my father hadn't come home for three days straight, or worse yet, when he had come home and spent the whole evening yelling nasty things at us, at six o'clock sharp there we were, all of us, eating food that tasted like wet cardboard. Slowly Judy put down the knife she was holding.

"Annie," she said softly, trying hard not to let her voice break. "Let's have a nice dinner together. Please. Afterwards we can go for a walk, okay?" Judy hoped her offer would appease Annie, since walking was one of Annie's favorite things to do, and Judy hated it.

"I'm out all day. After supper I like to be at home," she'd say to Annie. "Why don't you go by yourself?" And Annie would reply, "I don't like taking walks by myself. We hardly spend any time together. Can't you do this one little thing for me? You used to take walks with me all the time, in the beginning." In the beginning, Judy thought, I would have walked from here to Timbuktu with you. But unfortunately the honeymoon is over.

"Judy, after dinner there's this movie I want to watch on TV. And, anyway, I told you, I'm not hungry. What are you, my goddamn mother?" Annie flung up her hands and stomped out of the room, tears welling up in her eyes. My mother never even cooked me dinner, Annie thought, listening to the water running as Judy rinsed two tomatoes in the sink. She worked, my father worked, my brother was off with his hoody friends—I ate alone, every goddamn night of the week. Sure I'd love to sit down and have a romantic dinner with you, but when we start off fighting, I just lose my appetite. You know that about me, Judy, Annie thought. I'd just rather have a sandwich in front of the TV. Now you'll probably get on my case for watching a movie on our anniversary. Oh I don't care. Annie flopped down on the sofa and turned on the television.

Oh shit, not the TV. Judy filled a pot with water for the spaghetti, set it on the stove, and dumped sauce into another pot. I am not spending my anniversary in front of the television. She heard Annie switching channels until the news came on. Annie turned up the volume and Judy sighed. I'll probably regret this, she thought, as she broke a bunch of spaghetti in half, tossed it into the pot, and walked out into the living room.

"Honey, can you just turn it down a little? I have a headache." Annie didn't respond. "Annie?"

"Will you leave me alone? Just leave me alone. Goddamn it." Annie jumped up and switched off the TV. "Can't even watch the goddamn news around here," she muttered as she marched into the bedroom and slammed the door.

Now I've done it, Judy thought, sinking down onto the couch with her chin resting on her fists. Judy stared at the blank TV screen, eyeing her own reflection. You really blew it this time, she said to herself. You push her and push her until you get what you deserve—a typical Annie-and-Judy evening—no talking, no sex, no nothing. Well, as my mother would say, you made your bed, now you have to lie in it. Shit. Judy bit her lower lip trying not to cry, then jumped up at a noise she heard in the kitchen. The spaghetti was boiling over. She lowered the flame and set the table with the good cobalt blue plates they had bought together at Michigan last year. I'll wait until dinner's ready and then I'll try to talk to her, Judy thought, lighting two candles and setting them on the table. At least I'm trying.

Judy finished cooking, covered everything so it would stay warm, and walked through the apartment to the closed bedroom door.

Annie heard Judy's footsteps stop outside the door. Don't come in here, she thought, shutting her eyes tightly. Just leave me alone. Annie knew Judy hated when she retreated like this, but right now she didn't care. When she was upset, she found refuge by crawling into bed, with the blankets all the way up over her head. I know I should try to talk with her and work things out, Annie thought, but I'm just so sick of all this hassling. Can't a girl hang out with her friends and eat pizza and then come home and watch a little TV? Is that too much to ask?

Judy leaned her ear against the door. Not a sound. Was Annie asleep? If she would only let me in, Judy thought, raising her hand to tap at the door. Not just into the bedroom, into her heart. She always wants to be alone when she's upset. You'd think she would want someone to hold her and comfort her. Someone to tell her everything's gonna be all right. Not someone. Me. Her lover. God, if she wants to be alone so much, why doesn't she just break up with me?

This is probably a mistake, Judy thought as she knocked gently on the door. "Annie? Are you asleep? Can I come in?"

"No," Annie said from under the covers.

Judy pushed the door open. "Annie?"

"I didn't say come in." Annie popped her head out just long enough to deliver that one sentence before diving under the blankets again.

"I can't hear you." Judy took a cautious step into the room and turned on the light. Must we go through this, she thought as she approached the bed. "Annie, c'mon. You don't want the whole night to be like this, do you?" Judy sat down on the edge of the bed and laid her hand on Annie's back, hardly daring to breathe. Annie didn't jerk her body away or yell and scream at her to leave her alone. Judy relaxed a little. "Talk to me, Annie. Tell me what's wrong."

Annie sighed. It's no use now, she thought. Judy will nudge me and nudge me until we process this out. I always give in. Why can't she understand that I need a little breathing space? Just a little time alone.

"Annie." Judy started slowly pulling at the blankets until the top of Annie's head emerged. "C'mon honey. Tell me what's the matter."

"Will you please, please leave me alone?"

"No." Judy reached out and touched Annie's arm. "C'mon. You know we have to work through this. Are you sad? Do you want to cry? C'mon, I'll hold you." Judy lay down next to Annie and gathered her stiff body up into her arms as best as she could. "It's really okay, Annie," she crooned. "It's really okay."

Annie turned into Judy's arms and Judy saw she'd already been crying. She traced a tear track down Annie's cheek with her index finger and watched as Annie's eyes filled again. Annie cried quietly at first and then her whole body shook as Judy held her.

My poor baby, Judy thought, rubbing Annie's back up and down. So many tears. Judy half sat up and reached behind her to get Annie a tissue. Our spaghetti's getting cold, Judy thought, as Annie continued to cry. Judy turned her arm so she could see her wristwatch. Ten to nine. Well at least she won't be able to watch her movie now. She hates missing the beginning. God, what a bitch I am. Judy held Annie tighter and smoothed her hair away from her forehead. "Shh, it's all right now. It's okay, Annie. Tell me what's going on."

Annie blew her nose and looked into Judy's eyes. I used to see so much love there, Annie thought, focusing both her eyes on Judy's right eye, and then on her left. Now there's nothing. Annie rolled up the dirty Kleenex and tossed it over the edge of the bed. "I don't

know, Judy. It's just not the same anymore. You're always nagging
me about something—mud on the floor, the TV being too loud. I
never yell at you for putting rubberbands around the doorknobs or
making me save every plastic bag or bit of tin foil to use over again."

"Okay, okay." Judy removed her arms from Annie's back and re-
positioned herself so her body was no longer in any contact with Annie's.

Annie felt sad. "Don't go away," she said. "You asked. I thought
you wanted to hear how I feel."

"I didn't think I'd get another speech about how I always do everything wrong and you always do everything right."

"That's not what I said. You don't have to get so defensive."

"Annie, for the hundredth time, people get defensive when they
get attacked. I'm only human. Can't you say things in a different way
so I don't feel attacked?"

"Not this again." Annie turned her back to Judy and wiped her
nose on her sleeve.

"Don't turn away from me when we're talking." Judy touched Annie's back. "Annie."

"Don't whine." Annie half turned and spoke over her shoulder.
"Look, it's the same old thing. You ignore the issue and start in on
how I talk, and I wind up taking care of you instead of getting what I
need. I'm just not in the mood tonight." Annie turned back around
and lifted the covers over her head again.

"Annie, please come out and talk to me." Judy pulled at the blankets.

"No." Annie clenched them in her fists. "Just leave me alone."

"Leave me alone, leave me alone." Judy stood, threw up her
hands, and started pacing around the room. "How are we ever supposed to work things out if we don't talk to each other? I wanted to
make us a nice dinner, I come in here to talk to you, and what do I
get? Nothing. How am I supposed to work things out with you when
you're under the blankets like...like an ostrich with her head in the
sand?" Judy's voice had risen to a shrill pitch that grated in her own
ears. She stopped in front of the lump in the bed that was Annie with
her arms folded, listening to the silence around them.

Annie lay still, with her eyes closed, as if the darkness under the blankets would protect her. If I lie still enough long enough, maybe she'll go away. It used to work with my mother. I'd just pretend I was sleeping and we never talked about anything. All I want is peace and quiet, Annie thought, a tear welling up in her eye. I don't want to have to talk with anyone. Ever again.

"Annie." Judy bent down and uncovered Annie's face. "C'mon. Talk to me." Annie sighed and rolled over so her back was to Judy. Judy sighed too and walked around to the other side of the bed until she could look into Annie's eyes. "C'mon, Annie. You know we're gonna be miserable until we make up. Can't we talk?"

"No!" Annie slammed her fist into her pillow. "Do you understand English? N-O. No. Nyet in Russian, lo in Hebrew, non in French, o-nay in pig Latin. No, I do not want to talk with you now or ever again. Get it? Read my lips. No." Annie glared at Judy and then pulled the blankets over her head once more.

Shit, now it's a major fight, Judy thought. She's crossed the nastiness line. Maybe I should just go eat my dinner in peace. Judy started for the door and then stopped. No, it's not fair. She calls all the shots and I can't stand it. Now she'll be mean and withdrawn for at least a week. Or else she'll hide in front of the lousy TV and ignore me. I can't take this anymore.

Judy came back to stand in front of the bed. "Annie, c'mon. This is so unnecessary. It doesn't have to be like this." Judy reached for the blanket.

"Will you leave me alone? Just leave me the fuck alone!" Annie's voice exploded as she flung the blankets back and leaped out of bed in one motion. "You push me and push me until I never want to see your face again."

"Annie, you don't mean that."

"Yes I do. I want you out of this room and out of my life right now."

"It's my room too."

"Oh my God. Now we're two years old." Annie turned her back and folded her arms.

"Annie, please. It doesn't have to be like this."

Annie whirled around. "Will you stop saying that? It doesn't have to be like this, but it is like this. Now leave me alone before you force me to do something we'll both be sorry for."

"What?" Judy's eyebrows rose. "Are you threatening me? I don't believe it."

"Are you going to leave or not?" Annie's face was red with anger. Judy just stared at her. Is this my Annie, she wondered, too stunned to reply to Annie's question.

"Fine." Annie spun on her heels and walked out of the room.

"Annie, where are you going?" Judy tried to grab Annie's arm as she walked past, but she shook her off.

"To the bathroom, if you don't mind."

"Oh no you don't. You're not locking yourself in there again. No way." Judy ran after Annie and jammed her leg through the door just as Annie was closing it.

"Shit." Annie pressed her body against the door. "Move your leg, Judy. Move it. Now. I mean it."

"No. Annie, please come out of there. I want to talk to you. Annie, c'mon. I love you."

"Who gives a shit?" Annie leaned against the door harder as Judy tried to push it open. "Judy, stop it."

"You stop it."

"Move your leg."

"No!"

"I said move it." Annie pushed at Judy's leg with one hand while heaving her other shoulder against the door.

"Ow! Annie stop, you're hurting me. Annie!" Judy shrieked and maneuvered her shoulder inside the door. She's not going to win this time, Judy vowed to herself as she pushed harder. All of a sudden the door gave way, and Judy flew into the bathroom.

"Now c'mon Annie, this is getting ridiculous. I know we can work this out." Judy spoke softly, as she always did when Annie was in a rage. It was strange, but the angrier Annie got, the calmer Judy became. "We can work it out, Annie," Judy repeated, even though she wasn't sure what they were trying to work out anymore.

"Get away from that door! Leave me alone, leave me alone, leave me alone!" Annie was screaming now, her fists balled up in front of her face and her whole body clenched so tightly she was shaking.

Her voice was so loud inside the bathroom that Judy was afraid for a minute that the mirror would shatter until she remembered things like that only happen on TV.

"Okay Annie, okay. I'm sorry." Judy reached behind her and started turning the doorknob. Annie took her hands down from in front of her face and relaxed slightly. The two women stared at each other for a moment, hardly daring to breathe.

"I just want to say one thing," Judy said softly, "and then...."

"No!" Annie jumped up and down, screaming, "Get out! Get out! GET OUT!"

She's acting just like a child, Judy thought, and was just about to say so when Annie's hand came flying through the air, out of nowhere, and landed with a smack against Judy's cheek.

The silence that followed the slap felt ten times louder than Annie's raging and Judy's pleading put together. Time stood still as Judy's cheek stung and then went numb. She looked at all their things lined up on the shelf over the toilet—the baby powder, apricot shampoo, aloe vera moisturizing cream, and she felt embarrassed that all of them had witnessed her being slapped. Slapped by her lover. By her Annie.

"I'm sorry Judy." Annie's whisper was barely audible. She stared down at her hand. Her own hand that had hit her lover. Her Judy. How had that happened? She didn't mean to do it. Annie studied her hand as if it was a stranger, separate from her, with a mind of its own. "I didn't mean it," Annie said, not daring to look up.

Judy didn't answer; she slowly opened the door and backed out of the bathroom into the kitchen. This is where I live, she thought as she walked through the kitchen and living room, back into the bedroom. I live here with Annie. But why isn't the bed made? Is it time to get up or time to go to sleep? Judy's head began to throb and she wanted to lie down.

"Judy." Annie had followed her through the apartment and stood in the doorway of their bedroom watching her. "Judy, I'm sorry. It'll never happen again. I promise. Judy, c'mere." Annie opened her arms, and Judy fell into them sobbing. Annie held her, stroking her

back and looking over Judy's shoulder at the unmade bed, the pile of
dirty clothes on the chair, the fat lavender candle on the nightstand. I
hit my lover, Annie thought, as a tear leaked out of her eye. I hit my
lover.

Judy stopped crying and looked at Annie. "You're crying too?"
she asked, reaching up to touch Annie's cheek. "Come lay down. Let
me hold you." She took Annie's hand and led her to the bed.

"I'm the one that should be comforting you," Annie said as they
crawled between the sheets.

"Shh. It's all right now. It's over." Judy smoothed Annie's face. I
have to leave her now, I suppose, Judy thought, feeling strangely de-
tached, as if this were all happening to someone else. Don't I have to
leave?

Annie looked into Judy's eyes. "Judy, I love you. I'll never hit you
again. I promise." Annie put her arm around Judy's shoulder and
started massaging the back of her neck. I guess she'll leave me now,
Annie thought sadly. Well I can't blame her. I certainly deserve it.

Judy watched as Annie started to cry again. "It's okay, Annie. I believe you. I know you won't hit me again."

"But do you believe I love you?"

Judy hesitated. "Do you really love me Annie?"

"Yes. I do. Of course I love you. I"ll make it all up to you." Annie
leaned back a little to look at Judy's face. "Was it this cheek?"

"No, this one."

"Let me see." Annie stroked Judy's left cheek."Poor little cheek."
She began kissing it gently.

"Let me see your hand," Judy said, taking Annie's arm from her
shoulder. "Was it this hand?"

"No, this one." Annie gave Judy her right hand.

"Poor little hand. You got hurt too, didn't you?" Judy kissed each
one of Annie's fingers and then sucked on her thumb. She slowly
kissed her way up Annie's hand, wrist and arm until she was nuzzling
into Annie's elbow. Annie sighed and leaned down to kiss Judy's
neck.

"I don't want to ever fight with you again," Annie whispered into

Judy's ear, punctuating her words with her tongue. "I love you, Judy."

"I love you too." Judy's fingers swam through Annie's hair. "I'll never nag you again. I promise."

"I'll talk to you more, Judy. I won't hide under the blankets anymore."

"Shh. It's okay. Let's not talk about it now." Judy wanted Annie's mouth on her breast, on her belly. She didn't want any more words. She didn't want to think about what just happened, because she knew what she had to do and she didn't want to do it. Annie reached down and unzipped Judy's pants to find her wetness. Judy moaned. Maybe it was all a dream, Judy thought, as they quickly struggled out of their clothes. How could the same hand that was now giving her so much pleasure have hurt her less than a few minutes ago?

"Oh you're so beautiful," Annie whispered as her fingers flew in and out of Judy's cunt. "I love you," she said fiercely, her own body beginning to throb.

"I want you Annie. I want to come together." Judy reached down and entered Annie. Annie sighed and grasped Judy's free hand tightly.

She won't leave me now, Annie thought, moving her hips up and down. We're so connected, so good together. What happened before was just...just a fluke or something. It'll never happen again.

Annie and Judy rocked together until they came, and Judy burst into tears. "What is it, honey? Did I hurt you?" Annie held her close.

"No, I'm just so happy we made up," Judy whispered into Annie's shoulder. That might be the last time we ever make love, Judy thought, overcome with grief. How will I tell her? How will I leave?

"I'm happy too," Annie whispered into Judy's hair. I'm scared, Annie thought, stroking Judy's face. What if she leaves me? Maybe it would be better, just until I sort things out. But I would miss her so much. I don't know what to do. Annie leaned her cheek against Judy's forehead. I'm too tired to think about it, she told herself. I'll deal with it tomorrow. Right now I just want to be close to her. Even if it might very well be the last time. "Judy," Annie said softly. "Are you sleeping?"

"No."

"Are you hungry?"

Judy looked up. "Not really."

"I bet you haven't eaten since lunch, have you?" Judy shook her head. "You wait right here and I'll bring you dinner. You want me to heat it up?"

Judy shook her head. "No. Cold spaghetti is fine."

Annie climbed out of bed and tucked the blankets around Judy. "Now don't get chilled," she said, kissing Judy on the nose.

Judy watched as Annie's back disappeared around the corner. She has such a beautiful back, Judy thought. What am I going to do? I always swore I'd leave a relationship the minute anyone ever hit me. But she's not anyone—she's Annie. It's not that easy. Judy listened as Annie bustled about the kitchen, dishing out the spaghetti and ladling sauce on top of it.

I'll make it up to her starting right now, Annie thought, walking back through the house with the two plates. I'll show her how much I really love her. How much I need her. How much she means to me.

"Here, baby. Sit up." Annie handed Judy a plate and sat down on the edge of the bed, facing her. "Happy anniversary, sweetheart."

"Happy anniversary, Annie." Judy took the plate from Annie and set it on her lap as Annie crossed her legs. And then, even though neither of them was hungry, they both began to eat.

Right Off The Bat

My mother's a lesbian. That's the first thing I want you to know about me. I know it's not really about me, but it sort of is, and, anyway, I like people to know right off the bat so they don't get weird on me later when they find out.

Like Brenda for instance. Brenda used to be my best friend at my old school and then one day she just stopped talking to me. For no reason. I mean we didn't have a fight or anything, like the time she told Richard Culpepper I liked him which was a lie. We didn't speak for almost a whole week that time. But this time there was no reason. I mean she crossed the hallway when she saw me coming and everything. I finally cornered her in the bathroom between homeroom and first period and asked her what was wrong. She said, "Go away, my mom says I can't talk to you anymore. Your mother's a dyke."

Dyke is a bad word for lesbian, like Yid is a bad word for Jew. I'm Jewish too, which is another thing that makes me different. Being Jewish means I go to temple instead of church, only we hardly ever go anyway, and we have *Chanukah* and Passover instead of Christmas and Easter. Being a lesbian means my mom loves women instead of men. Not everyone knows these words. Sometimes my mom says dyke when she's talking to her friends on the phone or something, but she says that's okay. Lesbians can say dyke but straight people can't. I don't really understand that. I don't understand a lot of what my mom says or does. She's not like anyone else's mother I've ever met.

Like even what we eat. My mom won't let me eat school lunches,

though sometimes I save up my allowance and buy one and throw
out the lunch she's packed for me. At my old school I liked macaroni
and cheese the best with chocolate pudding for dessert.

My mom's not the world's greatest cook, and we always fight because she wants me to eat weird stuff like tofu which is this white
square that looks like soap and tastes like nothing. Just to get her to
make me a Swiss cheese sandwich is a big deal, because she always
has to give me a lecture about dairy products and how they clog you
all up.

If I'm lucky Linda will be around and tell my mom just to lay off. I
like Linda. Linda's the reason we moved here in the first place, so
my mom and Linda could be together. Linda's like, well she's part of
the family. She's my mother's, well, they use the word lover, but it's
not like she's Casanova or anything. Lots of kids have single parents
and lots of kids' moms have boyfriends. My mom has a girlfriend.

We have two bedrooms in our new house. My mom and Linda
have one and I have the other. When we moved here my mom said I
could paint my room any color I wanted. I said pink. She said any
color except pink, but Linda said that wasn't fair and anyway, I'd
grow out of it sooner or later. We have a kitchen and a living room
and a big yard, and a cat named Pat-the-cat. Pat-the-cat sleeps with
me and Linda sleeps with my mom.

Linda found us the house and then we moved here. I like it better
than my old house. My old house was really an apartment and I
didn't have a room. My mom had her room and I had half the living
room and my clothes were in the hall closet. I slept on a futon that
we folded into a couch during the day. A futon is a weird kind of mat-
tress my mom says is good for your back. Anyway, I like the new
house better—it's bigger and I have my own room, but I kind of liked
it when it was just me and my mom. Except Linda was there most
every weekend anyway, and once in a while we'd go to her house,
but I didn't like that so much. I couldn't see any of my friends, and
even though I packed things to do like books to read or records to listen to, it always worked out that what I really felt like doing was at
home. I mean, how should I know on Friday afternoon when I'm
packing up my stuff, that on Sunday morning I'd be just dying to
hear my new Whitney Houston album? My mom would just tell me to

stop *kvetching*—that's a Jewish word for complaining—but I never dragged her off to spend a weekend with one of my friends. Then she'd see what it was like.

Anyway, now we all live together and I know your next question—you don't even have to ask it—where's my father—right? Well this will probably shock you, but I don't have a father. I have a donor. A donor is a man who gives sperm to a sperm bank so a woman can have a baby. Oh I know all about the birds and the bees. My mom told me.

You see twelve years ago, no, make that twelve years and nine months ago, my mom decided that she wanted to have a baby. And she'd been a lesbian for a long time, so she certainly wasn't going to do it the old-fashioned way. That's what she calls it, you know how they do it in the movies and stuff. So she used alternative insemination.

She's into all kinds of alternative stuff—that's what people call her lifestyle—but that makes her kind of mad. How come straight people have a life and gay people have a lifestyle, she asked Linda once and Linda said, "I don't know, maybe because gay people have hair and straight people have hairstyles?" My mother thought that was hysterically funny. Personally I didn't get it at all, but she and Linda giggled for a good fifteen minutes over that one, until I rolled my eyes and said, "Children!" which made them laugh even more. I swear they can be so immature sometimes, much worse than me and my friends.

Anyway, what I was going to say was some people call it artificial insemination but my mom gets really mad at that. She gets mad pretty easy. She says it's not artificial, it's alternative. And there's nothing artificial about me. The way it works, see, is my mom got the sperm from the sperm bank and put it into a turkey baster and when her egg popped out, she popped the sperm in, and the rest, as they say, is history.

Only my mom would say herstory. She's always changing words around so they're not sexist but I forget sometimes. Anyway, I don't think it's all that important, but my mom gets mad when I say that. Like I told you, practically everything makes her mad. Like the fact that I want to wear make-up, for example. I'm not really ugly or anything, but I'm not exactly Whitney Houston either. It's bad enough being different in all the ways I've already told you about. It would really help to at least be able to look halfway normal. So just a little eye make-up and some blush, I asked her. I don't want to look loose or anything.

But my mom as usual had a fit, and went on and on about women's oppression, one of her favorite topics. She ranted and raved about how women are supposed to look a certain way and if we spent half the energy we spend on our bodies on our brains we could probably overthrow patriarchy, whatever that is, and really change the world.

Well, you know, by that time I was sorry I asked. It would have been a lot easier to just buy the stuff, put it on in the girls room at school and wash it off before my mom got home from work. But Linda was great. She's the only one who knows how to calm my mother down in these situations. "But Darlin'," she said—that's what she calls my mom— "Darlin', you're just laying your own trip on her, the same way your mother laid her own trip on you. Leave her be. She's got to make her own decisions about things. And besides, you wouldn't look so bad in a little lipstick yourself."

"Yeah," I said, "and anyway you're always saying how oppression is not having any choices so if you don't let me wear make-up, you're oppressing me."

I knew my mother wouldn't be able to argue with that one, and I felt pretty proud of myself for thinking of it, but she just shook her head and said that was different and I didn't understand. Anyway, it doesn't really matter because she finally gave in and Linda even showed me how to put eyeliner on straight.

My mom doesn't know about things like that. She never wears dresses or anything, but Linda does—just on special occasions. Like last year they got all dressed up to celebrate their anniversary, at a big fancy restaurant. I wanted to go too, but my mom said it was their special night, for just the two of them. She promised to bring me a surprise home from the restaurant if I wanted. I asked for something chocolate. Anyway, Linda got all dressed up in this royal blue dress with a big black belt around the waist. She even put her hair up on top of her head and wore these really cool silver earrings that have three interlocking loops and a ball in the middle. They kind of reminded me of an atom with a nucleus and protons and electrons orbiting around. Anyway, she looked really awesome.

My mom on the other hand, well she's not exactly the world's greatest dresser. All she ever wears are jeans and flannel shirts. And not designer jeans either—nerdy jeans from Bradlees. And in the summer she wears T-shirts with sayings on them like *I Am A Woman. I Can Bleed For Days And Not Die.* That's a white T-shirt she has with red splotches on it that stand for blood I guess. She made it herself. It's gross. Anyway, you get the picture. I mean her wardrobe is really pathetic. So that night she wore a pair of black jeans, a white jacket, a red shirt and a white tie. You probably think that's really weird, a woman wearing a tie, but lots of my mom's friends do. I'm kind of used to it I guess. Anyway, I can't imagine my mother in a dress. First of all she has these really hairy legs she refuses to shave, and second of all, what would she wear on her feet? She only has work boots, sneakers, and green flip flops for the summer.

So Linda and my mother got all dressed up that night. I took their picture and then off they went to have a good time. Only they didn't. Here's what happened: I guess they were in the restaurant eating their dinner and everything, and some punks figured out they were lesbians. They were probably doing something dumb, like holding hands. Anyway, while they were eating, I guess the punks scoped out which car was theirs, which wouldn't be too hard to do, since my mother has all these bumper stickers that say things like *I Love Womyn's Music*, and *You Can't Beat A Woman*, and one with purple letters which just says *We Are Everywhere*. It's kind of embarrassing when she takes me some place, but I don't know if I'm more embarrassed by the bumper stickers or by the car. It's not even a car really, it's a truck, a beat up old pickup because we aren't exactly rich or anything. So I bet my mother's old pickup with all her bumper stickers stuck out like a sore thumb in the parking lot of that fancy restaurant with all the Mercedes Benzes and Cadillacs and whatever other kinds of cars rich people drive.

Well, by the time these punks, or whoever it was got done, my mom's truck had four slashed tires. My mom was so mad she wanted to kill somebody. Linda just got really sad and started to cry. That's what always happens—my mom gets mad and Linda gets sad. I get both, but this time I got mad, just like my mom. I mean, it was their special night and they weren't hurting anybody or anything; they were just going out to have a good time. But then something happened inside of me, and I got really angry at my mother. I mean, if she would just shave her legs or put on a dress or quit holding Linda's hand on the street or something, these things wouldn't always be happening to her.

Me and my big mouth. As soon as I said it, I knew I shouldn't of. My mom tells me it's important to say how you feel, and then when I do, she always gets mad at me. "Haven't I taught you anything?" she yelled. Then she started pacing up and down the living room delivering one of her famous speeches about oppression and blaming the victim. And then all of a sudden she just stopped. Maybe she saw I wasn't really listening because she came over to the couch and sat down next to me and held my hand.

"Roo," she said, and I knew she couldn't be too mad if she was calling me Roo—that's my nickname from *Winnie the Pooh*. See, when I was a baby, my mom carried me around in a snuggly and she felt like Kanga with her baby Roo. My real name's Rhonda, after my grandma Rebecca, and my nickname's Ronnie. Anyway, my mom said, "Listen Roo, I know it's hard for you to understand why I live my life the way I do. You think if I just put on a skirt and shaved my legs everything would be okay. Well, your Great Aunt Zelda and your Uncle Hymie thought the exact same thing with their fancy Christmas tree on their front lawn, and still their neighbors in Poland turned them in to the Nazis for a buck fifty a piece. Remember Brenda, Ronnie? You don't need friends like that. Listen Roo," she said again, "if I only teach you one thing in your whole life, it's be yourself. Be straight, be gay, be a drag queen in heels, or a bulldyke like your old ma, but be whoever you are and be proud of it, okay? Life's too short to pretend you're someone you're not, and then spend all your time worrying about what's going to happen if you get caught. I spent too many years in the closet, and no tire-slashing assholes are going to push me back."

She made a fist and smacked it into her hand, hard. But she didn't hurt herself or anything. My mom studies karate, which is another weird thing she does. I watched her in her class once, where we used to live. It was pretty cool to see her punching and kicking and everything My mom's small, and kinda skinny, but she's a lot stronger than she looks. Her teacher was a lesbian too. I could just tell by her short hair and the way she shook my hand.

Which leads me to the next question I know you're thinking about—do I think I'm gonna be a lesbian when I grow up? I don't know. I know my mom wants me to be, even if she doesn't exactly say so. But one night I heard her talking to Linda when she thought I was sleeping. It was pretty easy to listen in on them in the old house because we only had the two rooms. Anyway, it was right after this boy Phillip called me up for the math homework because he was out sick. My mother handed me the phone with this who's Phillip look in her eye and later that night I heard her talking to Linda.

She said, "I hope Ronnie doesn't have to go through her teens and early twenties being straight like I did before she comes out. The thought of adolescent boys running around the house gives me the creeps. I haven't even talked to her about birth control yet. Or AIDS. Oh Goddess, (that's what my mom says instead of oh God) oh Goddess I feel like I just got her out of diapers and already boys are calling her up on the phone."

Then I heard Linda say, "Relax, Darlin'. Ronnie's got a good head on her shoulders. And besides, we know how to get rid of any fifteen year old boys we don't like. We just start with a little of this...and a little of this...and before you know it, they'll run home screaming to their mamas." Then I heard my mother laugh—Linda's the only one who can make her laugh—and then they didn't talk anymore.

Meanwhile, I didn't bother telling my mother that Phillip is a real nerd and I wouldn't go out with him if he paid me a million dollars. Well, maybe I would, just once, but he'd have to put the money up first—in cash. Anyway I wouldn't kiss him for all the tea in China, like my Aunt Myra would say. I've never kissed a boy. I've only gone out with a boy once, this guy Billy from my old school. We went out and he bought me ice cream and then he asked if he could kiss me. "Kiss me?" I said. "Are you kidding? We've only been going out for thirty-five minutes." We didn't go out again after that.

I don't know, kissing boys seems really gross and kissing girls seems really weird. Maybe I'll be a nun, except my mom says Jews can't be nuns. I don't know. I guess I'm kind of young to worry about it too much. That's what Linda says anyway. She says just be yourself and see what happens. I said to her, who else would I be, Whitney Houston, and she laughed—Linda laughs at my jokes most of the time, unlike my mom.

But really I kind of know what she means, because I used to pretend I came from a normal family. I even made up a father and pretended he was away on business trips a lot just so the other kids wouldn't tease me for being so different and all. I never told my mom that—I could just imagine what she would say.

So anyway, that's all about me. I wanted you to know right off the bat so I wouldn't have to worry about you pulling a Brenda. Do you think your mom will let us be friends?

Secrets

"Hi, Grandma, look at my picture, see, see? Miss Murray says it's the best picture I ever made ever, see?" Jeannie dropped her red schoolbag onto the kitchen floor and waved her painting in front of her grandmother's face.

"Very nice, Jeannie. Don't drop your things all over my kitchen now. Bring your schoolbag upstairs and go change your clothes."

"See, it's a house, just like ours, Grandma. And this is my room, right here." Jeannie spread her picture out on the kitchen table and pointed to a crooked window. "And this is Stevie's room, and this is Mommy and Daddy's room, and this is our car." Jeannie studied her picture proudly, as her grandmother got a carton of milk out of the refrigerator. "Can we hang my picture up on the 'frigerator, Grandma?"

"Why don't you take it upstairs, *mamela*, and put it in your room? Be a good girl and put away your things and then you can have your milk and cookies." Jeannie's grandmother put a glass of milk on the table with two chocolate-chip cookies on a paper napkin.

"Okay, okay." Jeannie took her things upstairs, walking up each step slowly. It was the best picture she had ever made, even if her grandmother didn't want to look at it. Miss Murray had even said so.

Jeannie took off her white blouse, crumpled it up and stuffed it into the dirty-clothes hamper in the bathroom under her brother's jeans and undershirts, hoping her grandmother wouldn't notice the ketchup stain on her sleeve and yell at her. She hung up her blue skirt and put on shorts and her favorite Minnie-Mouse T-shirt. Then she went back downstairs, sat down at the table and shoved one of the cookies into her mouth.

"Grandma, can we go for a walk?" Jeannie called into the den with her mouth full. No answer. Jeannie's grandmother was watching her soap opera which was turned up loud because she was hard of hearing. Jeannie finished her snack, swinging her legs back and forth and making designs with the cookie crumbs on the yellow oilcloth. The big crumb was the mommy duck and the three little crumbs were the baby ducks following her in a very straight line down to the drop of milk which was their pond.

Jeannie put her empty milk glass into the sink and went into the den. Her grandmother was drinking a cup of tea and staring at the television. "Did we get a postcard from Mommy today?" Jeannie asked.

"No, *mamela*. Maybe tomorrow. Come sit down and watch."

"Can't we go for a walk?" Jeannie hung back in the doorway. She hated her grandmother's soap operas. Everyone was always kissing each other on them. Yuck.

"Not now, *mamela*. Go upstairs and do your homework."

"Okay." Jeannie sighed and turned to go back upstairs. Just then the phone rang. "I'll get it!" she yelled, running into the kitchen.

"Hello?"

"Hello, is your mother home?"

"No, she's on vacation. Do you want to speak to my grandma?"

"No, Jeannie. I called to speak to you."

Jeannie's eyebrows shot up A man had never called to speak to her before. "Who are you?" she asked.

"I'm a friend of your mommy and daddy's. They told me to call you when they were on vacation to talk to you so you wouldn't be lonely. When are they coming back?"

"They're coming back on Saturday, after they visit Uncle Jack in Florida. And they're going to make a special stop at Disney World just for me so they can get me a Mickey-Mouse hat with my name on it."

"With your name on it? That's really special, Jeannie. Tell me, sweetheart, did you have a good day at school?"

"I made a picture." Jeannie turned around to look at her picture and then remembered her grandmother had made her take it upstairs.

"It's a picture of our house and our car and when Mommy gets home she's going to hang it up on the refrigerator."

"I bet it's a lovely picture, Jeannie. You're a very special little girl, so I bet your pictures are extra special too."

Jeannie sat down on a kitchen chair. "What's your name?" she asked the man on the phone.

"It's a secret," the man answered. "Do you like secrets, Jeannie?"

"Yes," she whispered, for secrets were told in whispers.

"Can you keep a secret?" the man asked.

"Yes," Jeannie whispered again.

"Well, I'm going to tell you a very special secret. But you have to promise first not to tell anyone. Not your mommy or your daddy or your grandma or Stevie. Because if they found out this secret, they might get hurt."

Why would they get hurt, Jeannie wondered. This secret, whatever it was, must be really important.

"What is it?" Jeannie asked, keeping her voice low.

"I'll tell you in a minute, sweetheart. But first you have to promise me you won't tell anyone. Can you promise?"

"I promise."

"Cross your heart and hope to die?"

"Cross my heart and hope to die." Jeannie closed her eyes and made an x with her index finger across her chest where she thought her heart would be, right under Minnie Mouse's ears.

"Jeannie, are you talking on the downstairs phone or the upstairs phone?"

Jeannie opened her eyes. "The downstairs phone."

"And where's your grandma, honey?"

Jeannie turned her head towards the doorway. "She's watching TV."

"And where's Stevie?"

"He's in the park, playing basketball."

"Good. Now Jeannie, I want you to listen to me, okay, sweetheart? Your daddy told me you were a very good girl and you always do what grown-ups tell you to. Are you a good girl, Jeannie?"

"Yes."

"Good. Now what I want you to do is hang up the phone and

then go upstairs. I'm going to call you right back, and you need to talk to me on the upstairs phone so I can tell you the secret. Okay?"

"Okay." Jeannie stood up to hang up the phone.

"You're a very good girl, Jeannie, you know that? And you know what else? You're also a very pretty girl. In fact, you're one of the prettiest girls I've ever seen."

Jeannie didn't say anything. No one had ever called her pretty before. Most of the time the other kids at school teased her about how she looked. They called her Four-eyes because she wore glasses and Tubby the Tuba because she was chubby. No one had ever called her pretty before; it made her stomach feel kind of funny. She waited for the man to say it again but he didn't, so she hung up the phone and tiptoed out of the kitchen and up the stairs. She walked into her parent's bedroom and sat down on the edge of their big double bed.

The phone was on a night table on her daddy's side of the bed. It was black and shiny, almost like her grandma's big patent-leather pocketbook. Jeannie sat with her back towards the middle of the room and stared at the phone waiting for it to ring. Maybe the man had lied. Maybe he wasn't going to call her back and she'd never find out what the secret was.

Jeannie looked up at the wall above her parents' bed. There were two big pictures hanging there, a picture of her as a baby and Stevie as a baby. In her picture, Jeannie had fat rosy cheeks and pudgy little hands and hardly any hair at all. She was holding a stuffed lamb which she still had, even though Stevie teased her about it. "Six-year-old one-year-old, six-year-old one-year-old," he'd chant whenever he caught her holding her Lamby. He never knocked on her door when it was closed, like he was supposed to, but always opened it to tell her that supper was ready or that it was time for her bath. Jeannie glanced at the picture of her brother. It was hard to imagine he was ever a baby. Even though he was only eleven, already he was almost as tall as their father.

Jeannie stared at the picture of herself again. I'm glad I'm not bald anymore, she thought, her hand automatically reaching up to touch her dark brown curls. They were tied up in two pigtails that were pulled way too tight. Jeannie hated the way her grandmother did her hair. She brushed too hard, until Jeannie was almost crying, and she never made her pigtails even. I wish Mommy and Daddy would come home already, she thought, looking at another picture in a stand-up frame on the night table next to the phone. This was her parents' wedding picture. It sort of looked like them, only her father wasn't wearing his glasses so his eyes looked a little funny, and her mother looked very thin, instead of soft and round like she was now.

The phone rang, and Jeannie jumped like she did when her Donald Duck alarm clock went off in the morning. "Hello?"

"Hello, Jeannie. Are you upstairs now?"

"Yes." Jeannie swung her legs up on her parents' bed and turned her body so she was facing the wall. She held the big black receiver tightly against her ear, all ready to hear the man's secret.

"Jeannie, now I'm going to tell you the secret just like I promised. Grown-ups always keep their promises. It's important that you remember that. It's important for little girls to keep their promises too. Do you remember what you promised me, Jeannie?"

"Not to tell the secret."

"Right. Now, are you in your mommy and daddy's room?"

"Yes." Jeannie wondered if the man could see her. She looked over to one window in her parents' bedroom but all she could see out of it was blue sky. Her belly was starting to feel a little funny, but she didn't know why.

"Jeannie, do you know what your mommy and daddy do in their bed at night when you and Stevie are sleeping?"

"They watch TV." Sometimes when Jeannie woke up in the middle of the night to pee, she could hear the muted voice of Johnny Carson coming out of her parents' bedroom.

"Do you know what else they do?"

"Sometimes they read books."

The man laughed. "You're a smart girl, Jeannie. Smart and pretty, I like that. Do you know, Jeannie, that your daddy loves your mommy very much? And sometimes when they're lying in bed he loves her so much that he has to give her a great big hug. Does your daddy ever give you a great big hug?"

"Yes, he does."

"Does he ever give you a goodnight kiss?"

"Yes, and he tells me a story."

"That's very nice, Jeannie. Well, your daddy kisses your mommy sometimes and then he hugs her very tight and then he loves her so much that he takes one of her breasts and he puts it into his mouth and sucks on it just like a little baby."

"Does milk come out?"

The man laughed again. "No, but something very special happens. What do you and Stevie call your mommy's breasts?"

Jeannie's belly tightened. She knew she shouldn't be talking to the man like this, but she felt confused because he was her daddy's friend.

"It's all right, Jeannie," the man said, as though he were reading her thoughts. "Your daddy told me to call you on the phone and talk to you so you wouldn't be so lonely, remember? Just answer my questions, sweetheart, and when your daddy comes home, I'm going to tell him what a good girl you were while he was away. Okay, darling? Now tell me what you and Stevie call your mommy's breasts."

"Her titties."

"When your daddy sucks your mommy's titties, his penis gets nice and hard. Have you ever seen your daddy's penis, Jeannie?"

"In the shower."

"And what did you call it?"

"His pee-pee." Jeannie spoke in a whisper and turned her body even more, so that she was completely facing the wall, with her back to the rest of the world. There was a smudge mark on the wall, shaped something like a spider. Jeannie stared at it while she talked to the man.

"When your daddy sucks your mommy's titties and his pee-pee gets big and hard, do you know what he does with it?"

"No."

"I can't hear you, sweetheart."

"No," Jeannie said louder. Her belly was feeling queasy now, like she had to go to the bathroom, and her left hand was starting to feel numb from holding the receiver so tight.

"Well, this is the secret, Jeannie. But first you have to tell me, what do you and Stevie call the place where your mommy pees from?"

Jeannie thought for a minute. They didn't call it anything, but she didn't want the man to think she was dumb. And besides, if she didn't answer his questions he wouldn't tell her the secret. "Her pee-pee."

"Oh no, Jeannie, your mommy doesn't have a pee-pee like your daddy. She has a cunt. Can you say that, sweetheart?"

Jeannie had never heard that word before. "Cunt."

"Say it louder, Jeannie."

"Cunt."

"Very good. I knew you were a smart girl. When your daddy's pee-pee gets big and hard, he sticks it right into your mommy's cunt and she wraps her legs tight around him and it feels so good, Jeannie. They rock back and forth, back and forth, and it feels so nice, baby, like nothing you've ever felt before. Back and forth, back and forth...." Jeannie felt her body swaying back and forth to the rhythm of the man's words. His voice was deep and lulling, almost like her father's when he told her a bedtime story. Jeannie stared at the spider-shaped smudge mark on the wall and felt almost like she was falling asleep, except that her left hand and arm were tingling in a strange way from gripping the phone too tight. Jeannie wanted to switch the phone into her other hand, but for some reason she was afraid to.

"Jeannie, are you still there?"

"Yes."

"Do you remember that new word I taught you for your mommy's pee-pee?"

"Yes."

"Can you say it for me, sweetheart?"

"Cunt." Jeannie said, dully.

"Say it again, sweetheart."

"Cunt." Jeannie's belly did a flip-flop when she said it The man was making funny breathing noises over the phone. Jeannie wondered if he was sick.

"Jeannie, you're such a smart girl, and so pretty too, just like your mommy. And someday you're going to have nice, big Jewish titties too, like your mommy and a big, hairy cunt. Arghh..." the man made a funny noise, like a cough, and then there was silence. Jeannie wondered if she should hang up the phone now, but she couldn't move.

"Jeannie, are you still there, love?" The man's voice was softer now, and tender, as though he were talking to a baby, or a brand new puppy. Jeannie nodded her head.

"Jeannie?"

"I'm here." Jeannie was surprised at the sound of her own voice. She hadn't meant to speak. It was as if her voice had spoken of its own accord, and it sounded strange, as though it belonged to somebody else.

"I'm going to hang up now, darling. But I'll call you tomorrow after school and tell you some more secrets, okay? I'll call you at three-thirty and I want you to pick up the upstairs phone right away, as soon as you hear it ring. Will you do that for me, sweetheart, so I can tell your daddy what a good girl you were while he was gone?"

"Yes."

"And remember, Jeannie, this is our special secret, just between me and you. As long as you don't tell anyone, everything will be okay and no one will get hurt."

Jeannie blinked her eyes. She thought she saw the spider on the wall move, but then she remembered it was only dirt. She waited for the man to fill the silence with his voice again, but he didn't, so she hung up the phone.

Jeannie sat very still, staring at the wall. Her left hand and arm felt numb, and only when she looked down at her body did she realize she was still holding onto the phone tightly, so tightly that her knuckles were white. She let go slowly then, and dropped her hand onto her lap, still sitting closely to the phone. Would the man call back? Was it okay that she had hung up the phone or was he mad at her? Did she do what she was supposed to do?

Jeannie looked at the phone. It looked bad, like a big black bullfrog with a scary face full of holes. She looked away and her eyes wandered to her parents' wedding picture. She wished they'd come home from Florida already with her Mickey-Mouse hat.

After a few minutes the front door slammed, and Jeannie heard Stevie's heavy footsteps running up the stairs and coming down the hallway.

"Hi stupid." Stevie switched on the TV and flipped the channels until a ball game came on. He sat at the edge of the bed with his legs spread and his elbows resting on his knees. The sports announcer's voice lulled Jeannie into a half-sleep, just as the man's voice on the telephone had done. She sat motionless, except for two big tears that rolled down her cheeks quietly, and the tingling of her left arm and hand as the feeling came rushing back. Jeannie knew that the pins and needles feeling was God's way of punishing her for talking dirty with the man on the phone.

"Hey dummy, what the matter, you in a coma or what?" A commercial for Mr. Clean was on, and Stevie turned around to face his sister. "Crybaby. What's the matter, you miss your mommy? She's only been gone three days, dummy. She'll be back Saturday. Boy, what a baby." He turned back to the television as the ball game resumed. "Grandma wants you to set the table for supper," he said over his shoulder. Jeannie didn't move.

"Jean-nie, what are you, comatose or something? Go downstairs and set the table."

Jeannie hesitated, then lifted her head, uncurled her body and lowered her feet to the floor. All of a sudden her body felt like it was filled with wet sand, and she moved slowly, like the slow-motion instant replays of the ball players Stevie was watching on the television. Jeannie stood a little shakily. Then rubbing her left hand with her right, she put one foot in front of the other and went downstairs to be a good girl and help her grandmother.

The next day Jeannie came straight home from school, took her books upstairs and changed out of her school clothes without being asked. Her best friend Angie had wanted her to come over and play Barbie dolls, but she had told her she had to go home and help her grandmother. Jeannie tiptoed out of her room and stood at the top of the stairs, listening. The television was on loud just like yesterday, so she knew she was safe. After her soap opera, Jeannie's grandmother liked to watch the Mike Douglas Show, which wasn't over until five-thirty. As long as her grandmother didn't hear the phone ring, everything would be okay.

Jeannie went into her parents' room and sat down on the bed to wait. It was quarter after three; both the big hand and the little hand were pointing to the three. Jeannie was proud that she knew how to tell time all by herself. Her daddy had taught her, and she had taught

Angie. Someday, when she was old enough she was going to have a real Mickey-Mouse watch. Maybe for her next birthday.

Now it was twenty after three. The man was supposed to call in ten minutes. What if he didn't call? What if he did call and her grandmother picked up the phone? Jeannie's belly began to feel funny, like she had to do a number two, but she had just gone to the bathroom when she changed her clothes. Actually, her tummy had felt a little funny all day. She didn't eat much of her lunch, and Miss Murray had asked her if she was sick and wanted to go home. Jeannie wouldn't let her call her grandmother. If she'd gone home sick, her grandmother would have made her put on her pajamas and get into bed and then how would she have been able to answer the phone? So instead of playing Dodge Ball at recess, Jeannie had sat in the quiet corner reading a book to herself. She hated Dodge Ball anyway—she always got stuck in the middle and the boys always threw the ball too high and she was afraid her glasses would get knocked off and broken.

The phone rang. "I'll get it," Jeannie said even though there was no one else in the room. She reached out for the receiver and tried to pick it up but somehow her hand wouldn't move. The receiver seemed very heavy all of a sudden. The phone rang and rang, each ring getting louder and louder. It rang so loudly that Jeannie thought for sure her grandmother would be able to hear it any second now, so she snatched up the receiver and waited for the man to speak.

"Jeannie, is that you?" the man asked, after a pause.

"Yes."

"Jeannie, I thought you were a good girl and always did what the grown-ups tell you to. You let the phone ring for much too long. Next time I want you to pick it up right away, do you understand, Jeannie? As soon as you hear the phone ring, you pick it up. It's very important, okay? I know you want me to tell your daddy what a good girl you were while he was away. So do as I tell you and everything will be all right, okay?"

Jeannie nodded. She felt awful. She hoped the man wasn't going to tell her daddy she'd been bad. Right before her parents had left, they'd sat her and Stevie down and told them how important it was for them to be extra specially good while they were gone and especially to listen to their grandmother.

"Are you still there, Jeannie?"

"Yes."

"Did you have a good day at school, sweetheart?"

"Yes."

"Did you make another picture?"

"No, we didn't have art today. We had music, and Mrs. Oliver taught us *Gray Squirrel, Gray Squirrel, Swish Your Bushy Tail.*"

"That sounds like a nice song. Do you want to sing it for me?"

"No." Jeannie felt shy about singing in front of people. Once she'd sung, *I'm a Little Tea Pot Short and Stout* for her parents, and her brother had teased her about being short and stout for weeks afterwards.

"Is gray your favorite color, Jeannie?"

"No."

"Tell me what's your favorite color, sweetheart?"

"Purple."

"Purple, huh? Purple is a pretty color. Do you want to know what my favorite color is, Jeannie?"

"Yes," Jeannie lied.

"My favorite color is red. And do you want to know why my favorite color is red?"

"Yes," Jeannie lied again.

"Because inside your mommy's cunt it's nice and red, a very pretty red, and sometimes big red drops of blood come out of her cunt too. Now do you remember what cunt means?"

"Yes." Jeannie gripped the phone tightly.

"Tell me what it means, darling."

"It's, it's...." Jeannie's voice dropped to a whisper. "It's where she pees from."

"That's right, honey. You're so smart and pretty. You looked extra pretty today in your green-and-white dress, did you know that? Now are you ready to hear another secret?"

"Yes." Her voice was dull.

"Okay, sweetheart. Are you still wearing your green-and-white dress?"

"No"

"Did you change your school clothes when you got home, like a good girl?"

"Yes."

"That's too bad, Jeannie. You're wearing pants, aren't you? Maybe next time we talk on the phone you can wear a dress, okay? Now listen, baby, I'm going to tell you a very special secret, because you're being such a good girl while your mommy and daddy are gone. Did you know that your mommy has a magic button? And that you have one too? All little girls and all big girls like your mommy have magic buttons that make them special."

"Does my grandma have one?" Jeannie asked.

"Yes she does."

"And does Angie have one?"

"Yes, but Jeannie, remember you can't tell anyone these secrets I tell you on the phone. They're very special secrets just between you and me, and you can't tell anyone, not your grandma, and especially not Angie. Angie wouldn't understand, she's not as smart and special as you. It's very, very important not to tell."

The man sounded mad, and Jeannie felt a little scared. "I won't tell, I promise."

"Good girl. I trust you, Jeannie. Trust is very important. Don't ruin everything now, okay? Are you ready to hear more about your magic button?"

"Yes."

"Well, your magic button is so special that you keep it deep inside yourself, all safe and warm. God put it there to protect you. And God told me to help you find it. It's all the way between your legs right near the place where you pee from. It's your magic button, and you can touch it any time you want, and say ABRACADABRA, and it will make you feel so good, like you're being tickled all over. It will make you feel so good that you won't miss your mommy and daddy anymore. Do you want to find your magic button now?"

"Yes"

"What I want you to do, sweetheart, is put the phone down and go close the door. Can you do that for me?"

Jeannie put the receiver down on her parents' bed and crossed the room to close the heavy door. She made sure it clicked shut before she sat back down on the bed and picked up the receiver again. "Are you there Jeannie?"

"Yes."

"Is the door closed?"

"Yes."

"Good girl. Now can you lie down on the bed for me like a good girl?"

Jeannie's belly tightened. She knew this was bad, but she didn't know what to do and she wanted the man to tell her daddy that she had been a good girl.

"Jeannie, are you lying down now?"

"Yes."

"Jeannie, don't lie to me now. I can see you, you know. Remember I told you God sent me here to watch over you and take care of you? Now lie down, sweetheart. There, that's better. Now all I want you to do is put your hand on your tummy and feel your belly button. Can you do that for me, sweetheart?"

Jeannie who was now leaning back against her parents' big fluffy pillows, half sitting up and half lying down, put her hand under her shirt and felt her navel.

"Can you feel it, Jeannie?" the man asked.

"Yes," she whispered. The phone was hard to hold while she was lying down, so Jeannie hunched up her left shoulder and gripped the receiver tightly.

"Do you have an inny or an outy belly button?"

"An inny."

"Oh, that's the best kind to have, Jeannie. I should have known that such a smart pretty girl like you would have an inny. Now what I want you to do is just take your hand and move it down your belly until you feel where you pee from. And then you'll feel a little soft place that tickles you all inside and that's your magic button. I'm going to wait right here until you find it, and remember Jeannie, I'm watching you."

Jeannie felt tears welling up in her eyes. What should she do? She knew this was bad and she was bad for talking on the phone like this. But if she hung up would the man tell her daddy that she was bad? Would God punish her if she didn't do what he said? And could he really see her?

"I'm watching you, Jeannie. Look out the window, do you see a fluffy cloud?" Jeannie's eyes moved to the sky outside her parents' bedroom. The blue sky was dotted with soft cotton candy clouds. "I'm standing on a cloud with God, watching you, Jeannie. Don't be afraid now. Just move your hand down your belly, into your cunt. It's just like your mommy's and it's a special secret, just between you and God and me. No one's going to get hurt, as long as you don't tell anyone. Now, look for your button, baby. Take all the time you need."

Jeannie did as the man told her. Her left hand, which was holding the telephone had fallen asleep and her right hand moved along her body to explore places she'd never touched before. When her little fingers landed on her clitoris, she jumped and gasped aloud.

The man laughed. "Was that your magic button, angel? You're such a smart girl, I knew you'd find it. Now sit up like a good girl and listen to me. I'm going to go now. I want you to go hang up the phone and wash your hands and help your grandma make supper. I'll call you again tomorrow and tell you more secrets, okay? Can you send me a goodbye kiss over the phone, darling?"

Jeannie made a smacking noise with her lips. "Bye." She took the receiver in both hands and hung up the phone. Then she sat still, waiting for the funny pins and needles feeling to fill her hand and arm. She knew God would punish her again for being so bad. She deserved it.

When her left hand and arm felt back to normal, Jeannie got up from her parents' bed and went into her own room. She lay down on her bed and hugged her Lamby tightly to her chest. Jeannie's room had two big windows and she looked out of first one and then the other, wondering if the man on the telephone was still watching her too. She lay there for a while, until she heard her brother's sneakers squeaking up the steps. She listened to him go into his room, come out again, cross the hallway and go into the bathroom. She heard him run the water and she could just see the dirt marks he'd leave all over the peach colored towels, and she imagined her mother yelling, "Stevie! How many times have I told you not to use those towels when you come in from the park?" Jeannie fought to keep back the tears that threatened to roll down her cheeks. I want my mommy, she thought, hugging Lamby even tighter.

Stevie's face appeared in the doorway "Grandma wants you downstairs," he said, looking down at her. "Are you crying again? What's the matter, dummy, you sick or something?"

"Jeannie! Stevie! Supper!" Their grandmother's voice travelled up the stairs.

"C'mon." Stevie turned and went back in his room again before going downstairs to the kitchen.

"Jean-nie! Come down this minute! Don't you hear me calling you?" Her grandmother's voice was on the verge of being mad. Jeannie sighed, gave her Lamby a little kiss, tucked her back under the blankets and went downstairs.

"Grandma, I have a bellyache," Jeannie said, coming into the kitchen.

"What are you talking about? Come here, let me feel your *keppie*." Jeannie walked over to her grandmother obediently and stood still in front of her, while she pressed her lips to Jeannie's forehead. "You don't feel so hot to me. Sit down and eat something, you'll feel better."

"She's faking. I can tell. She just doesn't want to eat her string beans," Stevie said, with his mouth full of mashed potatoes.

"I am not faking," Jeannie said, sitting down at her place and glaring at her brother.

"You are too."

"Am not."

"Are too."

"Am not."

"*Kinder*, that's enough!" Jeannie's grandmother put a piece of chicken on her plate. "Be still and eat now, *mamela*. Did you do your homework?"

"Not yet, Grandma."

"After supper, I want both of you to go upstairs and do your homework. And then I want both of you in bed early. It's a school night. And I want both of you to take a bath."

"Okay Grandma," Jeannie said, pushing her string beans around on her plate.

"Okay Grandma," Stevie said softly, mimicking Jeannie's expression, and sticking his tongue out at her.

After supper, Jeannie took her bath and got into her baby-blue nightie. She got into bed with Lamby and pulled her Mickey-Mouse blanket up to her chin. It was a warm spring night and she could hear the crickets chirping outside her bedroom window, interrupted occasionally by a car zooming by. The light in her bedroom changed from a light blue to a royal blue, and then to darkness. Jeannie was just about to fall asleep when she heard the phone ring and her grandmother answer it. Maybe it was her mommy and daddy calling from Florida. If it was, Jeannie hoped her grandmother would come wake her up so she could speak to them. But what if it was the man on the phone who told her secrets?

Jeannie listened and listened as hard as she could, but she couldn't understand what her grandmother was saying. Then she heard the click of the receiver being placed back in its cradle and hot tears welled up in her eyes and spilled down her cheeks. I want to talk to my mommy, Jeannie thought, as she began to sob. She had promised she'd call. She had promised. Jeannie buried her face in her pillow so Stevie wouldn't hear her crying and come in and tease her.

Grown-ups always keep their promises, Jeannie thought, wiping her nose with the edge of her blanket. The man on the telephone had said so. What if her mommy had gotten into an accident and that's why she hadn't called? But the man had said as long as she didn't tell anyone no one would get hurt.

I want my mommy, Jeannie thought again, burying her head under the blankets. I'm a furry rabbit in my rabbit hole, she thought, as she curled herself into a little ball and pulled Lamby down beside her. "Lamby-lamb," she whispered, to the the toy. "I have a secret to tell you. But you can't tell anyone, or else you'll be very, very bad and God will punish you, okay, sweetheart?" Jeannie shook Lamby's head up and down in agreement.

"I have a magic button and when I touch it and say ABRACA-DABRA, I won't miss my mommy any more." She slowly uncurled her legs and reached down to touch herself. As soon as she found her clitoris her whole body jumped and she took her hand away.

"Bad Lamby," Jeannie whispered to her toy. "You're a very, very bad Lamby. Now don't do that again. Only when the man tells you."

Jeannie wondered if the man could see her now under the covers. She made a little opening and stuck her head part way out. She could see the outline of her dresser, her clothes piled on her desk chair, and her school bag leaning against the wall in the corner. It was too dark for the man to see her, but God could see in the dark, couldn't he? He could see everything, so maybe the man on the telephone could too. What if he had heard her telling Lamby? "You're a very, very bad girl," Jeannie whispered shaking her toy roughly. Satisfied now, she tucked the stuffed animal under her arm and fell asleep.

The man called Jeannie every day after school that week. At first when she got on the phone he'd ask her how school had been, and he'd tell her how special she was; how smart and how pretty and how much he enjoyed talking to her and how he was going to tell her mommy and daddy what a good girl she was as soon as they got home. Then he would start talking about the things Jeannie didn't like; things like her mommy's *tushy* and her daddy's balls. And he always wanted to know about Jeannie's magic button—did she touch it? Did it feel good? Did she make sure and wash it nice and clean when she took her bath?

On Friday, Jeannie came home from school and went straight up to her room as usual, to change her clothes and wait for the phone to ring. She wasn't hungry, so she didn't drink the milk or eat the cookies her grandmother had left out for her. At exactly three-thirty the phone rang. Jeannie picked it up immediately so the man wouldn't yell at her.

"Hello, is that you, Jeannie?"

"Yes."

"How are you today?"

"Fine."

"That's good. What did you do in school today, sweetheart?"

"Nothing."

"Nothing? Didn't you have music or draw a picture?"

"No." Jeannie hadn't felt good again, so she had spent most of the day sitting at her desk, quietly copying the alphabet from her workbook into her new black-and-white notebook. When the other children had gone to art class, she had stayed behind with Miss Murray to help her wash the blackboard and clap the erasers.

"Jeannie, is your mommy coming home from vacation tomorrow?"

"Yes." Jeannie picked up her head as some energy rushed back into her voice. "And she's going to bring me my Mickey Mouse hat. And I made her a picture of me and Donald Duck. And I made my daddy a picture too."

"That's nice, Jeannie. Do you like Mickey Mouse better, or do you like Donald Duck?"

"Mickey Mouse."

"I like Donald Duck better, Jeannie. Do you know why?"

"No."

"Because duck rhymes with fuck and that's one of my favorite words. Do you know what fuck means, Jeannie?"

"No."

"Fucking is when your daddy puts his dick into your mommy's cunt. Do you remember what those words mean, Jeannie?" Jeannie nodded and heard a click on the other end of the phone, as the man went on. Jeannie's stomach tightened, and as usual, her left hand, which was gripping the receiver began feeling numb.

"Do you know, sweetheart, that your daddy fucks your mommy in the cunt sometimes, and sometimes ...."

"Who is this?" Jeannie's whole body stiffened and then started to shake as she heard her grandmother's voice on the downstairs phone. "Who is this? Jeannie, you hang up the phone this instant. Who is this?" her grandmother repeated. Then there was silence coming from all three phones. Jeannie heard a click and then another click and then she hung up the phone. After a few minutes, Jeannie heard her grandmother's footsteps starting to climb the stairs. She quickly ran down the hallway into her own room and sat down on the bed, putting her hands under her thighs and staring down at her sneakers, as her grandmother's footsteps got closer and closer.

"Jeannie, who was that on the phone?" Her grandmother was standing right in front of her, and Jeannie continued to stare down at her sneakers, though she could also see the heavy black toe of her grandmother's shoes. She wouldn't look up, for she knew if she saw her grandmother's face, she would start to cry. Jeannie didn't say a word and her grandmother didn't move. "Jeannie, what did he say to you?"

"Nothing"

"*Oy gevalt*, that I should live so long to hear such filth come out of a person's mouth. And to a child yet, *vey iss mir*." Jeannie's grandmother leaned down and took Jeannie's hand. "Come downstairs with me, *mamela*. The police are coming and they have some questions they want to ask you. *Oy vey*, that I should live to hear such things," her grandmother repeated as she took Jeannie's hand and led her down the stairs.

They sat in the kitchen, waiting quietly. Jeannie could hear the ticking of the clock and the humming of the refrigerator. Her grandmother had wiped the table clean of cookie crumbs and milk spills and was now sitting very still with her hands in her lap. The waiting seemed like forever. Jeannie felt like she had always been sitting in this kitchen in silence with her grandmother, and always would be. Her thoughts were interrupted by the sounds of a car pulling up in front of the house. Her grandmother jumped up, unlocked the door, and stood in the front hallway with her hands on her hips. Jeannie stayed in her seat, surrounded by a feeling of dread that wouldn't allow her to move.

Jeannie's grandmother stepped aside as two huge policemen filled the doorway. From where she was sitting, Jeannie could see they both wore hats with badges on them and they both had billy clubs hanging from their belts. Her grandmother was twisting her hands together, looking tiny beside them. Every once in a while her grandmother would wipe her hands on the apron tied around her waist that said *World's Greatest Cook* on it. Then she'd go back to twisting them. Jeannie watched her grandmother's hands and felt like her stomach was getting all twisted up as well. What were the policemen going to ask her? Was she going to get in trouble? Jeannie knew policemen only came when someone was in trouble, and she desperately wanted to stay out of trouble. Would they ask her questions about the man on the phone? Was he watching her right now? Would the policemen tell her mommy and daddy that she had been bad?

Jeannie watched one policeman ask her grandmother questions while the other one wrote things down on his clipboard. Her grandmother had to stretch her neck way up to look at the policeman. He looked towards the kitchen once and Jeannie quickly looked down at the table. She heard her grandmother say, "In here" and all of a sudden the three of them were coming towards her. But instead of coming into the kitchen they turned into the dining room. Jeannie was so surprised she forgot for a moment why they were there. No one ever used the dining room. The chairs still had plastic coverings on their seats and the rug was nice and soft The table was covered with a tablecloth her mother had embroidered with thousands of blue cross-stitches and the china closet was filled with special treasures that Jeannie wasn't allowed to touch—the clay *seder* plate, the red cut-glass wine goblets, and the bride and groom from her parents' wedding cake. Jeannie couldn't remember the last time anyone had sat in the dining room, but the two policemen were sitting in there now. Jeannie heard the plastic chair coverings crinkling underneath them.

"Jeannie, come in here a minute, *mamela*, the policemen want to talk to you." Jeannie's grandmother came into the kitchen and took her hand again, as if Jeannie was three years old. She led Jeannie into the dining room and stood beside her holding her hand.

"Hi Jeannie. My name is Officer Johnson, and I want to ask you a few questions." One of the policemen turned in his chair and bent down, resting his elbows on his knees until his face was very close to Jeannie's. His face was huge, bigger than the sun, and Jeannie backed away, as if she indeed could get burned by it. She turned away and hid her face in the skirt of her grandmother's housedress. It smelled old, like her grandmother, and when Jeannie burrowed into the folds of the cloth, it was nice and dark. She could pretend she was under the blankets up in her room, nice and safe with her Lamby.

Jeannie's grandmother stroked her hair. "Don't be scared, *mamela*. The policemen are here to help us. C'mon now, Jeannie."

The policeman cleared his throat. "Jeannie, can you tell us who the man talking to you on the phone was? Did he ever tell you his name?"

Jeannie stayed where she was and shook her head no.

"Did you recognize his voice? Was it someone who ever came to visit you here?" Again Jeannie shook her head.

The policeman leaned forward and touched Jeannie on the arm. "Now Jeannie, this is very important. Can you tell us what the man said to you?" The policeman spoke in a gentle voice, and Jeannie felt her lower lip start to tremble like it always did when she was about to cry. I can't tell, she thought, as she started to sniffle. I'll get in trouble. The man said so. But wasn't she in trouble already? That's why the police were there. Jeannie knew she was supposed to listen to grown-ups, but which ones? The policemen? The man on the phone? Her grandmother? They were all telling her different things and she knew that no matter what she did, her mommy and daddy were going to be mad at her when they got home.

"*Mamela*, come on now. Tell the policemen what the man said." Her grandmother moved back, and Jeannie looked up into the policeman's face. He smiled at her, but still he looked big and scary.

"Jeannie, would you like to blow my whistle?" the policeman asked, offering her the big shiny silver whistle that hung from a chain around his neck. Jeannie reached out her hand, but then just as suddenly, pulled her arm back and shook her head.

"Well, usually the whistle gets them." The policeman sighed and straightened up in his chair. "Got any lollipops, Joe?" The other policeman shook his head. "Look ma'am," the first policeman said to Jeannie's grandmother. "We can fill out a report, and when your son gets home we can talk about putting a tap on the phone, but to tell you the truth, there's not a whole hell of a lot we can do here. I suggest that you get an unlisted number and that will be the end of it. If you can get her to talk, give us a call." The policeman stood up and Jeannie stepped back. He had enormous black shiny boots on, and Jeannie knew her mother would be really mad when she found out he'd stepped on the dining room rug with them.

The next day Jeannie's parents came home. Jeannie heard the car pull into the driveway and she stayed in her room listening to the front door slam and her grandmother and parents greeting each other. Stevie was in the park, as usual playing ball. Jeannie was coloring in her Rocky the Flying Squirrel coloring book. She had just finished coloring Bullwinkle's ears a dark brown when she heard her grandmother call, "Jeannie, come on down, *mamela*. Mommy and Daddy are home."

Jeannie left her room and climbed down the stairs slowly. "Hi darling," her mother said softly, giving her a big hug and bending down to kiss the top of her head.

"How's my Jeannie?" Her father picked her up and swung her in the air. "I dream of Jeannie with the dark brown hair," he sang as he twirled her about. It was their song, and usually it made Jeannie dissolve into giggles, but now she just stared at her father with her big green eyes. Did they know about the man on the phone and the policemen? Was she going to get into trouble now?

Her father put her down. "Go upstairs and play, *tochterla*. I'm going to talk to Grandma and find out what a good girl you were while Mommy and Daddy were away. I'll come up in a little while to see you." Jeannie went back upstairs while her mother went into the kitchen to put up water for coffee and her father shuffled through a week's worth of mail.

After a while Jeannie heard her father's footsteps coming up the stairs. She started scribbling with her crayons very deliberately as he walked into her room. He sat down on the edge of her bed and said, "Jeannie, come sit next to Daddy," and from the way he said it, Jeannie knew that he knew.

Her father sighed and took Lamby in his hands for a minute. Lamby looked small in his big hands. Her father turned the toy over and over, then sighed again and put the stuffed animal back on Jeannie's pillow.

"Your grandmother tells me the police were here yesterday. Do you know why?"

Jeannie shook her head miserably.

"She said a man was talking to you on the telephone. Is that true?"

Jeannie shook her head. "I don't remember."

"Do you know who it was?"

"I don't remember."

"Did he call you more than once?"

Jeannie nodded.

"Did he call you more than twice?"

She nodded again.

"That bastard. I'll kill him. If I *ever* find out who that *schmuck* is, I'll kill the *momser*." Jeannie's father was yelling now, and she shrank back away from him. Was he going to punish her now? His face was bright red and his eyes were enormous behind his thick glasses.

"Jeannie, listen to me, *maideleh*." Her father's voice was quiet now. "Whatever that man said to you, you just forget all about it, okay? We're just going to pretend that it never happened, and starting Monday, we'll have a brand new phone number so he'll never bother you again, okay, Jeannie?" Jeannie nodded. "Now I don't want you to ever tell anyone that Mommy's not home when you answer the phone. Say that she's busy. Can you remember that, *mine tochter*? And I don't want you to tell anyone our new phone number. It's going to be a secret. Can you keep a secret?"

Jeannie nodded and looked up at her father. "Where's my Mickey Mouse hat?" she asked.

"Oh Jeannie, we didn't have time to stop at Disney World for you. But Mommy picked out something extra special." Jeannie's father reached into his pocket and pulled out a small white box. "Do you want to guess what it is?" He held the box out to her in the palm of his hand.

"No. I want my Mickey Mouse hat. With my name on it. Like you promised." Jeannie's shoulders began to shake as she started to cry. "Grown-ups always keep their promises," she said between sniffles. "It's very, very important. He even said so."

"Who, Jeannie?"

Jeannie stopped crying for a minute, horrified that she had spoken of the man on the phone. She hadn't told part of the secret, had she? She stole a look at her father and he smiled at her.

"Come on now, *mamela*. We brought you a pretty ring made of coral. Don't you want it?" Again he extended the little box.

"No!" Jeannie flung herself down on the bed and started sobbing. "I want my hat. You promised. You promised." Jeannie was shrieking now, and her father stood up in bewilderment.

"When you're ready to talk to me like a person, Jeannie, we can talk about it. Not every little girl is lucky enough to get presents like you. Some little girls don't even have enough to eat. When you're finished crying you can come downstairs." Her father put the little jewelry box down on the bed and left the room. Jeannie ignored the box and continued to cry. I want my Mickey Mouse hat, she thought, wiping her nose with the back of her hand. They promised. The man had said grown-ups always keep their promises. He kept his. He'd called back every day right after school at three-thirty just like he said he would but now her parents were home and they had a different phone number and the man was never going to call again and she was never going to have a Mickey Mouse hat, only a stupid ring. And the man told her secrets, and her daddy had told her a secret, and she was too tired to remember all these secrets and too scared to forget.

After a while, Jeannie stopped crying. She wiped her runny nose on her Mickey Mouse pillow case and pulled her stuffed lamb close to her. "Lamby, I want my Mickey Mouse hat," Jeannie whispered. She looked into Lamby's shiny green marble eyes and saw a faint reflection of herself. Lamby had seen and heard everything. "You're a bad Lamby. A very, very bad Lamby," Jeannie said, spanking the toy with the back of her hand. "You're a bad girl and you don't deserve anything." Jeannie flung Lamby across the room, but still the toy stared at her with its green eyes. "No," Jeannie shrieked. "You are a bad, bad girl!" She rose then, and kicked Lamby under her bed where the toy stayed for many years, collecting dust and almost, but not quite forgotten.

What Happened to Sharon

When I dropped my contact lens into the kitty litter, I knew it was going to be a bad day, but even that didn't indicate how bad. I mean, it could happen to anyone, right? One minute I was standing in front of the sink and the lens was balanced on the tip of my finger, and the next minute I was on my hands and knees searching the bathroom floor with a flashlight. I didn't want to admit, even to myself, that my hands were shaking, but they must have been, and why the hell do I keep the kitty litter under the sink anyway? I shone the flashlight all around the floor, illuminating dustballs, a stray marble and other such interesting items, until it dawned on me to look in Pan's box, and sure enough, there, shining like a diamond on a black velvet cushion, was my ticket to twenty-twenty vision, perched on piece of poop.

Well, there was no way I was going to pop that piece of plastic back into my eyeball. I'm not a Virgo for nothing, you know. I barely managed to fish the lens out of there and drop it back into its little plastic case without losing my breakfast. Yeah, I was nervous all right. The day before I had put both contact lenses into the same eye and that hurt like hell, you better believe it, sister. But after about an hour I'd been able to wear the little buggers. Not today though. I'd have to sterilize them first. Nope, today I'd have to wear my glasses, and damn, today all days, I wanted to look good. This was the day I was going to see Sharon.

Hell, maybe I really didn't want to *see* her. You don't have to be a Freudian analyst to figure out the significance of all that contact lens jazz. Sharon. How could one little word, six little letters hold so much emotion for me? When I think about seeing her, I get angry and sad and excited all at the same time.

I guess that's what happens when you've been with someone for seven years. Seven years! We even used to joke about the seven year itch, how it would never happen to us, or if it did, we'd just scratch it. Ha ha, very funny. Well, the joke's sure on me, because it was exactly three days after our seven-year anniversary that Sharon said she wanted out. She said she'd been thinking about it for a while, but she didn't want to spoil our anniversary. She wanted us to have one last good time to remember. And didn't I feel like a fool.

That night was so awful—not our anniversary—that night was fine, or so I thought. I'd been sensing that Sharon felt a little off lately—she'd been a little distant, she hadn't been feeling very sexual—but I wasn't worried or anything. You know how it is after seven years, these things ebb and flow and it's no big deal. But still, I wanted our anniversary to be really special. So I told her to get all dolled up and I'd take her out to Sam's, this very fancy place complete with a piano bar, where we happened to go on our very first date.

Every year on our anniversary we'd go to Sam's, ask the gay boy at the piano to play As Time Goes By , drink too much champagne, eat too much food and go home and make love and fall asleep. I'd buy Sharon red roses and she'd wear this little black mini-skirt which still fit her the same as it did seven years ago. She'd worn it on our first date and that just about knocked me out—that this dyke would have the nerve to do something like that. I think that's when she got me. It was love at first sight with Sharon. She said what got her was the way I held the car door open for her and how I lit her cigarette. She thought chivalry was dead. Hell, I would have lain my jacket across a puddle for her if I'd had to. I'd have done anything, I was so taken with her. And I still felt the same way.

So imagine my surprise when three days later, Sharon said she wanted to break up. And before I could turn around, she was gone. Just like that. Now I may be a fool, but one thing I do know is that you don't find an affordable apartment in a safe neighborhood in three days. Not in this city. She must have been planning this for a long time. Shit. You'd think after seven years I would deserve a little more respect than that. She wasn't even willing to go to therapy, like any self-respecting dyke would do. She just didn't want to be with me anymore and that was that.

Maybe it was my gray hair. I looked in the mirror and started fussing with it. I look a lot older than Sharon, even though we're only a couple of months apart. Maybe my looking older reminded her she was getting older too, and who wants to be reminded about that? Maybe she wanted to be with a young chick, some suave hipless butch who mousses her hair or something. I doubt it, but then again who knows? You think you know someone pretty well after seven years and then they pull a fast one on you.

Speaking of fast—I had to move my butt along so I wouldn't be late. That would really piss Sharon off. Punctuality is not my strong point, but Sharon sure changed that. I was on time for our first date of course, and for a couple of weeks after that. But then, well, you know how it is. You try to get out of the house and then you remember the fish have to be fed and then the phone rings, and you spend ten minutes telling whoever it is that you can't talk, you have a date, and right as you're leaving, you pass the hallway mirror and decide that the shirt you're wearing doesn't really go with the pants you have on, so you pick out another shirt and of course it needs to be ironed...you get the picture. Sharon wouldn't stand for it. She got me a watch for our one month anniversary and wrote on the card, *Happy Anniversary from your new girlfriend who doesn't like to be kept waiting.* She can be tough, my Sharon. My ex-Sharon, I mean.

Getting dressed though, is easier said than done, because everything I own has some memory of Sharon attached to it. I hate buying clothes, but Sharon was born to shop. Sometimes she goes shopping just for the fun of it, if you can believe that. When I had absolutely nothing left to wear, I'd let her drag me to the mall and we'd buzz through JC Penney's, Steigers, and Jeans West and, before I could say Visa, I'd have a whole new wardrobe.

I wanted to wear something she hadn't seen, hadn't picked out, hasn't undressed me in, for Chrissakes. I wanted to show her I have a life without her. Hell, six months is long enough to get over anyone, right? Wrong. Anyone but Sharon.

All right, basic white shirt, jeans and sneakers—what the hell, it's not like this is a date or anything. I'll go casual, like, what do I care what I look like, I only have a few minutes anyway. We were meeting downtown for coffee in a "neutral" place. Shit, what did she think, I was going to rant and rave like a blithering idiot? I didn't even do that when she left. I didn't even cry. Not in front of her anyway. Except when she took Cakes.

See, for our three-year anniversary we got these two kittens and we named one of them Pan and the other one Cakes. Separately they were okay, a pan and some cakes, but together they were fabulous—Pancakes! Just like us. So when Cakes left, it really got to me. I've always been a sucker for animals. I tried to explain it to Pan, but she just moped around the house looking up at the door every ten seconds like she was waiting for Sharon and Cakes to come back. At night she slept in bed with me, under the covers even, like she was afraid I'd run out on her too if she let me out of her sight for even one second.

That was tough. God, I really feel for people who have kids—must be really hard to explain it to them. At least Sharon and I never had kids. We talked about it some. She used to bring it up more than me, all that stuff about our biological clocks ticking away. We were both pretty ambivalent about it, though. I mean, if we could just get pregnant by making love, we probably would have done it. But it was too complicated to figure it all out—known donor, unknown donor—it was just too much. And besides, we didn't have the money. And besides that, I wasn't too wild about the thought of having a boy. We decided we really wanted to be aunts, you know enjoy a kid but not be totally responsible for her. Though it was a pity that Sharon never had a kid—she'd be beautiful, just like Sharon, with long brown hair, big brown eyes, gorgeous full lips, and a body that just won't quit.

Okay, enough of that—I'm outta here. And no more crying. I took off my glasses to wipe a tear on my sleeve. I didn't know how I'd feel when I first saw Sharon. The *first* first time I saw her, my legs started shaking, my knees got weak—it was love at first sight like I told you. And sometimes I would still feel that way when I'd come home from work and she'd be sitting at the kitchen table talking on the phone, or standing at the sink doing dishes, or even sprawled on the couch pouting because I was late. I still got all trembly knowing she was mine.

Was. What a lousy word. Oh well, nothing lasts forever I guess. I sure thought these past six months would. This no contact stuff was all Sharon's idea. I mean, how could we go from seeing each other everyday for seven years to not seeing each other at all for six months? At first we tried getting together once a week and then we tried talking on the phone, but according to Sharon it didn't work because the conversations always turned into a fight about why we broke up. I mean, what did she expect me to talk about—the weather?

So six months ago, we decided we'd meet at the Eggshell Diner today at three o'clock. It was unlikely we'd bump into anyone we knew at that hour, so we'd really be able to talk, though what we had left to really talk about was beyond me. It was bizarre to think I literally hadn't lain eyes on Sharon in six months. I mean, we live in the same city even though she works in Westbrook, which is about half an hour away, and I work right downtown. I hadn't seen her at any dances, or dyke events, not even at the Alix Dobkin concert, and everyone who was anyone was there. I'd even taken this woman Dana, who I knew had a crush on me, but the only reason I went out with her was to make Sharon jealous but she wasn't even there. What a waste of twenty-four bucks.

I'd asked around a little, but no one seemed to know what happened to Sharon. No one had seen her at the bar or at the bookstore—hell, she hadn't even played softball this year. Maybe she was really depressed over our breakup and was just lying low. That's what I'd hoped anyway. It's not like I'd been Ms. Social Butterfly myself. Maybe Sharon had come to her senses over the past six months and realized that no one would ever love her as good as I would. Maybe she was going to beg me to take her back.

Well, there was only one way to find out. I got to the Eggshell early, for a change, slid into a booth way in the back, and ordered myself a cup of coffee which I hoped would dissolve the lump in my belly by the time Sharon got there. Boy was I nervous. After about ten minutes I felt Sharon come in. Felt, I say, because the whole energy of the place changed. Every single guy stopped what he was doing to turn around and gawk at Sharon. Like I said, she's quite a looker. Guys were always staring at her when we were together, and it used to make me mad, but she'd just laugh and toss her head and tell me I was too serious. Politics was not exactly Sharon's forté.

Even now I could swear she just winked at one of those guys.

I watched her make her way over to my table and I slid my hands onto my lap to hide their shaking. She looked gorgeous. She was wearing these white pants and a baggy red sweater with a black and gold scarf around her neck. Her hair was pulled back and she had some makeup on of course—Sharon would rather be caught dead than without makeup on in public. She looked, though I hate to say it, happy somehow. Happier than I'd seen her in a long time.

"Hi."

"Hi." I half rose out of my seat, then thought better of it. What were we supposed to do—kiss on the mouth, kiss on the cheek, hug, shake hands? Why hadn't anyone written the *Emily Post Guide to Lesbian Ex-Lover Etiquette* yet? Sharon, who never loses her composure, simply slid into the booth, planted her purse on the table, and stared at me.

"New glasses?"

"No, I dropped...." I stopped myself, remembering that when we were together, the only times I'd ever worn my glasses in public was when we'd been up all night long making love, and I was too tired to wear my lenses. "I just didn't feel like putting my lenses in this morning," I said, staring down at my coffee. Let her wonder.

We didn't say anything for a few minutes, until the waitress came to take Sharon's order, and of all things she ordered herbal tea. I looked up at her, puzzled, and she shrugged.

"Don't you drink coffee anymore?" I asked, as the waitress gave her her tea and poured me a refill.

"No I stopped." She picked up the honey bear from the table, turned it upside down and let a smooth golden stream flow out of the top of the bear's head.

"I suppose you've given up cigarettes too." Sharon, who, not unlike Bette Davis, was usually enveloped in a cloud of smoke, hadn't lit up yet.

"Yep," she said, still dribbling honey into her tea.

"Got enough honey in there?" I wondered if she had turned into a clone of Winnie the Pooh.

She put the honey bear down and made a face. "Actually I hate tea." She picked up a spoon to stir with, and it was then that I noticed something new on her finger.

"What's that?" I asked, leaning forward to stare.

"What's what?"

"That." I pointed to her right hand.

"This?" She turned her hand towards her and studied it as though she'd never seen it before. As if some fairy godmother had magically, out of nowhere, plopped a diamond ring on the fourth finger of her right hand.

"Yeah, that."

"Just a ring." She said it as if I couldn't see her hand in front of my face. My vision isn't that bad, even without my glasses. Sharon continued stirring her tea, and I knew by that that something was up. To Sharon, nothing is "just" a ring or "just" a coat, or "just" an anything. Everything Sharon owns has a story. Take that black and gold scarf she has around her neck for instance. I remember the day she brought it home, and told me over supper, "Well, it was hanging in the window of this second hand store and I made the sales clerk get it out for me and she had to climb over all these mannequins and she got really miffed because there was this long line of customers waiting and then it wasn't really the style I wanted exactly, but I couldn't not buy it after she'd gone through all that trouble, and anyway it was only a dollar, so I thought I'd give it to my mother, but then I remembered she hates anything black, it makes her feel old she says, so I guess I'll keep it; I kind of like it actually...et cetera." So I knew this diamond ring had a story. A story she didn't want to tell me.

"Family heirloom?" I asked.

"No." She took the spoon out of her tea and put it down on her napkin.

"Is it real?" I wondered why I insisted on knowing what would probably kill me.

"Is what real?" She picked up her spoon and licked it.

"The honey," I said, my voice dripping with sarcasm.

She put the spoon down and looked at me then, and I wished she wasn't so damn pretty. I knew I still wanted her back, and I knew I'd never tell her.

"Well, if you must know," she gave her head a little impatient shake, "it happens to be an engagement ring."

"An engagement ring!" All of a sudden the piece of toast I'd eaten for breakfast that morning felt like a cinder block in the pit of my stomach. Very, very cautiously I asked, "Sharon, why are you wearing an engagement ring?"

"Because I'm engaged."

"You're engaged?" Ask a stupid question, get a stupid answer, I reminded myself. My eyes started blinking and I took off my glasses to rub them. Be cool, I told myself. I put my glasses back on and shoved them up my nose. "So, uh, not that I really care, but who's the lucky girl?" I tried not to let on I was dying of curiosity.

"Jo..." She hesitated for a split second.   "Jo, it's not a girl. It's a guy. His name is Rick."

I just stared at her, feeling the fist in my belly clench even tighter. Sharon was with a man? A person with a dick? A dick and a beard and a hairy chest and no tits? My Sharon? My Sharon who had buried her face between my legs more times than I could count, who had licked my breasts for hours, *hours* on end, who...but I didn't want to think about all that now.

"Hello?" She was waving her hand, her ringless left hand, thank God, in front of my face. "Earth to Jo, earth to Jo." I shook my head and she came back into focus. "So aren't you going to congratulate me?"

She always did have nerve.

"Hell no," I said, staring at her. She looked like Sharon. She sounded like Sharon. She even smelled like Sharon, and I should know; I'm the one who used to buy her perfume. Maybe this was her twin sister from another planet? This couldn't possibly be the same woman whose hair I braided every night, who'd slept right next to me for seven years, as if her head was velcroed to my shoulder. "No," I repeated, almost to myself. "I can't believe this. What'd you do, get it out of a bubble gum machine? Ha, ha, very funny, Shar. You almost fooled me."

"It's not a joke, Jo." She took her purse which is the size of a small valise off the table. She dug around until she fished out her wallet and flipped through her license and charge cards. She probably was still paying for a couple of my shirts, maybe even the one I was wearing, but, hell, I wasn't going to say anything. She held something out towards me. "Here."

I took the picture and looked. It was a guy all right, an old hippy type, complete with beard, drawstring pants (turquoise or purple no doubt, though I couldn't be sure because the picture was black and white), aviator glasses and a dog.

My belly lurched, and I knew it wasn't from the coffee. "You're not kidding," I said, barely managing to get the words out. "Where did you meet this guy?"

"At work. You remember, I told you about him. We had lunch a few times when I was still living with you."

Oh yeah, Rick. Another hippy-dippy-do-good-social-worker-save-the-world type. God, how could this be happening? I handed her back the photo, wondering if she still carried around a picture of me too. I still had one of her in my wallet, but not for long, that was for damn sure. "So what's so special about this guy, what'd you say his name was, Dick?"

"Rick," she said, like she was talking to a three year old. "You don't have to get nasty."

"I don't have to get nasty? You get fucking engaged to a guy six months after we split up, and I don't have to get nasty?" My voice was rising and people were staring so I got a grip and lowered my voice, which came out more like a hiss. "Sharon, that was seven years of my life, remember? Seven fucking years. And since your memory is so short, let me remind you, I wanted to get married too."

She sighed and shook her head. "Ah Jo, what good is it? A bunch of lesbians sitting in a circle passing a flower or a feather around, talking about how wonderful commitment is, and two years later they're all broken up and sleeping with someone else."

"How dare you?" I slammed my hand down on the table with more force than was really necessary, since unfortunately what she said had more than a ring of truth to it. "Straight people don't have such a great track record either, you know. One out of two break up. That's fifty per cent."

"You always were a whiz at math," she said dryly. Now I knew she was mad because Sharon hardly ever gets sarcastic. It's too unladylike.

"How's Cakes taking all of this?" I asked, trying to change the subject for two seconds anyway, to get some comic relief.

"She's fine. She just loves Rick. It took her a while to get used to Rufus, that's Rick's dog, and pretty soon...." Her voice trailed off.

"Pretty soon what?"

"Oh nothing." She didn't meet my eye.

"Don't oh-nothing me." All of a sudden I felt like we were a couple again. "Are you living together?"

She nodded, and it's a good thing the table was bolted to the floor or I would have knocked the whole damn thing over. I swear I felt my blood beginning to boil, as the saying goes, and I hoped I wasn't turning beet red all over, though why I should care about the way I looked now was beyond me. Sharon was living with this guy! Damnit, she had made me wait two lousy years before she'd move in with me—two whole years of "whose house should we sleep at tonight"; two years of "but we *always* sleep at your house"; two years of never knowing where half my shit was, at home or at Sharon's. And she's living with this guy after only being with him for six months? Or...suddenly I felt a little sick.

"Sharon..." I was holding onto the edge of the table for dear life. "Tell me the truth now. Did you start seeing this guy," (I still couldn't bear saying his name), "before we broke up?"

"No." She looked me right in the eye. "Only a few lunches and I didn't hide them from you." I knew she was telling the truth by the way she looked at me, and my gut loosened, maybe one thirty-second of an inch.

I loosened my death grip on the table a little bit. "Just tell me why."

She shifted her weight and started playing with the scarf around her neck. "I don't know, Jo. I always considered myself bi."

"That's a lie," I interrupted her. "You know I would never go out with a bisexual woman."

"I know. That's why I could never tell you."

I tightened my grip on the table again, until my knuckles turned white. "You lied to me? For seven years?" I stared at this stranger sitting across the table from me, who I thought I'd once known, as my whole world crumbled.

"Not exactly." She kept playing with her scarf, untying it and retying it and tucking the ends in just so, until I wanted to strangle her with it.

"Sharon." My tone of voice said I meant business.

"Well," she finally took her hands away from her throat. "Listen. I never lied to you. I felt like I was a lesbian. I mean, coming out was so wonderful, you know, and I was with Sal for four years and when we broke up I didn't think about going out with a man at all. I thought about going out with you."

My heart raced. I wished she hadn't said that. "So?"

"So, I didn't think it mattered, because I thought we'd be together forever. You know I always got mad when the Lesbian Alliance didn't want bisexual women in it. But I never said anything about it because I knew it would make you mad."

"Sharon, you said a lot of things you knew would make me mad."

She shrugged. "Look Jo, I know you're not going to like this, but something happened to me. For, oh, I don't know, the last eight months or so of our relationship, I kept dreaming about men. You know, it wasn't that different than coming out. I just felt my heart opening in that direction, and I knew I needed to explore it." She laughed a little and shook her head.

"What?" I asked, though I couldn't imagine what on earth could possibly be funny at this particular moment.

"You know before, when you said, 'Who's the lucky girl?' Well, I felt the same way as when people used to ask me if I was seeing anyone, and I'd say, yes, and they'd say, 'what's his name?' and I'd say, it's not a him. Her name is Johanna."

She smiled, but somehow I failed to see the humor of the situation. The irony however wasn't lost on me.

Sharon went on. "Don't you see Jo, it works both ways. You remember how exciting coming out was—everything you felt for the first time, like you were being born all over again. Well, this is the same thing. I hadn't been with a man for almost thirteen years. I forgot what it felt like to be held by a man, to look up at a man, to...."

"Spare me." I leaned back and crossed my arms. I couldn't stand seeing her look so...so goddamn dreamy about it. It wasn't the same thing at all, but I wasn't going to start that argument with Sharon. I didn't have to say anything though. It was like Sharon could read my mind. After all, even though it was hard to believe at this particular moment, we had been together for seven years.

"Johanna," she said, and I knew something important was coming, because no one ever uses my full name. "I know you're upset, but I wish you would try to understand. I'm not like you. I wasn't satisfied with women's this and women's that and half the world hating me and not even being able to walk down the street holding your hand."

That was the last straw. "Do you hold Rick's hand on the street?" I asked, amazed I didn't choke on his name. It had always been an issue between us. I didn't give a shit what people thought, unless we were in some dangerous situation like walking by a bunch of Skinheads or Neo-Nazis or something, which wasn't too likely in this town. Sharon, on the other hand, hated even the thought of people staring at us. So we compromised by walking side by side, touching arms from the shoulder down to the elbow. Sharon even felt funny about that. She wouldn't even hold my hand at night on a deserted street or even in Provincetown where you could hold hands with an octopus and no one would notice.

Sharon was very busily not looking at me, so I answered the question for her. "So, you walk around holding this guy's hand." I didn't wait for her acknowledgement. "And you kiss him hello when you meet him downtown and you let him put his arm around you at the movies and you're going to marry him and share health insurance and tax breaks and you expect me to be happy for you?" I unfolded my arms and leaned forward, as if I were about to make a speech. "Sharon, do you know, for seven years I worried about what would happen if one of us got hurt? I worried about how I'd get in to see you if you were lying in a hospital somewhere? Seven years of that, and now, all you have to do is say 'I do' and this man will be your next of kin?"

I sat back and then leaned forward again. "I bet your mother is thrilled, isn't she? Five years, and everytime I answered the phone she'd say, 'Hello, is Sharon there?' like she didn't even know who I was."

"Jo, I'm not denying anything you're saying." She was playing with her damn scarf again. "You're right. You're absolutely right. You have no idea what it feels like to be able to tell the women at work about Rick and have them get excited for me. I finally feel like I belong, and to tell you the truth, it's a big relief. They're even giving me a bridal shower, Jo. I feel so..." she thought for a moment, "...so *normal.*"

"Excuse me, I'm about to be sick," I mumbled, sliding out of the booth. I headed for the woman's room, where I did in fact lose my breakfast. It never fails. Whenever I get upset, it goes right to my stomach. When my grandmother died, I cried so hard I puked, and Sharon was really good about it, stroking my hair, putting a cold washcloth on my face. God, why did I have to have so many good memories about her? And I felt so weird about what she was saying. I felt relieved and normal and like I finally belonged when I came out, and for Sharon it was just the opposite. My head was beginning to ache, so I stayed in the bathroom for a while, washing out my mouth and trying to get it together. If there had been a back door I would have exited then and there, but unfortunately this wasn't the movies. This was my life.

Slowly, and against my better judgement, I made my way back to the table. Somewhat to my surprise, Sharon was still sitting there, her hands cupped around her tea, which she still hadn't touched. Just as well, since it probably had enough honey in it to curl her hair anyway. I slid into the booth and sort of smiled. "Did you think I fell in?" I asked.

She smiled back, because despite herself, Sharon always did appreciate my junior-high sense of humor. "Are you okay?"

"Better now. I did get sick though."

"Poor baby." She almost reached for my hand. Out of habit, I suppose. Her right hand, the one with the ring on it, edged towards my end of the table, stopped, and then retreated. "I got sick this morning, too."

I was touched. "Were you that nervous about seeing me?" I asked, and this time it was my hand that started creeping across the table, as though it had a mind of its own.

"Well..." She hesitated, and my intuition told me to brace myself. "Not exactly. Jo, I'm pregnant."

"Whoa." I lurched back as if I'd been punched in the face. Pregnant! She was really going the whole nine yards with this guy.

"You're pregnant?" I stared at her face, and then my eyes travelled down her body, which still looked exactly the same to me, though of course a good part of it was hiding under the table. Maybe I was on a bad acid trip. I hadn't taken drugs in over fifteen years but still, maybe this was a flashback? I couldn't seem to comprehend the fact that there was not one, but two people sitting across from me, one inside the other.

The one who was visible to the naked eye (behind my glasses of course) was now really smiling. I could see she'd been holding back, because happiness was just oozing out of her now. That pregnant glow, I suppose.

"You're having a baby?" I asked like an idiot, since that is, after all what being pregnant implies. "I never knew you were that serious about having a baby."

"I wasn't. It just happened."

"It just happened?" All I could do, at this point, was repeat everything she said.

"The rubber broke." She sort of giggled, and I could have killed her. I couldn't believe the words that had just come out of her mouth. The rubber broke. Rubber meant dick. I could not for the life of me, bear to imagine her beautiful cunt with all its delicious folds and crevices being hammered away at by some prick. Not to mention all the lesbians I knew who spent month, years even, trying to get pregnant. And then to Sharon, it "just happens."

"Aren't you happy you're finally going to be an aunt?" she asked. I saw the waitress out of the corner of my eye start to approach the table and then think better of it. You probably could have cut the vibe between me and Sharon with a knife.

"An aunt?" I still couldn't manage much more than being Sharon's echo.

"Of course." Sharon leaned forward, pushing her tea aside so she wouldn't drag the end of her scarf through it. "You were the most important person in my life for seven years. Of course I want you to be an aunt."

Were. There it was again, that lousy past tense. You were. Boy did that hurt. I couldn't believe she thought we could just let bygones be bygones and live happily ever after, her and the kid and the husband, and good old Aunt Johanna.

"What about what's-his-face? Does he approve of his child having a lesbian aunt?"

"Of course." Sharon chose to ignore my temporary memory loss concerning names. Or rather one name. His. "I've told him all about you."

I groaned. I could just see the two of them lying in bed side by side, with Sharon telling him all about me. All about us. Some guys get turned on by that stuff you know. Sharon would probably tell him what we used to do, and then he'd get a hard-on, and then...Oh God, I felt like I was going to get sick again.

"He's very understanding, Jo. In fact, he even had an affair with a man once."

"He's bi too?" My voice and eyebrows shot up. "Has he been tested for AIDS?"

"Of course." Sharon waved her hand as if she was shooing away a fly. "That was right after high school, when he was just playing around. But, yes, he did get tested, and everything's fine."

Just playing around? Is that what Sharon considered the last seven years?

"Jo." Now her hand was definitely seeking mine. I slid my hands off the table onto my lap, safely out of reach.

"Shit," she mumbled under her breath. "Jo," she said again. She always was persistent. "Listen to me. I'm still the same person. I'm still woman-identified. I still love women. In fact, I still think women are smarter, more creative, more passionate, more...more everything than men. You don't have to be a lesbian to be a feminist you know. It's just...." She let out a deep sigh. "Never mind. You wouldn't understand."

"Sharon." I decided to try the voice of reason. "If you think women are better than men in every way, how can you have your most intimate relationship with someone you think is inferior to you?"

"I never said inferior. Men are human beings you know." I knew it. I was just waiting for the men-are-people-too line. "Besides," she went on, "it's not what I *think*, it's what I *feel*." She pointed to her heart with the hand that had that damn ring on it. "When you were a teenager, you thought you had to be with men, right, but you *felt* you wanted to be with women. No one made you change. You couldn't *force* yourself to be attracted to men. Well, it's the same thing. During our last year together, I knew I should want to be with women, but I felt myself changing, being drawn towards men. And I couldn't stop it or deny it. I wanted to be with a man."

"It's not the same thing." My voice was coming out low and even. "It's not the same thing at all." I looked down at my lap and ran my fingers through my hair. For a second I felt like Sharon had been brainwashed by some cult, and I was the hired deprogrammer, out to save her. I knew logic wasn't going to work, but I had to try it anyway. "Sharon," I looked up at her. "Everyone tried to make me change. My parents, my teachers, hell, even some of the women I slept with."

"Exactly." She looked triumphant. "You see Jo, you're different than me. I'm not a fighter. *You pays your money, you makes your choice*, that's what my father used to say. You made your choice, I'm making mine, and each one has its price." She looked down at her hands then which were folded on the table. "The price of being a lesbian was just too high for me," she said, and I swear I thought I saw a tear leak out of her eye.

"Sharon." I leaned forward, resting my elbows on the table and trying to meet her gaze. "Don't you see?" I asked gently. "If the world didn't make it so hard for lesbians, you'd still be with me." I even reached across the table and stroked her arm. "We can make it, Babe. Sure it's tough, but if we love each other enough, it doesn't matter. Just because the world hates lesbians is no reason to deny your own happiness. That's way too high a price." I squeezed her arm and waited. Two fat tears definitely streaked down her face. I decided to go all out. "Hey, listen. Ditch the guy and I'll be your co-mother."

"No." She jerked her arm away. "I'm not going to have my kid go through this. I can just see her bringing her little friends home and they'll ask a few questions and the next thing you know it'll be all over her school and no one will be allowed to play with her. No Jo," she shook her head, "I made my choice."

Well, at least I had tried. I studied her face, tempted to wipe the tears from her cheeks, as I had done so many times before. "But won't you miss women?" I asked.

She shrugged. "I'm bi, not straight, remember? Maybe I'll have an affair. Married people do all the time."

Now I was confused. "Didn't you say a minute ago that you weren't attracted to women anymore?"

She shrugged again. "Things can change you know."

"But what about your husband?" I asked, pronouncing the two syllables distinctly.

She waved her hand, brushing aside that invisible fly again. "Rick lets me do whatever I want."

"He *lets* you?" God, she was even talking like a straight woman. "Sharon, Sharon, Sharon." Oh I just wanted to shake her. "What are you going to do, put an ad in the classifieds: 'Married woman looking for same, for discreet afternoon pleasure?' What do you think, Rick's gonna watch the baby while you trot off to Michigan next summer to have an affair? You're getting *married*. That means a lifetime commitment."

"So? You think lesbians have cornered the market on non-monogamy?"

"Sharon, you can't have everything. You can't live a straight life and have one foot in the lesbian world too."

"Jo, you're just as bad as my straight friends who dumped me when I came out, you know that? It's the same exact thing."

"Will you stop saying that? It's not the same thing." My voice rose, and this time I didn't care. "Sharon, do I have to give you a crash course in Oppression 101? You are joining the dominant culture. Are you still going to fight for gay rights? No. Are you going to make a statement at your wedding about straight privilege? No. Are you going to take your child to gay pride marches? It sure as hell doesn't sound like it. So have a nice life." I rose to go but I was stopped by Sharon's hand on my arm. I hate to admit that even now the touch of her skin still sent electric shocks through me, but it did.

"Don't leave," she said, and I made the mistake of looking into her eyes. "Jo, I miss you."

My heart started pounding and I slid back into the booth. Once a fool, always a fool, I suppose.

"Sharon, for the last time, listen to me. I still love you. I'm still *in*

love with you. I would take you back in a minute. You and the baby."
I'd never felt so vulnerable in my entire life.

She looked right at me and our eyes filled at the same time. She
reached for my hand and I let her take it. Her skin was so soft and
warm, I almost kissed her palm. Bi my ass, I thought to myself. Sharon was a woman's woman through and through.

"I can't Jo," she said, her voice barely a whisper. "But I'd like you
to be my baby's godmother."

I sighed deeply. That's some consolation prize, I thought, taking
my hand back and standing to go, for real this time. I fished around
in my pocket for some cash and tossed a buck on the table for my
coffee, hearing Sharon's words echo in my brain: *"You pays your
money, you makes your choice."*

"Jo?" She looked up at me.

I held my hands out, palms up, and lifted my shoulders, as if I was
pleading for mercy. "Sharon, how in the world can you expect me to
answer that question right now?"

She didn't give an inch. "Jo, it's important to me."

I lowered my hands in defeat. "I don't know, Sharon. Maybe. I
have to think about it. Hey." A lightbulb went on over my head.

"What?"

"What if you have a daughter and she grows up to be a lesbian?"

Sharon's eyes filled again. "I'd be awful proud," she whispered.
And I tell you, I left a mighty big piece of my heart sitting at that table
as I turned and walked out the door.

Perfectly Normal

Nice to meet you, Dr. Polansky. My name is Harriet. Oh you know that already, of course. I wasn't expecting a woman doctor. Well, life is full of surprises, isn't it? Yes, everything is fine, my room is just lovely. I love the light blue walls—robin's egg blue, they call it. It's the same color as our bedroom at home; isn't that a funny coincidence? Steve and I just painted it ourselves. See that tree outside my window? Just a minute before you came, a bird was singing in the branches—a robin I think; maybe she thought my walls were her eggs. Just a joke.

I bet you weren't expecting to find someone so cheerful and healthy, were you, Doctor? There's nothing wrong with me; I'm fine really. I'm perfectly normal in every way, as you can see. It wasn't my idea to come here, you know. It was Steve's. He wants me to put on a little weight. I don't think I really need to, but you know husbands—you've got to please them. Anyway, I could use a little rest—who couldn't?

Tell you about my weight? I'm five foot, seven inches and I weigh ninety-seven pounds. I've weighed ninety-seven pounds for three years now, ever since we got married. Was I thin before we got married? Of course—why do you think Steve married me in the first place? Steve would never date a fat girl. Never.

I wasn't always this thin. Before we got married I weighed one hundred and fifteen pounds, and then, once we set the date, I went on a diet so I'd look good on our wedding day. A girl only gets married once in her life—hopefully anyway, you never know these days—so of course I wanted to look my best. I got down to one hundred and seven pounds, and I wore a size three/four wedding dress. It was a beautiful dress—white lace sleeves, a low neckline, little pearl buttons going all the way down the front. Everyone said I looked just like a little doll. I'd wanted to get down to one hundred and five pounds, but somehow I couldn't get rid of those last two pounds.

When I was younger, dieting was easier somehow. I don't know, maybe your metabolism changes as you get older; it's much harder now for me to take off the weight. If it's like this at twenty-seven, imagine what it'll be like when I'm fifty! That's why I work so hard to stay thin. See this roll of flab around my stomach? It used to be much bigger. I know my stomach isn't as flat as it should be. I can't get rid of this roll for love or money. I do three hundred sit-ups every night and I still don't have a flat tummy. I keep trying, though. Never give up; the Lord hates a quitter. That's what I always say.

My relationship with Steve? Oh, he's wonderful. Really. I couldn't ask for a better husband. He lets me do whatever I want, and as long as the house is clean and his dinner's on the table, he doesn't complain. I like cooking for him—he's a real meat and potatoes man. When he comes home from work I sit and watch him eat. Do you know that man can consume a thousand calories in one sitting? Really. A hunk of steak, a baked potato with butter, salad and ice cream for dessert. Men have it so much easier than women. Steve never has to think about his weight, and I can gain five pounds just watching him eat dinner! I never eat with him. Usually I just drink black coffee or diet soda. I don't eat much for supper. A hard boiled egg and a raw carrot sometimes, or steamed spinach with half a cup of cottage cheese. I never eat breakfast or lunch. There's just no time. There's so much to do—I have to clean the house, do the laundry, shop for food and go to my aerobics class, of course. Steve says it's good for me to get out. He's afraid I'll get lonely in the house by myself all day, so I go to aerobics every afternoon. I usually do two or three classes. I know how important it is to stay fit.

Oh, those kind of relations. Well, Steve and I really don't have sex all that much. We did in the beginning of course—everyone does— but I don't know, I don't really think about it. I can't remember the last time Steve and I had sex. I think Steve's afraid he'll crush me or something. Sometimes in the night I'll roll over to hug him, and his hipbones will clank against mine, and it hurts. I think maybe that's why he wanted me to come here, so I'd gain weight and we could have sex again. Eventually we want children of course, everybody does. I haven't told Steve this, but I haven't got my period in a long time. I don't know why. Maybe you can run some tests, as long as I'm in here anyway.

Sometimes I think Steve goes to a prostitute once in a while. I wouldn't blame him if he did—it's different for men, you know. They have needs, not like women. I just don't care that much about it. Steve would never have an affair or anything, he simply adores me to pieces, but he might go to a prostitute every now and then, you know, to satisfy himself. I don't really mind. It's perfectly normal, that's what those places are for.

He reads *Playboy* and *Penthouse*, you know, men's magazines. He keeps them in the bottom drawer of his dresser. Sometimes when he's at work, I look at them. Pages and pages of gorgeous women, I'd give anything in the world to look like. I still have a lot of potential, you know. I'm not that old, and I have nice features, don't I? My eyes are pretty, everyone says so. You know, I would start eating a little more if you could guarantee that I'd gain weight in all the right places. I know everything would just go right to my stomach, and if there's one thing I cannot stand, it's a flabby belly. Ugh. I wouldn't mind a little padding on my derrière. That's why I'm sitting on this pillow—my bones hurt when I have to sit on a hard chair like this. At home I just sit on the couch or on the bed.

Siblings? Oh yes, I have a sister. Boy, do I have a sister! She's a real problem in our family. I don't talk about her all that much. She lives all the way across the country in San Francisco, so we don't see her very much, which is fine with me. You see, well, I don't tell many people this, but well, you're a doctor, I suppose it's all right to tell you our family secrets. Well, my sister is a lesbian. I know, it's a real tragedy, isn't it? At first I thought about it a lot; I mean, she is my baby sister. We grew up in the same house, and why one of us should turn out perfectly normal and the other one so sick is beyond me.

I think I know what happened, though. I think it's because she's fat. She always was a chubby kid, and then she was pretty big as a teenager, but now she's fat. And I mean fat. She's really let herself go the last couple of years, and I wouldn't be surprised if she weighed close to a hundred and fifty pounds by now. She's only five foot three, she takes after my mother's side of the family, so you can just imagine.

Maybe she's slimmed down recently. I doubt it, but you never know. I haven't seen her in three years, not since our wedding. She left home when she was seventeen, and moved to San Francisco. I was twenty at the time, so that was...oh, seven years ago. She never came to visit—she said the air fare was too expensive—so I didn't get to see her for four years, not until the night before our wedding.

To tell you the truth, I really didn't want to invite her. I know that's a horrible thing to say about your own sister, but anyone would feel the same way. I mean, how was I going to explain her to Steve's relatives? I had hardly even mentioned her to Steve, but how long could I keep my baby sister a secret? Steve was great about it though. I didn't want to tell him, but finally I got all my courage up, and told him my little sister was gay. And you know what he said? He said, "Oh, that's why you never talk about her," and then he changed the subject. He's so good that way—he never dwells on the bad things in life. He has a real positive attitude—that's one of the things I like about him.

He did look kind of shocked when he finally met my sister though. I guess I should have told him she was fat, but it was hard enough to tell him that she was queer. I was hoping that she'd slimmed down some, but I should have known better. She sends my mother pictures every year—my sister's really into photography. For the past few years, she's sent pictures of herself and a woman named Bev, who's her *friend*, if you know what I mean. And get this—Bev is even fatter than my sister is. Thank God the two of them found each other, that's what I say. I mean, who else would have them? Still, I know, it's very sad.

Oh, I tried to help her lose weight when we were growing up, but she never could stay on a diet. I taught her how to add up the calories of her food, how to use smaller plates so her meals would look bigger, how to drink a diet soda before she ate so she would be full before she started—you know, just basic common sense, things that everybody knows. But it never worked. So then I tried to teach her how to dress so at least she could look thinner than she was, even if she couldn't be thinner—you know, dark colors, no horizontal stripes, a necklace or a pretty scarf to draw the eyes away from her hips and up to her face. She really does have a pretty face—it's a shame, a crime really, that she's let herself go like that. She just doesn't seem to care.

I had so much to do before the wedding, I just didn't think about my sister coming until it was time to pick her up at the airport. I volunteered Steve and me to go because I don't really trust my sister— she's not too bright, and she doesn't know when to keep her mouth shut. Steve's brother said he would go, but what if she told him she was gay? I would just die. When she called to tell me she was coming, she said she was sorry but Bev couldn't make it—they couldn't afford two airfares. Thank God for that! Imagine having to explain the two of them.

Anyway, there we were, waiting at the United terminal, and out walks my sister, big as life. I could see all my years of fashion advice had been a complete waste, in one ear and out the other. My sister was wearing—get this—purple pants and a white, button-down blouse with these big purple irises splashed all over it. And, if that wasn't bad enough, she had her blouse tucked in! I could have died. Really, I couldn't believe it. I know Steve was in shock, because, like I said, I didn't warn him, and everyone else in my family is nice and thin, of course. And she had done something really awful to her hair, cut it very short in the front, almost like a boy's, and left one piece hanging long in the back and part of it had been bleached. Oh, I tell you, she was a sight. I wanted to get her out of there as quickly as possible—I'm sure people were staring—but she took her own sweet time. She had to introduce us to some girl she had met on the plane and then we had to wait while they exchanged phone numbers and hugged and kissed goodbye like they had known each other for years.

One thing that's strange about my sister is she makes friends wherever she goes. I've never understood it. I think people just feel sorry for her. Women mostly. She doesn't have any men friends, of course—you know why. I don't like women all that much myself. Oh, nothing personal, Doctor. It's just that men are, you know, more interesting. I have one or two girlfriends I go shopping with, but mostly I like being with Steve. When he goes out with the boys, I stay home alone. He goes out, not that much, oh, I don't know, maybe three times a week.

To tell you the truth, I'd rather watch a good TV program and improve my mind than hang out with a bunch of women. Mostly they sit around and gossip, and I'll tell you a little secret—some of them are very jealous of me. I mean Steve's a very handsome guy, and we're pretty well off, and I'm about the only one on the block who's kept my figure. All the girls want to know how I stay so thin. It's very easy. Willpower, I tell them, that's all. When you see something you want, you just don't have it. You feel much better about yourself that way. Also, I tell them, try and lose a few extra pounds—that's so you can have a little leeway. I'd like to weigh ninety-five, so I'd have five pounds to play with. That way, if I let myself go, for some reason and gained a pound or two, God forbid, I still wouldn't weigh over a hundred. But it doesn't work for everyone, I guess. It seems so simple—I don't know why. I used to think it depended on your type of genes or something, but then how would you explain my sister?

When Steve dropped us off at my parent's house that night, my sister went inside, and I stayed in the car to kiss him goodnight. He took me in his arms and—I'll never forget this—he said, "Promise me one thing." "What?" I asked. "Promise me you'll never get as fat as your sister." I was shocked. "You know I wouldn't," I said to him. "I'd rather die."

After Steve left I went into my old room, the room I shared with my sister when we were growing up. This would be the last night I'd ever sleep in it—the last night I'd sleep anywhere without Steve. Oh, I was so happy! Of course we'd slept together already; we even had our apartment by then, but we decided to be old-fashioned and not see each other until our wedding day. I think Steve went out with the boys to a strip joint or something. I don't mind. That's just the way men are.

My sister stayed downstairs to talk to my parents for a while and then she came upstairs to go to sleep. I didn't know what to say to her. When we were little we'd talk all night long—brush each other's hair, tell each other stories. She always wanted to be a famous photographer and travel all around the world taking pictures of everything. I wanted to be a ballerina. I took ballet lessons for a while—I still have my pink toeshoes with the satin laces—but then I stopped. I just got too fat. Ballerinas have to be really thin, much thinner than I'll ever be. I always had at least five extra pounds to lose, mostly around my belly, no matter how many sit-ups I do. It's a problem I've had all my life.

My sister still takes pictures though. It's not such a big deal. I mean she doesn't work for *Time* or *Newsweek* or anything. She works on a newspaper for people like her; I forget the name of it. Sometimes she sends pictures home to my mother. She's had some on the front page even, but I don't know, I don't think they're very good.

So there we were in our old bedroom, and my sister just got undressed, like she had nothing to be ashamed of. I couldn't believe it. I tried not to stare at her, but my God, I couldn't exactly ignore her; she took up half the room. And, I have to admit it, I wanted to look. Morbid curiosity, I guess. I won't go into the gory details, but take my word for it, Doctor, if you ever get a chance to look at a fat, naked woman, do yourself a favor. One look, and I guarantee, you'll never go off your diet again.

I'll never forget the sight of her as long as I live. Especially her breasts—they were positively vulgar, hanging down like, like...I don't know, eggplants or something. And her belly was so soft and round—if I didn't know better, I'd have sworn she was pregnant. She looked like she could bounce, she was so soft, like the Pillsbury Dough Boy, for God's sake. Really. You couldn't see a bone anywhere in her entire body.

I felt so bad for my sister, but she didn't seem to mind. She's used to it, I guess. She...you'll never believe this, but she sat down on her bed, stark naked, for half an hour, polishing her fingernails and toenails bright red. "Where'd you get the polish?" I asked her. "From Mama," she said. "I'm getting all dressed up for tomorrow." I felt so awful then, I didn't know what to do. I mean, I never dreamed she cared about her appearance at all—you certainly wouldn't know it by looking at her—so, to see her painting her nails as if that would make a difference was just absolutely pathetic.

I wanted to say something to her, you know, to help her. I thought Steve and I could offer to pay for some kind of operation. She could get her stomach stapled or her jaw wired shut or they could take out part of her intestines. Really, there are so many options these days, there's no excuse for anyone to be fat. But I was scared she'd take it the wrong way—you know how sensitive fat people are. So I just kept my mouth shut.

I was dying to ask her how much she weighed, but I couldn't figure out how to fit it into the conversation. I mean you can't just ask someone a thing like that, especially a fat person. It's like asking a woman her age. Some things are too private to talk about, even between sisters.

Later though, when she went to the bathroom, I did look at the labels in her clothes to see what size they were. She'd folded her pants and her blouse neatly and put them on top of her suitcase. Her shirt was an extra large, can you imagine? I'd rather die than wear a large anything, let alone an extra large. And her pants were a fifteen/sixteen. I felt horrible when I saw that. The least she could do was rip out the labels so she wouldn't have to be embarrassed.

Finally I asked her what she was going to wear to the wedding. I should have known not to ask. White pants and a red silk blouse that matched my mother's nail polish. I didn't know what to say. First of all, everyone knows fat people shouldn't wear white. I must have told her that at least a million times. And I could see right away she was planning on tucking her blouse in, which would be a disaster with her stomach and everything. But what could I do? We certainly couldn't take her shopping at eleven o'clock at night. I told her her outfit was very nice with my fingers crossed behind my back. One thing I've learned is that a little white lie to someone who's less fortunate than you isn't such a bad thing if it makes that person feel better.

While she was waiting for the second coat on her nails to dry, I opened the window. To get some fresh air, I told her, but really I was hoping the room would get drafty so she would cover herself up. A person can only take so much. Then I started hoping she would catch a cold and then she wouldn't be able to come to the wedding. I mean, how was I ever going to explain her to Steve's relatives? I know you're thinking that's a horrible thing to say about your own sister, but Doctor, I had spent months getting ready for my wedding. Months. Everything matched perfectly—the flowers, the bridesmaids' dresses, the ushers' tuxedos, and then my sister has to come along and ruin everything. Thank God I had sense enough not to ask her to be a bridesmaid. I mean, can you imagine with her punk hairdo and everything? My mother really wanted me to, but I just put my foot down.

I was hoping the photographer would have enough sense not to get her in any of the pictures, but no such luck. There she is, big as life, smiling all over the place. My sister is not shy, that's for sure. And she does have a beautiful smile—I'll give her that much. I used to be jealous of her smile, but now, well, there's nothing to be jealous of. Sure she seems happy, but everyone knows fat people are always jolly on the outside.

So finally she put on a long T-shirt, thank God. And then she asked me if I wanted to see some of her pictures. I said sure. What the hell. I mean, she probably doesn't have anyone else to show them to and, after all, she is my sister.

Well, first she showed me pictures from the newspaper she works on. They were pretty boring. A lot of them were from some kind of parade for people like her, and none of them knew anything about how to dress, believe me. Then she showed me about a million pictures of her and Bev, her friend, remember? My sister and Bev in their apartment, down at Fisherman's Wharf, on top of some mountain they'd climbed, cross country skiing, paddling a canoe, flying a kite, you name it, they've done it. There was even a picture of them at the beach. In bathing suits yet. They were lying side by side on a big purple towel, leaning up on their elbows, and all I could think about was whales. They looked like two beached whales.

Well, thank God they've found each other, that's all I can say. I mean, who else would have them, and anything is better than being alone. One thing bothered me though. My sister kept referring to Bev as her lover. I don't know why she just couldn't say friend. You see what I mean about not letting her around Steve's relatives? You never know what she's going to say next. What if she started talking about her lover to Steve's mother? I mean can you imagine? And can you imagine two women having sex together? Two fat women? Ugh.

I asked Steve about it, and he told me they use dildos. He showed me a picture in *Playboy*. One of them straps it on and then climbs on top of the other one. I can't imagine my sister doing that. I used to look at that issue of *Playboy* a lot when Steve wasn't home. On the page after the dildos, they showed two women doing sixty-nine. Really. I know you think I'm making this up, but I can show you. It's so disgusting, I just couldn't get over it. Steve has never put his thing in my mouth. Never. He puts it, you know, right down there where it belongs. And he's never put his mouth down there either. Ugh. We have perfectly normal sex, at least we used to, and I'm sure we will again.

My sister had pictures of other women too. Her friends. They were all like her, you know, I could just tell, but, thank God, not all of them were fat. There's still hope. She showed me pictures of her last birthday party—there must have been about fifty people there. All women of course. No man would be caught dead near her I'm sure. She says she doesn't like men, that she and Bev are really happy together, but I know she's just saying that. I know she'd give anything to be normal like me. Anyone would.

She asked me if I had any pictures, but all I had was one of Steve that I carry in my wallet. I never let anyone take my picture, everyone knows the camera adds at least ten pounds. And I certainly would never let anyone take a picture of me in a bathing suit. I haven't worn a bathing suit since junior high. Of course I had to let the photographer take pictures of me at the wedding. I learned a trick though, from a woman who went to modeling school. You lift your hands over your head like this, see, and you automatically look five pounds thinner. See how my stomach flattens and my ribs stick out? So that's what I did every time the photographer came near me, I just lifted my hands and pretended I was adjusting my veil.

After we finished looking at the pictures, my sister got kind of sappy. She took my hand and said, "Harriet, are you sure you're all right?" I could tell she wanted to have one of those heart-to-heart talks with me—she's very emotional, my sister. I told her of course I was all right. She just kept looking at me kind of funny, and then she said, "But Harriet, are you happy?"

"Of course I'm happy," I told her. Who wouldn't be happy the night before their own wedding?

"I'm worried about you," she said. "You've gotten so thin, you've lost so much weight. Have you been sick?"

Well, then, I realized she was just jealous. I wanted to tell her I was worried about her, she'd *gained* so much weight, but I didn't want to make her feel bad. So I just patted her hand and told her I was perfectly fine, just a little tired.

"You look tired," she said, putting her other hand on top of mine. "Are you sure you're taking care of yourself? Is there anything you want to tell me?"

"Of course I look tired," I told her. "Who wouldn't be tired with all the running around I've been doing lately? A wedding doesn't just happen all by itself. Let's go to bed," I said to her, "tomorrow's going to be a big day." She didn't say anything, but all of a sudden two big tears welled up in her eyes, and I just turned away. If there's one thing I can't stand, it's seeing a fat person cry. As soon as she fell asleep, I got down on the floor and did an extra three hundred sit-ups. I vowed that very night to get thin and to stay thin once and for all.

I didn't see my sister much the next day. Of course we had breakfast together with my parents. I had my usual black coffee and my sister had a piece of toast, an egg, and some orange juice. Funny, I thought she'd eat a lot more, but I guess she's too embarrassed to really eat in front of anyone. I know I would be if I looked like that. I didn't even get a chance to say goodbye to her. There were so many people at the wedding, and of course Steve and I left right afterwards for our honeymoon.

I did catch sight of my sister out of the corner of my eye a few times though. She'd brought along her camera, even though I'd told her not to—we'd hired a professional photographer—but she really seemed to want to, so I said okay. She probably knew no one would talk to her, so at least with her camera she'd have something to do.

She sent me some copies of the pictures she took, but they weren't very good. I wasn't even smiling in any of them. It's almost like she was just lurking around, waiting to catch me at my very worst, and then she'd snap her camera. It's just because she's jealous, that's all.

The pictures the photographer took are a hundred times better.

Do I want my sister to come visit me here? You've got to be kidding. Unless you mean to be a patient. Now that I could understand. She could really use a place like this to help her lose weight. Wouldn't that be funny—she'd lose weight and I'd gain. Though I only want to gain a pound or two at the most, and she could stand to lose a good fifty. Maybe if she got thin she could find some man to marry her. I'm sure that Bev would understand. I mean, I wish my sister could just be happy like me and Steve. I know I have a few problems—who doesn't—but at least I'm normal. Perfectly normal. I really do pity my sister.

Lunch time already? Oh, I never eat lunch. Just black coffee will be fine. I haven't had lunch in years. One thing I did want to ask you though—do you think I could get a VCR for my room? I brought my Jane Fonda workout tape along—I don't want to get flabby while I'm in here. If it's not possible, don't worry, I'll manage. I brought her workout book too, just in case. I put my membership at the aerobics club on hold, I can renew it as soon as I go home.

So I guess I'll get some rest now. It was nice meeting you, Doctor, I'm sure we'll speak again. I hope I didn't talk your ear off, I can be a real chatterbox. But as you can see, there's nothing at all the matter with me. I'll probably stay here a week, ten days at the most. I'm sure Steve misses me already. Of course I miss him terribly, but it's nice to just relax and not have to worry about things for a change.

Will you close the door on your way out, Doctor? I'm just going to do a few exercises, since I won't be going to aerobics this afternoon. I don't like to miss a day—before you know it, one day turns into two, then three, then four, and then it's all downhill from there. I don't want to wind up fat like my sister. Can you imagine me, dressed in horizontal stripes or bright purple pants, like I didn't care about anything, smiling right in front of the camera for all the world to see? Laughing on the outside and crying on the inside? Not me. I've been very lucky. I've got Steve, I've got my health, my looks. I've got...well, that's enough, isn't it? I mean, what more could any woman possibly want?

The Dating Game

I
The Party

"*Mazel tov.*" Chelsea kissed Darlene on the cheek and handed her a big bouquet of wild irises. "Where's the other half of this celebration?"

"She's in the kitchen getting more burgers. These are beautiful. Thanks Chelsea."

"Sure." Chelsea sat down on the chair nearest Darlene. "Irises are for seven years. Your next anniversary you get mums."

"What's after that?" Rachel called from across the yard. "Roses?"

Chelsea looked up. "I don't know. I'm running out of kinds of purple flowers."

"How about violets? Those are pretty." Jessie flopped onto a lawn chair with a paper plate full of food.

"Chelsea, do you know Jessie? Jessie, Chelsea. Chels, Jess."

"Hi." Jessie balanced her plate on her lap and reached over to shake Chelsea's hand.

"Hi, yourself." Chelsea smiled.

"You know everyone else, Chelsea, don't you?" Darlene asked.

Chelsea looked around. Phyllis and Rachel were playing frisbee, and Sunflower was turning some tofu hot dogs on the hibachi. "This is nice Darlene. I think it's great that you and Alice are throwing a party for your seventh. It should only happen to me."

"It will." Darlene patted her arm. "Have some food, Chels."

"Right. A girl's got to keep up her strength."

"That's right. You don't want to be all skin and bones when Ms. Right comes along."

Phyllis came over to the picnic table and picked up a paper plate. "No, you wanna be big and tough like me. You gotta be strong enough to sweep her off her feet, scoop her up in your arms...." She made a muscle, first with her left arm and then with her right.

"Oh Phyl, you're so butch." Rachel came up behind her and squeezed her biceps.

"So that's why you study karate," Darlene said.

"Sure." Phyllis heaped a small mound of potato salad onto her plate. "Watching those girls change in the dressing room every Thursday is the high point of my week."

"I'm telling your Sensei." Sunflower put a plate of tofu dogs on the table. "Who wants one of these?"

"No thanks, Sunflower, I'm waiting for the chicken," Chelsea said.

"Got any burgers for us real dykes?" Phyllis asked.

"Coming right up," Alice called. She walked across the yard with a paper plate covered with tin foil, squatted in front of the hibachi, and put on some hamburgers.

"Oh there's the other anniversary girl. *Mazel tov.*"

"Thanks, Chelsea."

"Hey, you shouldn't be cooking, Alice. It's your party," Jessie said. "Go sit down next to your girl. I'll watch these."

"Yeah, honey. Come sit next to me."

"Okay." Alice sat down on the grass in front of Darlene's chair with her back leaning against her legs.

"Look at that. The happy couple. Smile now." Sunflower held up her hands and clicked a pretend camera in front of her face.

"A match made in heaven." Chelsea sighed wistfully.

"How did you two meet, anyway?" Phyllis asked.

Alice swiveled around to face Darlene. "How did we meet, sweetheart?"

"You don't remember?" Darlene folded her arms. "Cancel this party."

"Now, now, just wait a minute. Let me think. It was in Michigan, wasn't it, at the Butch/Femme workshop, no, no, that was Emily...."

"Alice!" Darlene leaned forward, threatening to spill her beer over Alice's head.

"Only kidding, only kidding." Alice covered her head with her hands. "Of course I remember where we met. It was at Annie and Ellen's fifth-year anniversary party."

"Tell us what happened," Sunflower said.

"Yeah, did you know right away?" Chelsea asked.

"Well, I definitely thought Alice was cute right away," Darlene said, running her hands through Alice's hair. "She was wearing these tight black pants and a white button down shirt, with her brown shoes and one rhinestone earring in her left ear."

"You remember what I was wearing?" Alice turned sideways and leaned her elbow on Darlene's knee.

"Of course I do, sweetheart," Darlene said lovingly. "You've worn that outfit to practically every party we've been to in the last seven years." She laughed. "Of course I didn't know that then." Darlene paused. "Don't you remember what I was wearing?"

Alice ate some coleslaw, trying to think. "No."

"Well I do," Darlene said. "I was wearing my black sequin top and my hot pink skirt, you know the one that goes straight down, and black fishnet stockings and high heels."

"Wow." Phyllis rolled her eyes. "Too bad I wasn't at that party, Darlene. I would have snatched you right up."

"I had a date for the evening anyway," Darlene said.

"Well, that usually doesn't stop Phyllis," said Rachel.

"What do you mean?" Phyllis asked, indignant.

"Go on with your story," Chelsea said. "So you met at this party; then how did you two get together?"

"Wait a second, I want to hear this." Jessie came over and set a plate of burgers down in the center of the circle. When everyone had their food, Darlene continued.

"As I remember it, I called up Alice and asked her on a date."

"You did?" Rachel asked.

"That was brave," Sunflower said.

"But did she know it was a date-date, or did she just think it was a date?" Chelsea asked.

"How do you know the difference?" asked Phyllis.

"What is dating anyway?" Jessie asked.

"Dating means no sex," Sunflower said.

"Not always," Phyllis said.

"Especially in Phyllis' case," Rachel added.

"I think you're dating someone until you have sex with them," Chelsea said thoughtfully.

"Then what happens?" Jessie looked interested.

"Then you're going out with them."

"What does seeing someone mean?" Sunflower asked.

"That definitely means sex." Chelsea nodded her head.

"But how do you know if you're having an affair or a relationship?" asked Jessie.

"Or a non-committed relationship," Chelsea added. "I've had plenty of those."

"Alice, did you know it was a real date when Darlene asked you?" Rachel asked.

"Well, yeah, sort of," Alice said.

"There's a definite answer." Phyllis said.

"I always know when I'm going out on a date," Chelsea said.

"How?"

"Well, I have two barometers."

"Oh yeah? Do you keep them in your living room?" Alice asked.

"No Alice, listen. The first is how old I feel before she gets there. If I feel between twelve and sixteen, it's a sure sign. And the second is, how many times I change my clothes before I go."

"It's all in the inflection of your voice when you ask," Jessie said. "Like, for example, you could say, 'Would you like to go out on a date?'" Jessie voice was expressionless as if she were asking about the weather. "Or you could say," this time she spoke in a low Marlene Dietrich voice, "'Would you like to go out on a *date*.'"

Chelsea turned towards Jessie. "Ooh, I like that, I like that. Say that again."

"Oh I couldn't." Jessie looked down shyly.

"I went out on a date a few months ago," Rachel said.

"You did, Rach? You didn't tell me. That's great," Darlene said.

"What happened, Rachel?" asked Alice.

"Well, we went out for a drink, only she doesn't drink, so we had seltzer," Rachel said. "Then afterwards we took a walk down by the river and the moon came up and it was really romantic."

"Ooh, sounds hot!"

"Then what happened?"

"Then she took my hand and we stopped walking," Rachel said. "So there we were by the river, listening to the water and looking at the stars, not another soul in sight. Then she turned to me and I shut my eyes, all ready for her kiss...." Rachel shut her eyes and tilted back her head.

"And then what happened?"

Rachel opened her eyes and threw her hands up in the air. "Then she told me she was committed to being celibate for a year."

"Oh no!"

"Yep." Rachel sunk back into her chair.

Sunflower shook her head. "Only us lesbians."

"And she wanted to keep dating," Rachel added.

"What did she mean by celibate? No sex, no kissing, what?" Darlene asked.

"No nothing," Rachel said gloomily. "Just seltzer."

"I had a date recently," Chelsea said. "Only I didn't really know it was a date until halfway through."

"What happened?"

"I bumped into this friend of mine at the bookstore. She wasn't a good friend really, just a casual friend, you know? And we were both reading this notice about a Ferron concert and I said 'Wow, I'd really like to go to that,' and she said, 'Wanna go together?' and I said, 'Sure.'"

"So?"

"So halfway through the concert she just reached into my lap and started holding my hand."

"Oh no!"

"What did you do?"

"I didn't know what to do. What would you do?" Chelsea asked, looking around. "I waited a minute and then I let go of her hand to scratch my face and then I folded my arms."

"Did you talk about it?"

"Of course not. Then she called me the next day and we had to process the whole thing for two hours."

"Yuck," Alice said.

"That's weird," Phyllis said, "when friends start having crushes on you. That's happened to me."

"Everything's happened to you," Rachel reminded her.

"Well I can't help it if I'm so charming, right?" Phyllis shrugged her shoulders. "It was a woman on my softball team. She kept asking me for a ride home every Tuesday night after practice. And every week she'd sit closer and closer to me in the car."

"And then what happened?"

"Well, I didn't want to assume anything."

"Phyllis never assumes anything," Rachel said.

"Well maybe her car was broken."

"All summer?" Darlene asked. "C'mon, Phyllis."

"I wasn't sure. You know."

"Did she ask you to come in when you dropped her off?" Sunflower asked.

"Yeah, she always wanted to fix me dinner or something to drink, but I don't know, maybe she was just trying to be friendly."

"You don't fix someone dinner at nine-thirty just to be friendly," Darlene said.

"Especially after you've gone out for pizza already," Rachel added.

"Did you ever go out with her?" Chelsea asked.

"Well, then softball season ended. But she did call and invite me to go out to Tanglewood with her next week."

"Tanglewood—that's a sure sign."

"Yeah, lying on a blanket under the stars, listening to music— that's really romantic."

"Yeah, she's making a whole picnic—wine, cheese, apples. I don't know, though. You guys really think she's interested?"

"I'd say she's pretty interested," Sunflower said.

"I'd say she has a pretty high interest rate," said Chelsea. "But I don't know. I can't imagine sleeping with friends."

"That's what I always do," said Sunflower.

"Then what happens?" asked Chelsea. "I mean, do you stay friends with them?"

Sunflower thought for a moment. "No. Then we become lovers."

"And then what?" Chelsea asked. "I mean, assuming you break

up eventually."

"Not everyone breaks up eventually," Alice pointed out.

"That's right, sweetheart," Darlene added.

"Wow," Jessie said. "Do you realize that all of us, except you two are single? That's pretty rare at a lesbian party."

"I rest my case." Chelsea brushed a potato chip crumb off her skirt. "So, Sunflower, do you think it's easier to remain friends with someone after you break up if you were friends first?"

"Well, let's see. Yes. No. Well, not necessarily. I guess it depends."

"On what?"

"On how clear you were from the beginning about what you both wanted. Like if one of you wanted to have a fling and the other one wanted to get married, it could be trouble."

"It's hard to have a fling in this town." Jessie sighed and rested her chin on her fist.

"You have to go out of town for a fling," Phyllis said.

Rachel looked at her. "You don't."

"Tell us, Phyllis." Chelsea leaned forward in her chair. "Have you really had an out-of-town affair?"

Rachel choked on her beer and Phyllis glared at her. "Yeah, I've had maybe one or two."

Rachel gasped. "One or two?"

"Tell us about one. The last one."

"Well, let's see." Phyllis thought for a minute. "It was at this teacher's convention in Minneapolis last year."

"Minneapolis? I thought we were talking Boston here."

"Or New York."

"Or Northampton. I can't afford to go all the way to Minneapolis."

"So what happened?"

"Well, you know how these things are. We sat at the same table the first night at dinner, and it was pretty clear we were the only dykes there, so we took a walk after dinner and then we just slept together."

"Wait a minute, wait a minute," Chelsea said. "What do you mean, you just slept together?"

"Well we were in a hotel already, you know for the convention. So one thing just led to another, you know.... "

"No I don't know," said Chelsea. "That's the problem."

"It's just an organic process, Chels," Sunflower said.

"You mean like gardening?"

"Yeah, sort of." Sunflower picked a dandelion from the lawn and started playing with it. "I mean, first you have this feeling and then another feeling grows, and then another one grows, and then...." she shrugged her shoulders. "And then you just know."

"I disagree," Chelsea said. "I mean this just knowing stuff assumes an awful lot. I went to this JoAnn Loulin workshop last week, you know, she wrote that book *Lesbian Sex*?"

"Ooh, that was brave of you to go," Darlene said.

"Yeah, tell us about it," said Phyllis.

"Well, she said that lesbians have to talk to each other more about sex and dating. I mean, straight people always know when they're going out on a date, right? So she had us practice. We had to have lunch with three women we didn't know and talk about what we like in bed the whole time."

"Over lunch?" Darlene asked. "How did you eat?"

"Very s-l-o-w-l-y," Chelsea said with a laugh.

"I can tell you what I like in bed," Jessie said. "Soft flannel sheets, my teddy bear, a nice hot cup of tea...."

"Oh Jessie, you're hopeless, Phylilis said, "The woman means S-E-X."

"Give us an example, Chelsea," Rachel said.

Chelsea looked down into her lap. "Oh no, I couldn't."

"Oh c'mon."

"Yeah, c'mon Chelsea. You're among friends."

"Okay, let me think." Chelsea took a deep breath. Then she took another one. "Oh I can't."

"I know," Jessie said. "If Chelsea says something, we all have to say something."

"Yeah," Chelsea said. "That's fair. Okay you guys?"

"Okay."

"Okay." Everyone nodded.

"Well," Chelsea looked down into her lap again. "Someone in my group said, she said..." Chelsea paused and then her words came out all in one breath very fast: "...she-said-she-liked-having-both-her-breasts-sucked-at-the-same-time. Oh my God, I can't believe I just said that." Chelsea covered her face with her hands.

Darlene looked down at her chest. "Can you do that?"

"Obviously some of us can." Jessie stared at Chelsea who was blushing furiously.

Phyllis reached under her T-shirt which announced *an army of ex-lovers can not fail* on it, and squeezed her breasts together trying to get her nipples to meet a mouth's width apart. Her attempt failed. "Of course, you could be in bed with more than one person."

"Only you would think of that," Rachel said, shaking her head.

"You could be nursing two babies," Sunflower added.

"Or you could suck one of your own breasts and have your lover suck the other one," Alice said.

"Okay, okay, who's next?" Chelsea asked.

"Wait a minute, you said it was someone in your group. You didn't say it was you," Jessie said.

"Oh come on Jessie." Chelsea gave her a long look until she too was blushing. "Besides the workshop was confidential. I couldn't tell you what anyone else said."

"I think Phyllis should go next," Rachel said. "She's had the most experience."

"C'mon Rachel. It's been a long time."

"How long?"

"Oh, I don't know. Let me see." Phyllis started counting backwards on her fingers. "August, July, June, May, April. Five months. No, wait a minute. Do one night stands count?"

"I think Darlene and Alice should go next," Sunflower said, turning towards them. "Let us in on some secrets about how you two manage to stay together."

"No way!" Darlene said.

"Well, first of all, Darlene likes her back scratched," Alice said with a little smile. "And then she likes me to...."

"Alice!" Darlene clapped her hands over Alice's mouth. "Is nothing sacred?" She looked up at the darkening sky. "Hey, do you think we could get in one more game of volleyball before the sun goes down?"

"I'm too full to move," Rachel said.

"I gotta get going," said Phyllis.

"Got a date?" Sunflower asked.

"I'll never tell." Phyllis stood up and threw her paper plate in the trash.

Chelsea folded her arms. "Hey, wait a minute. You guys promised."

"Uh-oh. Now she's going to pout," Alice said.

"At our tenth year anniversary party, Chelsea," Darlene said, patting her on the shoulder. "I promise, everyone will tell all."

"Great," Phyllis said. "That gives us plenty of time to practice."

"Thanks for the party." Sunflower gave Darlene a hug. "It was really fun."

"Hey, it's only nine. How come everyone's leaving so soon?" Chelsea asked.

"Pssst. This is an anniversary party, Chelsea," Rachel said in a stage whisper. "Darlene and Alice want to do a little private celebrating."

"Oh, I get it." She got up from her chair and straightened out her skirt. "Well, come to think of it, I've got to get going myself." She hugged Alice and gave Darlene a kiss on the cheek. "See you."

"Bye."

Chelsea walked across the lawn and paused for a minute, leaning back on her car. The stars sure are pretty tonight, she thought, trying to pick out the Big Dipper.

"Hey, there's a girl with stars in her eyes," Sunflower said, putting her pack in the back seat of her car. "See you Chelsea." She pushed the driver's seat forward so Rachel and Phyllis could get into her car.

"Goodnight."

Chelsea watched them drive off, then reluctantly got into her own car. Just before she pulled out of the driveway, she was startled by Jessie tapping on her window. She rolled it down and smiled.

"I just wanted to tell you," Jessie said, leaning her forearm along the car door, "I thought it was really brave of you to say what you said, and I'm sorry no one else said something after they said that they would."

Chelsea looked up into Jessie's eyes. "Thanks." She paused. "Do you think I made a fool of myself?"

"No. Sometimes it's important to take a risk, that's all." Jessie kicked at the driveway with the toe of her sneaker without saying anything. Chelsea waited for a minute, feeling that Jessie wanted something, but she didn't know what. "Well goodnight, Jessie," she said.

Jessie didn't move. "Chelsea," she said softly, staring down at her own arm. "One thing I really like is sucking both women's breasts at the same time too. I mean one woman's both breasts. Ah, you know what I mean." Chelsea looked up to see Jessie blushing furiously before she turned and disappeared into the night.

II
The Phone Call(s)

It was Sunday morning around eleven. Chelsea sat at the kitchen table staring blankly into her bowl of yogurt. She hadn't slept very well. All that talk about sex and dating had made her lonely and restless. She'd tossed and turned, tried counting backwards from one hundred, and drinking catnip tea (one of Sunflower's suggestions for insomnia). Around four in the morning she'd finally given up, snapped on the light and begun to read. The words swam around the page though, and rearranged themselves into the profile of a face that looked remarkably like Jessie's.

"That woman is completely cute," Chelsea said aloud, dribbling some honey from a plastic bear into her yogurt. "God, I'd love to ask her out on a date."

Do it, a voice inside Chelsea's head urged her.

But I don't have her phone number, she answered it.

Ever hear of the phone book? the voice shot back.

Chelsea abandoned her yogurt for the moment, walked into the living room and picked up the phone book from the telephone stand. She started flipping through it and then remembered that she didn't even know Jessie's last name. "Damn." She put the phone book down and went back into the kitchen. I could always call Darlene, Chelsea thought, as she started to eat. She glanced up at the clock above the kitchen table. It's only eleven-twenty though. She's probably still in bed with Alice. That's what girls with girlfriends do on Sunday mornings.

Chelsea ate slowly thinking about last night's party. *I can't believe I said that about my breasts in front of everyone.* She stared at her rounded reflection on the back of her spoon. *So much for my reputation,* she told herself. *And what about what Jessie had said? Was she being nice, or was she interested? She certainly didn't have to say what she said. And furthermore, she went out of her way to say it.* "And furthermore," she told the Swedish ivy hanging in the window, "I just love it when a tough butch blushes like that."

Chelsea looked up at the clock again. All of seven minutes had passed. Almost eleven-thirty—how to fill up the day? Sundays were hard on a single girl living alone. *I wonder what Jessie's doing right now—just getting up, going out for a run maybe.* She seemed more the athletic type than the sit-at-home-with-bagels-and-the-New-York-Sunday-Times type. *Though she did seem pretty intellectual too. Or maybe it was just her wire-rimmed glasses.*

Maybe she's thinking about me this very second, Chelsea thought. *Maybe she's even contemplating giving me a ring. I'll send her some vibes.* Chelsea closed her eyes and placed her hands on her lap, palms facing up. *Earth to Jessie earth to Jessie,* she mouthed silently. *Call Chelsea Klein. Call Chelsea Klein. Five-five-five-two-three-seven-oh. That's five-five-five-two-three-seven-oh.* Chelsea waited but the phone didn't ring. She opened her eyes and sighed. "Oh well," she said.

Chelsea finished her yogurt, went into the living room again and dialed Darlene and Alice's number. The phone rang and rang. *They must be either fighting or fucking,* Chelsea thought, remembering her last relationship. *Of course, there always was the remote possibility that they really weren't home.*

She took a shower, watered the plants, *putzed* around the apartment for a while, and tried to call some friends to see if anyone wanted to go swimming. Since there was no one around to play with, she decided to be productive. She did her laundry and her food shopping for the week and even wrote a few letters, one to her brother who lived in New Jersey, and one to her Great Aunt Rose.

At six-thirty Chelsea tried Darlene again. After the third ring Darlene answered.

"Hello?"

"Hi Darlene."

"Hi Chelsea. What'cha doing?"

"Oh nothing much. Just sitting here fantasizing about that Jessie girl."

"Really, Chelsea? Do you have a crush on her?"

"I got it bad, Darlene. You know me, I always go for those strong silent butchy types." Chelsea paused. "I was, uh, thinking about asking her out on a date."

"That's a great idea, Chelsea. You want her phone number?"

"Oh I thought you'd never ask." Chelsea balanced the receiver between her ear and shoulder and picked up a pen. "Got it?"

"Wait a minute, I'm looking. Hey honey, guess what?" Chelsea heard her call, "Chelsea's going to ask Jessie out on a date."

"All right. Way to go Chelsea!" Alice called from across the room.

"Darlene, for God's sake, don't tell anyone," Chelsea said.

"Why not?"

"I don't know. You know how rumors spread all over this town."

"Faster than peanut butter," Darlene said. "Oh here it is. Five-five-five-three-two-three-one. Are you going to call her right now?"

"I guess so."

"Well, call me right back and tell me what she says."

If you only knew what she said, Chelsea thought, but she couldn't bring herself to say it. Instead she said, "Darlene, what if Jessie doesn't want to go out with me?"

"Why wouldn't she? You're a wonderful woman, Chelsea. She'll probably be flattered that you asked. And besides, Jessie's nice. You don't have to be afraid of her."

"But is she the kind of nice person that would go out with me just because she feels sorry for me?"

"Chel-sea," Darlene drawled. "You are being ridiculous."

"Okay, okay. Listen, I better call now before I lose my nerve."

"Okay. Don't forget to call me back."

"I won't. Bye." Chelsea hung up the phone and started pacing around the apartment. What should she say to Jessie on the phone? "Hi Jessie, this is Chelsea and I'm calling to ask you out on a date."

That sounded pretty good. A little formal maybe. Maybe I shouldn't say it right off. Maybe I should make a little small-talk first. You know, how'd you like the party last night, what'd you do today, wanna come over and suck both my breasts?

Chelsea walked back over to the phone, picked up the receiver and dialed. After one and half rings, Chelsea heard a click and then Jessie's voice. "Hi, you have reached five-five-five-three-two-three-one...."

Oh no, Chelsea thought, not an answering machine. Maybe I'll just hang up. No, I can't do that, I'm sure she'll know it was me. Oh my God, what should I say?

"...And leave a message after the beep." *Beep.*

"Hi Jessie, this is Chelsea and I'm calling to ask you to go out on a date. With me, I mean. That's date as in date, capital D-A-T-E, date. My number is five-five-five-two-three-seven-oh, and I'll be home all night. Bye." Chelsea hung up the phone and immediately called Darlene back.

"Hello?"

"Hi it's me again. I did it."

"So fast? What happened?"

"She wasn't home, but I left a message on her tape."

"Did you say you were calling about a date?"

"Yep."

"A date-date?"

"A date-date."

"Good for you. Well let me know if she calls you back."

"Okay, I will. Bye."

"Bye."

Chelsea hung up the phone again and stared at it. Now what should I do? Suddenly she felt very hyper. I could go for a walk, she thought. Or a bike ride. But I told her I'd be home all night. If she calls and I'm not here, she might think I'm a pathological liar or something. Then again, if she knows I'm just sitting here waiting by the phone, she'll think I'm a real jerk. I mean, that's about the most politically incorrect thing a feminist can do. Chelsea settled herself down on the living room couch with a new collection of lesbian short stories to try and distract herself. Every once in a while she'd look up at the clock —seven thirty, seven forty-five, eight fifteen, eight thirty-five....

At nine-forty Chelsea got into bed. So don't call me back, she thought, taking out her turquoise earrings and setting them down on her night stand. See if I care. Just as she got all settled in and cozy, the phone rang. "Coming, coming," Chelsea called, leaping out of bed, half excited and half annoyed. She picked up the phone anxiously.

"Hello?"

"Hi, is Chelsea there?"

"This is me."

"Hi Chelsea, this is Jessie."

"Hi." Chelsea wondered if she could hear her smiling.

"Well I got your message. You're a pretty brave woman."

"Well, you're not so timid yourself." Chelsea twirled the telephone cord around her finger. "So, um, would you like to go out on a date with me?"

"Yes, I'd love to."

"You would? Really?"

"Sure I would. Why do you act so surprised?"

"Oh, I don't know. You really want to go?"

"Yes, I really do. Do you?"

"Yes." Steady now, Chelsea old girl, she thought to herself. Just try and hold it together here. Details, she reminded herself. Time, place, activity. "Well, what's your schedule like?"

"Pretty booked until the end of the week. How about Saturday night?"

Bingo—date night. "Let me look in my calendar," Chelsea said, glancing around for her purse. Her Great Aunt Rose always told her to play hard to get. She flipped through her calendar to the current week and saw what she already knew; Saturday night was completely empty.

"Looks good," Chelsea said. "I'm writing you in."

"What should we do?" Jessie asked.

Chelsea sighed. "Oh God, I don't know. I didn't get that far."

"What do you mean?"

Chelsea ran her fingers through her hair. "Just thinking about calling and asking you out on a date took most of the day," she said, thinking, why am I telling her this?

"I love how honest you are," Jessie said.

Oh, that's why. "Thanks," said Chelsea. "Well, what do people do on dates? They eat dinner, they go to the movies...."

"I don't want to go to the movies," Jessie said. "That's not a good way to get to know each other."

She wants to get to know me, Chelsea thought happily. "Want to do dinner then?"

"Okay."

"I'm a lousy cook though."

"Me too."

"Wow, we have so much in common," Chelsea said with a laugh. Then she blushed, remembering what else they had in common. "Let's go out then. And then maybe we can go hear some music. How about six-thirty?"

"Fine. Should I pick you up?"

"That would be great. I live at sixteen Grove Street. A big brown house, second floor."

"Got it." Jessie paused. "You know, Chelsea, I was thinking of calling and asking you out on a date myself."

"You were? You really were?"

"Yes I really was. Why do you sound so surprised again?"

"You really were? You're not just saying that?"

"No. Why would I just say it?"

"To be nice. Darlene said you were nice."

Jessie laughed. "I'll have to thank her next time I see her."

"Oh I feel much better now," Chelsea said.

"Why?" Jessie asked. "Didn't you know I'd say yes?"

"Well, I didn't want to assume anything."

"Like Phyllis," Jessie said, and they both laughed. They talked a little longer then—about work, about what they'd been doing all summer, and before Chelsea knew it, it was eleven-fifteen. Jessie was really easy to talk to, and besides, her voice was incredibly sexy. She could seduce me by reading me her shopping list, Chelsea thought, as Jessie went on about a canoe trip she'd taken a month ago. Pomegranates, Chelsea thought. Strawberries, whipped cream. Dried

pears. Cat food. Applesauce. There was a pause and Chelsea realized that Jesse had stopped speaking and was waiting for her to answer a question she hadn't heard her ask.

"I'm sorry Jessie, what did you say?"

"Am I boring you?"

"Oh no, not at all. I'm just sort of spacey. I didn't get much sleep
last night."

"Me neither. Well I guess I'll let you go then. Sweet dreams."

"Yeah, see you Saturday. Thanks for calling back."

Jessie laughed. "Well thanks for calling."

"Okay, bye."

"Bye." Chelsea hung up the phone and drifted back to bed as
though she were walking on stars.

III
The Pep Talk

Darlene sat on the edge of Chelsea's bed watching her friend
rummage through her closet. Chelsea turned around to face Darlene
with a red jumpsuit in her hands. "How about this?"

"Ooh, that's nice, Chels. But do you want to be that dressed up?"

"I don't know Darl. Is Jessie the dress-up type?"

"No, not really. I mean, she'll look nice and everything, but she
won't be dressed up. She'll probably wear jeans and your basic white
button-down shirt. Ironed though. She's a great ironer."

"Oh God," Chelsea groaned. "Jeans and plain white shirts for the
next twenty years?"

"Twenty years? Chelsea girl, get a grip. We're talking about one
date, remember?"

"I remember, I remember." Chelsea hung the red jumpsuit back
in her closet. "Maybe this then, what do you think?" She held up a
bright blouse with flowers and tropical birds printed on it.

"I like that. Try it on."

Chelsea slipped her arms through the sleeves and buttoned it up.
"What do you think?"

Darlene stood up, walked over to Chelsea and straightened her
collar. "Ooh, maxi pads," she said, squeezing the shoulder pads over

Chelsea's shoulders. "Very convenient, in case you start to bleed."

"Or find yourself involved in a football game. Okay, now what pants?"

Darlene inspected Chelsea's closet. "These, I think," she said, taking out a pair of red pants, "and your red shoes."

"Okay." Chelsea unbuttoned the blouse and hung it back on a hanger.

"Now what accessories?" Darlene mumbled to herself as she opened the jewelry box on top of Chelsea's dresser. "Wow, look at these. Can I borrow them sometime?" She held some dangling rhinestone earrings up to her ears and admired herself in the mirror.

"Sure." Chelsea came over and stood behind Darlene. "I was thinking about these turquoise earrings," she said, lifting them out of the box.

"Yeah, wear those," Darlene said. "Blue's her favorite color. Now what about underwear?" She stepped back and opened the top drawer of Chelsea's dresser.

"Underwear is irrelevant. We're not going to sleep together right away. We're just going out on a date to get to know each other better."

"To see if you want to sleep together or not," Darlene added.

"Right. Oh my God, is that what we're doing?" Chelsea began to pace around the room.

Darlene turned towards Chelsea and held up a pair of bikini underwear in a black-and-orange jungle motif with Garfield on the front of them, baring his fangs. "Let's see now. How about these?"

"Give me those!" Chelsea lunged for her underwear which Darlene was holding high over her head, before tossing them over her shoulder.

"Or how about this?" Darlene pulled a black lace bra out of the drawer. "This is really pretty." Darlene put her hands in the cups of the bra to inspect the lace better. "My God, Chelsea, this is a cut-out bra." Her fingers slipped through the nipple hole. "You little slut! I didn't know you had one of these."

"Darlene! Give me that!" Chelsea's face was bright red as she grabbed the brassiere and shut the drawer. "Now come sit down with me before I have a heart attack." She pulled Darlene across the room and flopped down on the bed. "What time is it?"

"Three-thirty."

"Oh my God, she'll be here in three hours. Darlene, I'm going on a date—a real date. How am I going to live through it?"

"Relax, girl. You've survived worse things."

Chelsea threw herself down flat on her back and flung one arm over her head. She stared at the ceiling. "Darlene, do you think Jessie is really interested in me?"

"Well, I didn't want to tell you this, but she did call me up to tell me you had asked her out."

"She did? She did? Why didn't you tell me?" Chelsea sat up and grabbed Darlene's arm. "What'd she say? Did she sound happy?"

"Yeah, she sounded happy. And she said she was scared."

"Scared? Why would she be scared?"

"I don't know. Because she's going out on a date with you."

"Well I won't bite her or anything. Not on the first date anyway." Chelsea let go of Darlene's arm and lay back down on the bed again. "Now, if she said she was scared, that means she must like me, right? Because if she didn't like me, she wouldn't be scared."

"Such logical thinking." Darlene leaned back against Chelsea's pillow and stroked her friend's hair. "What are you going to do, anyway?"

"We're going out to dinner and then we're going to hear some music. That sounds pretty romantic, don't you think?" Chelsea asked anxiously. She reached for Darlene's hand and held it against her cheek. "Darlene, do you really think there's a teeny-weeny chance that she just might be interested in me?"

Darlene shook her head. "We are hitting an all time low in the area of self-esteem here. No Chelsea, I don't think she's interested in you at all. I think someone is paying her off to go out with you. Probably your mother."

"Don't even say that!" Chelsea shrieked. "You know how paranoid I am."

"Okay, okay. Only kidding."

"Oh God, what are we going to talk about? What'll I do when she gets here? This is exhausting," Chelsea moaned, curling up on her side.

"She's picking you up, right?" Darlene asked.

Chelsea nodded.

"So, it's very simple. You open the door," Darlene stood up and pantomimed opening a door, "and you take the flowers she's brought you...." Darlene reached for an imaginary bouquet of flowers.

"Darlene, she's not going to bring me flowers."

"What if she does?"

"What if she does?" Chelsea mumbled. "If she does, I say 'Flowers for me?'" Chelsea spoke in a high-pitched squeal. "But," she went on in a normal voice, "now I have something else to worry about. What if she doesn't bring me flowers?"

"You open the door," Darlene said, "and you say...."

"Jessie, where are the flowers?"

"Right." They both laughed.

"Okay, so we go out to dinner, we go hear the music, then what happens?"

"Then she brings you home."

"And then what? Do I kiss her goodnight?"

"It depends."

"Depends on what?"

"Well, do you think you'll hold hands?"

"I don't know." Chelsea moaned, moving over to rest her head on Darlene's lap. "So many decisions."

"Well you can't hold hands over dinner. You have to eat."

"Oh God." Chelsea looked up into Darlene's eyes. "What if I get food stuck in my teeth and I don't know it?"

"You better not eat any corn or chicken."

"No chicken or corn," Chelsea repeated. "What else is there?"

"I don't know Chels. Bring lots of toothpicks and go to the bathroom frequently."

"Darlene," Chelsea asked anxiously, "is she the kind that would tell me if I had food stuck in my teeth? I'd be so embarrassed, I would die." Chelsea stared up at the ceiling thoughtfully. "But would she not tell me to be polite and then I'd have made a fool of myself the whole time? Oh God, Darlene, I don't know if I can go through with this."

"Of course you can, Chelsea." Darlene looked down at her. "Relax, girl. Let me rub your head a little." Darlene started massaging Chelsea's temples with her fingers in a small circular motion.

"Umm, that feels good. Now, what were we talking about?"

"Kissing goodnight."

Chelsea's body jumped. "What did we decide?"

"Well, you made the first move by calling," Darlene said, stroking Chelsea's forehead. "So it's her move. But then again, if you hold hands....."

Chelsea opened her eyes to inspect her hands. "My hands are a mess," she groaned. "I knew I shouldn't have worked in the garden today."

Darlene ignored Chelsea's remark. "Let's say, for some reason, you go out to dinner, you go to the concert, you drive home, without holding hands...." Darlene paused to think. "Got it." She looked down at Chelsea. "Listen. If she brings you flowers you can kiss, but if she doesn't, you can't."

"Okay. Flowers, kisses, no flowers, no kisses. I can remember that." Chelsea furrowed her brow. "But I'll die if I don't kiss her."

Darlene smoothed Chelsea's forehead. "You won't die."

"Maybe I should kiss her when she comes to pick me up, just to get it over with?" Chelsea asked, hopefully.

"Nothing doing. God, it's amazing you ever got a girlfriend before you had me around to coach you."

"What if she honks? Is she the honking type?" Chelsea asked.

"She's not a goose, silly. She'll definitely come up. I don't know, Chelsea, you'll have to play it by ear."

"Do you think I should invite her up after the date, when she drops me off?"

"Depends."

"On what?" Chelsea threw up her hands in exasperation. "Everything depends on something."

"Well, it depends on whether she shuts the car off or not when she pulls into the driveway."

"Right. If she shuts it off, it's a good sign. What if she doesn't shut it off?"

"You tell her you had a nice time and you'd like to go out with her again."

"But what if we have a lousy time?"

"You tell her you had a lousy time and you don't want to go out with her again." Darlene gently nudged Chelsea's head off her lap. "Speaking of time, girl, it's almost five. I have to go. And you have a date to get ready for."

Chelsea sat up. "Don't remind me."

Darlene bent over and kissed Chelsea on the cheek. "Now call me Sunday morning and tell me everything. And don't worry. It'll be fine. Just be yourself."

"Okay I will. Thanks for coming over, Darlene."

"See you later."

"Bye." Chelsea watched Darlene's back disappear through her bedroom doorway, then leaped up, grabbed her clothes and rushed into the bathroom to take a shower.

IV
The Date

Six o'clock. Chelsea stood in front of the bathroom mirror, inspecting her face. "Bags under my eyes," she moaned, staring at herself. "Well what do you expect from someone who hasn't slept all week?" Chelsea ran a brush through her hair, trying to tame it into some kind of presentable shape. "I knew I should have gotten my hair cut," she groaned, tucking a stray strand behind her ear. Chelsea's hair was at its unruly length—long enough to part, but not long enough to pull back into a braid or do anything else to keep it out of her eyes. "Oh well, too late now," she said. "And besides, what if they'd really butchered me? Then I'd have to call and tell Jessie I couldn't go out with her."

Chelsea sighed. "C'mon, girl." She shut the bathroom light off, took herself by the hand and sat down on the living room couch. "It's enough already. You'll make yourself sick." She had, in fact, had the runs twice this week, though she'd barely eaten a thing. "This is not normal," she told herself, hugging a lavender pillow to her chest. "Not that I ever thought I was normal," she went on, "but this is ridiculous. I hardly know this woman." Chelsea stood up and started picking dead leaves off the spider plant hanging in the window. Her apartment was immaculately clean. Maybe too clean. Chelsea looked around and frowned slightly. Maybe I should mess it up a little, she thought. I don't want her to think I'm compulsive or anything.

She walked over to her bookshelf. Maybe some books scattered around. That'll impress her. She's the intellectual type. Chelsea studied the titles; *Lesbian Psychologies,* no, too dry and academic. *Lesbian Sex*—definitely not. How about some fiction, then? Dostoevsky? No, too morbid. Jane Rule, I think, but for God's sake not *Desert of the Heart.* That's too obvious. Chelsea selected a collection of Jane Rule's short stories and set it down on the coffee table.

Six-twenty. She'd be there in ten minutes. Chelsea wondered if she'd be on time. She seemed the punctual type. And Darlene said she wouldn't honk. What to be doing when she arrived? Listening to music? No, then she might not hear her knock. Oh God, music, Chelsea thought. What if she asks me to find a station on the radio and I pick out something nerdy? Chelsea walked back into the kitchen, grabbed a sponge from the sink and started wiping the table. I can always clean, she thought, picking at a drop of wax with her thumbnail. I could always scrub the stove. Or polish the toaster.

Six twenty-five. What if she was early? She could be here any second. Sit down, Chelsea, before you make yourself sick. Oh my God, what if I get car sick, she asked herself. What if I open my mouth to say hello and I vomit? Chelsea threw the sponge into the kitchen sink and sank down into a kitchen chair. Oh God, please just don't let me make an ass of myself, she prayed, holding her head in her hands.

There was a knock at the door. Chelsea jerked her head up and looked at the clock. Six-thirty exactly. She took three deep breaths which didn't calm her down at all, and ran to open the front door.

"Hi."

"Hi. Come on in." Chelsea stepped aside making room for Jessie to pass. She felt her face break into a wide open smile at the sight of her. She was wearing just what Darlene had predicted—jeans, a white shirt and black Reeboks.

Chelsea realized she was staring, and looked down shyly. Then she forced herself to look up. "Hi," she said again and then blushed. "Oh, I said that already."

"You can say it again if you want," Jessie said, smiling at her.

"Oh, I couldn't," Chelsea turned away shyly.

Jessie looked around."Nice place you got here. What a great toaster." She walked over to the counter and inspected Chelsea's 40's toaster that had two side doors that opened and only toasted bread one side at a time.

Chelsea leaned her back against the stove and folded her arms. "Yeah, it was my mother's. She was gonna throw it away but I nabbed it. She couldn't believe I wanted it. My mother thinks the microwave is the greatest invention since the wheel."

Jessie made a face. "Yuck. I'm an old fashioned girl."

Chelsea smiled. "Me too." They held each other's gaze for a moment, and then simultaneously started moving towards each other. They stopped about two feet apart. Now what? I am going to die, Chelsea thought. Should I give her a hug? I have never felt so graceless in my entire life.

"Well, should we go?" Jessie asked, not moving any closer, but not backing away either.

"Yeah, I'm ready," Chelsea said without moving. "Jessie," she said, taking a deep breath. "I'm really nervous. I mean really, really, really, *really* nervous. I don't know why, and I probably shouldn't be telling you this, but I just wanted you to know."

"I'm so glad you said that." Jessie shoved her hands into her pockets and looked down at her shoes. "Listen, I probably shouldn't tell you this either, but I spent about two hours trying to decide whether to bring you flowers or not. I almost did, but then I thought it would be too obvious. Now I wish I had."

Oh no, Chelsea thought, remembering the guidelines she and Darlene had come up with: flowers, kisses; no flowers, no kisses. But she almost brought me flowers. Does that mean I can almost kiss her? "Well, it's the thought that counts," Chelsea said, trying to comfort them both.

"Next time, I'll bring a dozen roses," Jessie said, looking up. "How's that?"

"Great." Chelsea looked down shyly. She said next time. Does that mean there'll be a next time? "Well, I'm ready," Chelsea said, grabbing her purse. "Are you?"

"Yeah. Let's go." Jessie moved towards the door and Chelsea followed her out and down the steps. Once they were outside, Chelsea felt a little more relaxed. Jessie opened the car door for her which endeared her to Chelsea's heart forever. I love old fashioned butches, she thought, as Jessie slid behind the wheel. They really know the right way to treat a girl.

"So, where are we going?" Chelsea asked.

"How about Monaco's? Do you like Italian food?"

"Yeah, that would be great."

Jessie backed out of Chelsea's driveway, looking over her shoulder and resting her arm across the back of the seat, letting her hand lightly touch Chelsea's upper arm. Oh my God, if she leaves her hand there I am going to die, Chelsea thought, scarcely daring to breathe. Luckily her life was saved by the fact that Jessie had to use her right hand to shift the car into first.

"So, um, how many times did you change your clothes before you came over?" Chelsea stared at Jessie's profile as she drove.

Jessie laughed. "You sure don't pull any punches, do you?" She took her eyes off the road to look at Chelsea for a minute, and Chelsea felt her belly jump. "Oh I considered, two, maybe three shirts. But I did spend about an hour ironing."

"You did a great job," Chelsea said, following the crease that ran down the arm of Jessie's shirt with her finger. Oh God, I'm touching her. Stop, she told herself, pulling her hand away and dropping it into her lap. "Well, I'm not much of an ironer myself, but I did spend most of today trying on my entire wardrobe in front of Darlene."

"You look really nice," Jessie said, turning to look at Chelsea again. "Darlene's got good taste."

"So do you."

"Why do you say that?"

"Because you're going out on a date with me."

They both laughed. She's nice, Chelsea thought, as they pulled into the parking lot of the restaurant. She's really nice. I can be myself with her. Well who else would you be, asked a voice inside Chelsea's head. Greta Garbo? Amelia Earhart? Gertrude Stein?

They entered the restaurant and sat down at a corner table with a burning fat red candle and a small bouquet of zinnias on it. The restaurant was fairly empty, much to Chelsea's relief. She didn't want this hitting the dyke grapevine. Not yet, anyway, she thought, as Jessie handed her a menu. Now, nothing with garlic, she reminded herself. And no spaghetti, that's too hard to eat. And eat slowly. You don't want to burn your mouth.

Jessie watched Chelsea with a little smile. "You look pretty in this light."

Chelsea forced herself to not lower her eyes. "You don't pull any punches either," she mumbled. "I mean, thank you."

"Thank you," Jesse said.

"For what?"

"For being pretty. For being you. For asking me out on a date."

"Thank you for coming. For coming out, I mean. With me. On a date I mean. Oh, you know what I mean." Chelsea shook her head. "I feel so incredibly awkward. Do you? I mean, why is this so hard?"

"Because we're being honest with each other," Jessie said.

"Because we're not jumping right into bed," Chelsea added, wishing they were.

"Right," Jessie said, tapping her fork lightly on the table. "It's easy just to go to bed with someone."

"It is?" Chelsea asked.

"Yeah. I don't want to do that anymore."

"You don't?" Then why are we out on a date, Chelsea wanted to add.

"No, I don't. I mean, I do. I'm very attracted to you Chelsea, you know that, don't you?"

Chelsea nodded, thinking, I can't believe she just said that.

"I just want to take my time and get to know you better, and see what kind of relationship develops."

Chelsea gripped the table. Oh my God—the R word. She used the R word. I am going to die.

"I really like courting," Chelsea said. "Flowers, love letters, you know, the whole bit."

"Oh, so you're a romantic, huh?"

Chelsea nodded. "Incurably. Completely."

Jessie smiled. "A woman after my own heart."

"You'd better believe it," Chelsea said, looking right into Jessie's eyes.

Luckily the waitperson came just then to take their order, for Chelsea's smile was so big she was afraid her face would fall off. Chelsea ordered a cold tortellini salad, and Jessie ordered shrimp scampi. After the waitperson left, they sat in silence for a few minutes. Chelsea sipped her water and Jessie fiddled with the perfectly ironed cuffs of her shirt. Every time one of them looked up, the other one would look away, only to look back again a few seconds later to see the other one glancing away again. Finally Chelsea cleared her throat.

"So, um, do you come often? I mean, do you come here often? To eat, I mean. You know, food. Oh God, Jessie, I didn't mean it, it just slipped out, you know what I mean?" Chelsea hid her face in her hands and took a deep breath before she dared look across the table. "Am I impressing you with my articuless-ness? Is that a word? I mean my ability to articulate?"

Jessie laughed. "Chelsea, you're lovely."

Lovely. Had anyone ever called her lovely? It was such a well, such a lovely word. "I am?"

"Yes you are. Lovely and funny and charming and I really like you."

"You do?"

"Yes I do."

"I like you too." Chelsea reached across the table for Jessie's hand which was slowly sliding towards her. They held hands and gazed at each other until their food arrived. Thank God for food, Chelsea thought, spreading her napkin on her lap. She began to eat, and though the tortellini salad was wonderful, it could have been sauteed wood chips, for all Chelsea noticed.

"So, um, what is your thesis about anyway?" Chelsea asked, remembering Jessie had told her over the phone she was a doctoral student.

"Spiders."

"Spiders?"

"Yeah. I mean, it's a little more complicated than that. That's my one word answer. I don't want to bore you about it."

"Oh I wouldn't be bored," Chelsea reassured her.

"But I would. After five years, I get pretty tired of talking about it."

"Well, I hate spiders myself," Chelsea said. "I try not to kill them, but they really creep me out. Do you do experiments on them and stuff? Oh, I'm sorry," she put down her fork. "Chelsea, the woman said she didn't want to talk about it. Don't you listen?" She shook her head. "Jessie, I really am a good listener and I do respect boundaries. Really. You can ask Darlene. She'll vouch for me."

"She already has."

"What do you mean?"

Jessie shifted her weight. "Well, I, um, called Darlene to ask her about something else, and we talked a little bit about you."

"You did? What did she say?"

"Let's see." Jessie paused, a piece of shrimp in mid-air. "Well, she said you were very funny, a mediocre cook specializing in peanut butter sandwiches, and a lousy driver."

"A lousy driver? Oh no. Jessie, did she tell you how we met?" Jessie nodded. "Oh no, I am so embarrassed." Chelsea put down her fork and touched Jessie's arm. "It's not true. I'm not a lousy driver. I mean, I've never had an accident or anything. I'm just a lousy parker."

Four years ago Chelsea had gone to see Sweet Honey In The Rock. In front of the theatre she had spent about ten minutes in four vain attempts trying to parallel park her little Toyota. Finally, Darlene had stepped out of line, rapped on Chelsea's window and volunteered to do it for her. Chelsea had stepped out of the car, embarrassed but grateful.

"She said the space was big enough for a bus," Jessie said.

"A bus? It was not." Chelsea frowned. "A small truck, maybe. Oh, I am going to kill her the minute I get home. Well, maybe not the very minute," she added, remembering that she still didn't know what the night had in store for her. "But tomorrow for sure." She put a tortellini into her mouth and paused.

"So, um, Jessie, you were asking Darlene questions about me?"

Jessie swallowed a bite of shrimp and nodded.

"Well, I never assume anything, but could that mean that you're interested in me?"

Jessie took a sip of water. "I'd say there's a pretty high interest rate on this side of the table."

Chelsea laughed. "You really listen, don't you? God, I love being quoted to myself." She wrinkled her nose. "Do you think that's a really weird thing to say?"

They finished their dinner, eating slowly, talking and not talking, looking and not looking at each other. After they paid the check they left the restaurant and got into the car. Jessie hesitated before starting the engine.

"Chelsea, I have a confession to make."

Uh-oh. She has another girl friend. I knew it. Chelsea felt the tortellini shift in her stomach.

"Well, there are two things. First of all, I didn't call Darlene to talk about anything else. I called to ask about you."

One down and one to go, Chelsea thought. "And?"

"And, I don't really want to go listen to music."

"You don't?" Oh well, Chelsea thought, glumly. The night is still young. Maybe I can catch a late movie on TV or something.

"No. Would you like to take a walk down by the river instead?"

Chelsea looked up hopefully. "And look at the stars maybe?"

"You have this knack for saying just what I'm too scared to say." Jessie smiled at Chelsea.

"What else are you too scared to say?" she whispered.

Jessie looked into her eyes. "Can I kiss you?"

"Yes."

Jessie moved towards her then and took Chelsea in her arms. They hesitated for a moment, each feeling the pounding of her heart. Then they moved at the same time and bumped noses.

"I don't believe this," Chelsea mumbled, tilting her head to the side and touching Jessie's lips lightly with her own. Gingerly at first, and then a little more forcefully, they kissed for a few minutes.

"Hey, I thought you were a lousy parker," Jessie whispered, pulling back a little to look at Chelsea.

"You're lovely," Chelsea answered, moving forward to kiss Jessie again. She felt electric desire shooting through her veins and pulled away gently.

"We better stop," she murmured, "or I won't be able to."

Jessie nodded. "Right. We're courting, remember?"

"How could I forget?" Chelsea took Jessie's hand and started playing with her fingers. Such strong hands, she thought. "Um, ac-

cording to the official Guide to Lesbian Dating, how long does courting usually last?"

"About three hours." Jessie interlaced her fingers with Chelsea's.

Chelsea looked up. "You got a watch?"

"No," Jessie answered. "You got time?"

"I got all the time in the world, angel." Chelsea leaned back
against the seat, so happy she thought she would burst. Jessie started
up the car and pulled out of the parking lot, heading for the stars.

V

Postscript: Three Years Later

"So that's how you two really got together? I always wondered,"
Sunflower said, chopping up a giant zucchini from her garden. "Because of Darlene and Alice's party three years ago?" She was standing in Darlene and Alice's kitchen along with Rachel, Phyllis, Chelsea
and Jessie. It was Alice and Darlene's tenth year anniversary party,
and since it was raining, the party had to be indoors this year. Darlene was in the living room picking out some music to put on, and
Alice was rummaging around the pantry, looking for a corkscrew.

"God, I remember that party," Rachel said. "I still haven't been
able to find anyone to suck both my breasts at once."

"Watch your language," Alice said, emerging from the pantry,
corkscrew in hand. "I am shocked."

"You could always do it yourself," Phyllis said.

Rachel nodded. "That's true. We lesbians are so independent. I
should write the lesbian do-it-yourself sex book. Goddess knows, we
lesbians do everything else ourselves—tune up our own cars, build
our own houses...."

"Grow our own food," Sunflower held up a fat juicy tomato from
her garden.

"Deejay our own anniversary parties," Darlene said, coming into
the kitchen as Linda Tillery's voice came blasting out of the speakers.

"Well, not everything," Chelsea said, putting her arm around Jessie's waist and kissing her on the cheek.

"You newlyweds are disgusting," Phyllis said, making a face.

"You're just jealous," Jessie said, squeezing Chelsea to her side.

"And anyway, we're not newlyweds. It's been three years."

"And the honeymoon isn't even over," Chelsea said, looking directly into Jessie's eyes.

"Oh Goddess, gag me with an organic cauliflower," Sunflower said, breaking the vegetable into little flowerettes.

"Just how long did you two actually court?" Phyllis asked.

"Oh, not long," Jessie said.

"Not long? It was practically forever." Chelsea disengaged herself from Jessie's embrace and started counting the months on her fingers. "Let's see. Our first date was in August. August, September, October, November, December. Five months."

"Five months! That's a world record," Phyllis exclaimed.

"Who made the first move?" Alice asked.

"I did," Chelsea said.

"She said if she didn't make love by the end of the year she'd forget how," Jessie said.

Darlene hooted. "And you believed her?"

Jessie looked over at Chelsea. "Not really. But I didn't want to take the risk."

"How did you guys wait so long?" Phyllis asked, munching on a carrot stick.

"My God, Phyllis. Five months isn't all that long. Some of us have been waiting for years," Rachel said.

"We had a few things to work out first," Chelsea said.

"Like what?"

"Jessie wanted a fling and I was looking to get married."

"So what did you do?"

Chelsea shrugged her shoulders. "Well, first we flung and then we got married."

"So much for dating." Sunflower set the platter of chopped vegetables and hummus on the table.

"Who needs to keep dating when you've found what you're looking for?" Jessie asked.

"You two are really nauseating. That's the last time I ever match up two of my friends," Alice said.

"You didn't match them up. I did," Darlene said. "Anyway they're both just hopeless romantics."

"We matched ourselves up," Jessie pointed out.

"And that's not hopeless. It's hopeful. Hopeful romantics." Chelsea added.

"I'm still looking for Ms. Right," Sunflower said. "I hope I'm not the only single girl at this party next year."

"You won't be." Rachel handed out paper plates to everyone. "If I'm invited, that is."

"Rachel, of course you'll be invited," Darlene said.

"Well, I never assume anything," Rachel said. "I learned that at one of your parties."

"Wasn't that the party when Chelsea said she assumed that everyone broke up eventually?" Phyllis asked, piling some tabouli onto her plate.

"Phyllis, you know I hate being quoted to myself." Chelsea poked her with her elbow. "Besides, Alice and Darlene are still together."

Darlene handed Alice a plate. "We sure are."

"I rest my case." Chelsea filled a glass with iced tea.

"I guess some couples do stay together," Phyllis admitted, sitting down with her plate.

"I think it's wonderful," Rachel said.

"A toast! A toast!" Sunflower popped the cork on the champagne, filled seven glasses and passed them around.

"To the happy couple," Sunflower raised her glass.

"To thirty-eight more years of celibacy," Rachel mumbled.

"Rachel, it hasn't been thirty-eight years." Phyllis laughed. "You haven't been celibate since you were born."

"It sure seems that way," Rachel said with a sigh.

"To our friends." Darlene looked around smiling.

"Hear, hear," Alice added.

"And to true romantics everywhere." Chelsea clinked her glass against Jessie's.

"I'll drink to that," Darlene clinked her glass against Alice's.

"I won't," said Phyllis.

"You will too." Rachel lightly punched her.

"To all romantics and cynics," Sunflower said. "Is that better?"

"Yeah." Phyllis touched her glass to Sunflower's. "May they continue to find each other."

"And may one of them find me," Rachel added.

Everyone laughed. "Here's to all of us and our happiness," Jessie said, "whether we're single ...."

"Or double," interrupted Sunflower. Then laughing, everyone clinked glasses, downed their champagne and moved into the living room to enjoy the rest of the party.

Holding On

May 1st

Dear Nicky;
   Now that you're finally gone, I can tell you how I really feel (and don't give me shit about waiting until you're gone to tell you). I am pissed! How could you move to Colorado and leave me two thousand miles behind? I can't believe you're gone. I'm glad I didn't help you load up your van and I hope it breaks down in the middle of nowhere and you see what an idiotic mistake you're making and you turn around and COME HOME where you belong. Nicky, I don't even care that we're not lovers anymore—don't flatter yourself—six months is long enough to get over anyone. Nicky, you're my friend, and I need you here. New York just isn't the same without you.
   Now that I've gotten that off my buxom, hairy chest— how are you? I bet Athena is happy to be out of the city, poor puppy. Make sure she wears her seatbelt!
   Your plants are fine (I know it's only been two hours, but you know how I am with plants). I don't know what I'm going to do today, maybe take a walk up to Central Park, or maybe catch a movie. There's a dance tonight, but I doubt I'll go—who would I dance with? You spoiled everything by being such a good dancer, you know that? Maybe (and I'll only admit this because by now you're at least a hundred miles away) maybe I'm not completely over you.
                                        Love, Lainie
   P.S. Don't kid yourself, I'm still pissed as shit (but I wouldn't be if you came home).

May 2nd

Dear Nicks;

I checked my mailbox today but nothing from you. So what if you haven't even been gone twenty-four hours and there's no mail on Sundays anyway? I can still hope, can't I? Why am I asking your permission anyway? I thought I stopped that when we broke up. Correction: when you broke up with me.

Guess I'm still pissed. Last night I went to Jocelyn and Wanda's house for supper and they're so goddamn happy I could have shit. Remember they got together a week after we did, and we laughed and said it would never last? Well, look who's laughing now. They barely took their eyes (and hands) off each other all evening, which is pretty rare in the lesbo community after two and a half years. I kept thinking that that's how we could be, but no-o-o-o, you had to break it off. Why? I still don't get it. I know you explained it a million and one times, but it didn't seem so bad to me. No relationship is perfect. We could have worked it out. I didn't drink or do drugs or run around or hit you or anything. No big no-no's. I thought we had it pretty good. And I know you still love me—why else wouldn't you be able to look at me when you told me you were leaving? I saw that tear leak out of your eye.

All this bullshit about finding yourself—Nicole, you're not seventeen, you're twenty-seven years old for God's sake. So what if you've never lived out of New York before. Why start now? It's time for you to grow up and settle down. And you'll never find anyone better than me.

End of lecture. I wound up crashing on J & W's couch because it got late and I wasn't up for dealing with the subway or spending half the grocery money on a cab. Maybe you're right, maybe leaving New York is a good idea, but Colorado? What's out there besides mountains and cowboys? Any dykes?

Give Athena a smooch for me, and keep her collar on. I've seen too many Lassie reruns, where Lassie walks hundreds of miles searching for Timmy after somehow they got separated. I'd hate to see Athena wandering around the Bowery looking for you.

Love, L.

May 3rd

Dear Nicks;

I'm typing this on the word processor at work—made a file this morning: LETTERS: NICK. Office work is such a drag. I know, I know, if I hate it so much, why don't I quit complaining and change my life? Shit or get off the pot? Well Nicky, some of us can't just up and leave our jobs, friends and lovers at the drop of a hat. Some of us are constipated I guess, that's why we're stuck on the good old proverbial pot. But I got news for you. Some of us are proud that we've stayed in the same place for all of our lives.

Advantages:

1) Rent-controlled apartment

2) Four weeks paid vacation (which I just might spend in Colorado if you beg me)

3) Seniority (in other words, I don't have to make the coffee for the entire office any more)

4) Long time friends

5) know where the best and cheapest restaurants are (including Chinese)

6) no one laughs at your New York accent

7) your mail doesn't get lost because you're always changing your address

Disadvantages:

1) my mother always knows where to find me

So want to come up to the office for lunch today? We can go to that health food store around the corner and get some sandwiches and take them to the park.

Oh God, Arthur just came in with a box of cannolis for Estelle. This is always the high point of my day. Have I ever told you about Arthur and Estelle? (Of course I have, but one advantage of being pen pals, which is how I'm currently defining our relationship, is that you can't say "Lai-n-n-n-ie, you told me that story already." You, my dear, are a captive audience.) (Unless of course you throw my letters away without reading them and I'd never know I suppose, but what a waste of great literature that would be.)

Anyway, Arthur. He is so fucking pathetic. He comes in everyday
and brings a box of cannolis for Estelle. He puts them on her desk
and he goes, "I brought you some cannolis, Estelle." And she barely
looks up from her keyboard and goes, "Thanks Arthur, but I don't
like cannolis." (Who knows, maybe she's not doing her work either.
Maybe she's writing a letter to her ex-lover, but can you imagine Estelle with an ex-lover? No, you probably can't, since you've never
met her, but take my word for it, anyone who wears polyester blous-
es with bows attached at the neck in the 1980's probably doesn't
have an ex-lover.) Listen to me, Ms. Judgmental. Maybe old Estelle
has a wilder sex life than I do, which wouldn't be too hard these days,
because..... Well, I won't go into it since it's none of your business
anymore anyway and just in case my boss would ever break into this
file.

Anyway, so Arthur just stands there like a lost puppy (no offense,
Athena) and Estelle doesn't say a thing. So he finally goes, "I'll just
leave them on your desk, maybe the girls will want some with their
coffee." (The girls being me, who everyone knows doesn't drink coffee or eat sugar, and Shirley, the anorexic, who wouldn't eat a cannoli if her life depended on it, which it probably does.)

Anyway, an hour later Arthur comes back and he goes, "So Estelle, did you try a cannoli yet?" And she goes, "No Arthur," so he
goes, "Can I try one?" and she goes, "Yes Arthur." So he unties the
red and white string on the box and eats a cannoli, which, in case
your memory is shot and they have no Italian bakeries in Colorado, is
kind of like an eggroll filled with sweet vanilla cream (or is it cheese?
I'll ask next time I'm in Veniero's, which won't be till hell freezes
over, as you can have a sugar rush just by walking by the place). I
know, I know, "how can someone so conscious about her health live
in New York City?" Spare me.

So Arthur (remember Arthur?) finishes the cannoli and peers into
the box. "Got any chocolate ones in there, Estelle?" he asks her. And
Estelle goes, "I don't know, Arthur, take a look." He looks and takes
one out of the box. "Mind if I have it Estelle? I mean, I'll leave it if
you're gonna eat it, but it would be a shame to let it go to waste."

Estelle finally looks up and she's pissed. "Don't bust my chops,
Arthur. You don't mess with the redhead. Take the whole lousy box

of cannolis and get lost."

Which is what Arthur wanted all along, of course.

I know you think they're crazy, but somehow I get a kick out of seeing them go through this every day. It's kind of comforting, you know, to be able to count on something, Monday through Friday at ten o'clock sharp every morning. It's been going on for five years now. Hell, who's to say? Their relationship (or whatever you'd call it) outlasted ours.

Well, lunchtime. Time sure flies when you're having fun. Thanks for spending the morning with me, kiddo. No one gets any work done on Monday mornings anyway. Where are you by the way? Ohio? Indiana? I'm not too good at geography. I mean I know Brooklyn, Queens, the Bronx, Manhattan, and Staten Island.... Florida is south of here, Maine is north.

Lock up that van good and tight when you sleep. I worry about you. I'm glad you've got Athena along— she would tear anyone to pieces if they tried to hurt you. Remember the first time we did it and she kept whining and yelping? And you had to keep climbing down from the loft bed to comfort her, and then she'd quiet down, but as soon as you got to the top of the ladder, she'd start crying again. God, I thought I'd crawl out of my skin, you were such a tease. Worth it though. I didn't say that.

> Love,
> Your pen pal, Lainie

May 4th

Dear Nickers:

I don't know why I'm writing to you every day. Maybe I'm lonelier than I'd care to admit (especially to you). I vowed I wouldn't write to you today, especially at the office where the work is piling up, but here I am stuck in the subway, so what the hell? I could either read the ads for Rice-a-Roni above my head (in English or Spanish) or stare at the people across from me (who look as bad as I feel) or take a little nap (which I wouldn't advise if you value your life).

Everyday's an adventure in this town. You wouldn't believe what happened to me before I got on this train. A guy comes up to me and says, "Hello, I hate to bother you, but may I ask you for a dollar to buy a cup of coffee?" Now what's so strange about this? First of all, a *dollar* for a cup of coffee? I haven't been in Chock Full of Nuts lately, but is inflation that bad? Second of all, I wanted to say to this guy, "I hate to bother you, but may I ask you where you bought your pants?" I mean this guy was making quite a fashion statement. He was wearing a perfectly pressed white shirt with brown wool pants, alligator shoes...he looked like he should be buying me coffee—at the Russian Tea Room! When I didn't respond he said, "Do you speak English?" and then he asked me again, in Spanish! I decided he must be from the New School (I was in that neighborhood) and maybe he was doing research for a sociological paper or something. Uh-oh, we're starting to move, I think. I'll finish this later.

Later:

Well, the train did move, and I made it home, but guess what happened on the train? This guy comes on, and he's holding a cup, and he goes, "Can I have your attention, ladies and gentlemen?" (Panhandlers seem to be very polite these days). "I have AIDS. My wife has AIDS. I lost my job. We lost our apartment. Won't you help us?"

I couldn't believe it. New Yorkers have absolutely no shame. What a fucking line. These guys will do anything for money.

I know you would have probably believed him. That's why you had to leave this city ("If you can make it here, you'll make it anywhere"— just ask Frank Sinatra). You were getting too soft, Nicky. Good thing you weren't with me. We would have probably had a fight about it. Maybe there are some advantages to being single.

1) no fighting

2) can leave dirty dishes in sink (even though I don't. Too tempting for the roaches)

3) can eat whatever I want

4)

Well, that's a pitiful list.

Are you ever going to write to me? Or call me? Is no news good news? Should I be worrying that you got lost or hit by a drunk driver or something? I know you said you were gonna take your time driving across and all, and you haven't gotten my letters yet. (I hope General Delivery keeps them for you. I never did trust the P.O.)

It's a lousy life. Just when we started speaking to each other again, you decide to move to Colorado. We could have been such good friends, Nicks. We like a lot of the same things—movies, museums, walks in the park. I would even have gotten another lover, so you wouldn't think I was hanging around you, just to try and get you back. I know, I know, it's a great sacrifice, but really, I would have done it, just to make you feel better.

Listen, I'll make a deal with you (and Monty Hall). If you come back, I'll let you and Athena crash here as long as you want. I'll even go out for croissants (whole wheat) and the New York Times in the morning. Please?

Oh God, you've reduced me to begging.

Love, Lainie

May 5th

Dear Nick (wherever the hell you are);

You know, I like having a pen pal. It gives me the security of being in a relationship without the hassles of really being in one. It's perfect. Why didn't we ever think of this before? There is one problem though. No sex. Oh well. There's always something. We could try phone sex, that seems to be pretty popular these days. Or auto-sex— that's the new term for masturbation. Pretty space age, huh? The first time I heard it, I thought it meant having sex in the car.

Well, you know where my mind's at these days. You know how I get right before my period. I was thinking, Nicky (you'll appreciate this) what if food and sex traded places? What I mean is, what if we had to do it three times a day to survive, and food was something very intimate and pleasurable and you only ate with someone you really trusted, and you didn't need it to survive (though of course some would argue that fact).

So, the morning fuck would be the most important one of the day. If you left the house on an empty cunt, you'd be sluggish, you wouldn't be able to concentrate, etc., etc. Lunch time—well, instead of restaurants, there'd have to be little rooms for "eating in" if you catch my drift. And for the evening meal, I guess most people would just go home. I haven't worked it all out yet, but it does have interesting possibilities.

Think I've finally lost it? Well you always did say I was a sex maniac. I'm just an average gal who likes to have a little fun (and who gets a little horny before her period). All right, all right, I know you hate the word horny—too male—how about randy? That's what my friend Bev from England says. How about full of desire? Full of arousal? Full of shit? God, Nicole, you could be such a snob sometimes.

After work today I went down to the gym to try and do something with, shall we say with this energy. At least I got to sweat and grunt and see some naked women in the locker room. But it wasn't very satisfying. I swear half the women in New York are anorexic and the other half are jocks. And then there's me, the Renaissance woman. I was born in the wrong era—Renoir would have loved me. No one appreciates a real womanly woman anymore. I'm a soft girl in a hard world.

I guess you appreciated me. Sometimes, that is, but I never really believed that you didn't think I'd be better off ten pounds lighter. You never said it, but I could just tell. Oh, you liked my body all right, but you were glad you didn't have one just like it. Just wait till you're thirty-eight years old. Think you'll be a bean pole forever? Wait till you've been stuck behind a word processor for ten years.

Oh yeah, you're not going to have an office job. You're gonna teach kids to climb mountains so they can feel their feelings or something. Well, anyway....

I guess I just got the blues tonight. I even listened to some Billie Holiday albums and looked through old photos of me and you. We looked happy. We smelled happy. We were happy (some of the time anyway).

My favorite picture was the one of you and me on the bench in Central Park and all the pigeons are surrounding us because you thought it would be a great idea to feed them the bag of wholewheat bagel chips we had just bought. Remember you asked that guy to take our picture, and I was sure he was going to run off with the camera, or a pigeon was going to shit on my head before he got the thing focused. Then we had a fight afterwards because you said I didn't trust anyone and I said you were just lucky that time. Anyway, it's a great picture.

Well, I'm going to bed and a little auto-sex. I hope it doesn't make me cry.

Love, Lainie

To: <u>Nicole P. Foley</u>
Date: <u>May 6, 1989</u>
          WHILE YOU WERE OUT
<u>Ms. Lainie Wilson</u>
of <u>Letter Writers Anonymous</u>
Phone: <u>212-555-9076</u>

Telephone	Returned your call
Called to see you	Please call
Was in to see you	Will call again
Wants to see you XXX	URGENT XXXXXXXXXX

Message: <u>If a letter arrives in a mailbox and nobody</u>
<u>reads it does it really matter what it says?</u>

(Smooth) Operator:<u> L.W.</u>

May 7th T.G.I.F.!!!!!

Dear Nickeroo:

Well, everyone's in a better mood on Friday, natch, since the weekend is coming up. What are your plans? Want to check out that new woman's bookstore in the village, Judith's Room? Then we can just hang out. There's some films playing at N.Y.U. I wouldn't mind seeing.

Oh, you're busy? Well never mind, Rita's coming over tonight. We'll probably just bring in some Chinese food and watch a movie on the VCR. Now that you're gone, I can finally not feel guilty about having one, and I can even use the damn thing every once in a while without someone (I won't mention any names) giving me a lecture on the alienation of the American public. I'm just more comfortable in my own home than in a crowd of strangers, any of whom could mug me in the woman's room at a moment's notice. Besides, the popcorn here is better—you can't get it in the theatre with Brewer's yeast and tamari.

Well, I'm running out of things to tell you, can you believe it? Getting my hair cut tomorrow—that's exciting. Though I don't have anyone to run their fingers through it. Maybe Rita and I will do it once more for old time's sake. I doubt it. I couldn't even masturbate the other night. (I can't believe I'm telling you this. Well, I guess letter writing is a safe place to tell secrets. Did I ever tell you that Yoko Ono thought people were more intimate over the phone than they are in person? She and John Lennon used to talk on the phone for hours everyday. All right, all right, I know I told you. You even bought those cute little toy phones for us to keep on either side of the bed and talk into when we were feeling shy.)

So where was I? Oh yeah, sex (for a change). Well, I haven't made love with anyone since you, so I couldn't help but think about you and remember how much you used to like kissing for hours and hours, and how you liked to nuzzle into my breasts, and how wild you would get when I licked your ear and pulled your nipples. Well, then I got really sad, and then I got mad at you, and then, try as I might, I just couldn't get it up, to coin a phrase that I know you hate.

I can't believe I just wrote all this at work. I better destroy this file before I go home today. Or better yet, change the names (to protect the guilty) and leave it on Estelle's desk. Give her something to chew on besides Arthur's cannolis.

Quitting time in half an hour—yippee! The trick is to look busy so the boss doesn't zap you with a letter that has to go out yesterday, and will keep you going until five-fifteen.

And that's the story, toots. If I don't hear from you tomorrow I'll kill myself.(Is that a promise or a threat, my brother, Mr. Charming, used to say.)

> Love, your pen pal (or should I
> say your word processor pal?)
> Lainie

May 8th

Dear Ms. Foley:

One week exactly since you've been gone and I've written more letters (seven to be exact) this week than I have in my entire adult life. Maybe I've found my niche at last—I could be a professional letter writer. I could charge ten bucks a letter— what the hell, fifteen, and throw in the stamp for free. What do you think—Lainie's Letter Writing, or maybe just Lainie's Letters— that's kind of catchy.

But what if my customers (or clients, that's more professional, don't you think) ask for a guarantee—your money back if your letter isn't answered in one week? I'll go broke—I sure have a shitty track record. You haven't even sent me one lousy postcard. Not even "Weather's fine, wish you were here" or even "weather's fine, glad you're not here." I just wanna hear from you.

My mother called this morning— talk about a fine way to start the day. She gave me the rundown on the family—weddings, births, promotions, mortgages, etc., etc.—I won't bore you with the details. And then she ends the conversation with, "So when are you coming home?" As if I'd want to, after hearing the heterosexual roll call. Of course, she doesn't ask me anything about my life (what you don't know can kill you I suppose). Anyway, it was a lousy way to start my Saturday.

Rita and I had a pretty interesting evening last night.

We didn't even use the VCR by the way, you'll be happy to know, though I may use it this afternoon—it looks like rain. No, Rita and I played Rehash the Relationship, which I suppose you and I may do some day, after we've been broken up for five years. Five years. I couldn't believe we'd been ex-lovers for that long. Lesbians are the only people I know who go out for six months, spend a year and a half breaking up, and then become friends for life. Rita and I came up with this theory that lesbian relationships work on the dog-year principle (just ask Athena about it, and while you're at it, give her a Milkbone for me). You know how one year in a dog's life equals seven years in a person's life? Well, it's the same for lesbian relationships. So, Rita and I were together for about two years, which is really fourteen years, and we've been apart for five years, which is really thirty-five years. So that makes a total of forty-nine years. Add in thirty more years, which is how old I was when I met Rita, so all in all I am actually seventy-nine years old, which is about how I feel at the moment.

I bet you're bored to death by all these letters. I bet you got some long-legged athletic-type blonde hitchhiker making goo-goo eyes at you around a romantic campfire somewhere and Athena is stuck in the van while you two are whooping it up in your sleeping bag under the stars. You would never put Athena in the other room for me. I'm never having a lover with a dog again. Hey, I bet they don't have pooper scooper laws in Colorado. You won't have to follow Athena around with a pail and shovel anymore. They probably don't have alternate side of the street parking either. How will you stand it?

Don't you miss me even a little? I am sort of cute, in an older woman way. I know thirty-eight isn't really older, but it's older than you. Old enough to be called handsome by some. By you. I know what handsome means. Not pretty. Well at least you never called me distinguished.

All right, Nickers, laundry calls (think I'll "shout it out"), and other such odds and ends that make up a life, though it obviously wasn't exciting enough for you. See any bears out there? Or snakes? Be careful! (But if you can't be careful, at least be good).

Love
L.

May 9th

Nick, Nicky, Nicole, Nickeroo!

It was *SO GOOD* to hear your voice! I could have killed you for calling at 11:00 on a Sunday morning—you know I don't open my eyes until noon on Sundays. Of course you don't remember those itty-bitty details —oh hell, never mind. I'm too excited to get mad at you this morning.

I can't believe you got a flat tire your first day. What a drag! Good thing Monica taught you the fine art of changing a tire, else you'd still be stuck in New Jersey, waiting for AAA to come fix it. I can't be-

lieve you made it to Colorado. I bet Athena's glad to get out of the
van and stretch her little paws.

I hope the weather holds till you find a place to live. You have the
van though, you'll be all right. It would be kind of romantic, I bet, to
hear rain beating on the roof at night, kind of cozy. Be careful if
there's a thunderstorm—don't go out without your shoes! I hear light-
ning can be very intense out there.

I'm sure you'll find yourself a job pretty quick—you're a woman of
many talents (some of which you better not start charging for). And
you'll probably make lots of friends and fall in love soon and before
you know it Lainie Wilson will just be a fading memory on the wings
of time (get out the violins please).

Well, guess what— I wrote you a letter every day this week—how
do you like that? No, I didn't forget to put stamps on them. The reason you didn't get them is that I didn't send them. Nope. I read them
all over this morning after we got off the phone, and I decided that I
really wrote them for me, not you. You should understand. You keep
a journal and all. I was saving them until you had an address. (I never
did like that General Delivery idea.)

So I got kind of maudlin and I read them and you know, there
were some good times and some bad times, but I guess you did the
right thing when you broke up with me. I mean, I could never get
you to settle down with me, and you'd have to use more than a shoe
horn to get me out of New York. I was surprised at how I sounded in
the letters—angry, sad, whiny, depressed—sort of reminded me of
those five stages of grief they teach you in Intro to Psychology classes—what are they again? Denial, Depression, Anger, Bargaining—
and what's the fifth? Don't tell me, it'll come to me. While I'm trying
to remember, let me tell you (or tell me, since I don't know if I'll mail
this letter either) that when I reread the letters I realized that I do love
you, even though you broke my heart (sorry, I couldn't resist). But seriously, Nicky, I really do. Otherwise I wouldn't be going through
these five stages of grief—I wouldn't be so pissed at you, I wouldn't
have refused to believe you were really going until the very last minute, I wouldn't have offered to move to Brooklyn (maybe) if you
would only stay. You don't grieve over something or someone unless
you care about them.

So let it be known, that I, Lainie Wilson, will always love and care about Nicole Foley and that the latter will always be welcome to stay with the former whenever she may find herself wandering around the well-worn streets of New York. In other words, kiddo, you're always welcome here (Athena too).

So all right, I had to call Evelyn, my friend the social worker to remind me the fifth stage of grief is acceptance. Funny that's the one I'd forget, huh? I guess that means I haven't really accepted the fact that you're gone from my life. Maybe that's my way of holding on to you.

> I love you Nicky,
> Lainie

Retreat

"Hey, didn't I see you at Michigan last summer?" A woman with short dark hair, wearing aviator glasses and a tiny silver woman's symbol around her neck was studying Joyce and waiting for a reply.

Joyce put down her soup spoon and chewed over the woman's comment. Notice, she said to herself, she didn't say *in* Michigan, as in the state of Michigan, but *at* Michigan, as in at the Michigan Womyn's Music Festival. Someone else might have missed this subtle difference—as a matter of fact a few years ago Joyce herself wouldn't have known that the woman was really saying to her; *I'm a lesbian, are you one too?*

"I've never been to Michigan," Joyce said, buttering a piece of homemade bread. She knew her answer could either mean A—I don't know what you're talking about, or B—I do know what you're talking about but I've never been to the festival. After a minute she added, "I may have seen you at NEWMR though," assuring the woman that yes, indeed, she was a dyke.

"Maybe." The woman visibly relaxed and extended her arm across the table, almost dragging her sleeve through the bowl of tahini. "I'm Sue."

"Joyce."

"Where you from, Joyce?"

"Boston."

"I'm from New York." Sue held onto her hand just a tad longer than Joyce thought necessary, and then released it. "Ever been on a meditation retreat before?"

"No, have you?"

"Yeah, I've been meditating about ten years now." Sue dipped a hunk of bread into her soup. "Zen, Tibetan, Vipassana, I've tried them all. I can't seem to stick with anything for very long though. I just get too strong an urge to cut loose and get a good dose of wine, women, and song. Know what I mean?" She bit hungrily into her bread and threw Joyce a long, meaningful look.

Joyce looked down into her own soup bowl, hoping no one else had heard. Even though her best friend Rhea, who had been at this meditation center many times before, said it was fine to be out at the retreat, Joyce felt really shy about letting people know she was a lesbian. Why, the woman sitting next to Joyce who had snow white hair and bifocals hanging from a chain around her neck, looked old enough to be Joyce's mother. What on earth would she think? Besides, all this was so new to Joyce. She'd been a goody-goody all her life complete with a husband, two kids, and a station wagon in the garage. "Don't make waves," she'd always been told, and and her life had been as smooth as a clear blue lake on a cloudless summer day until two years ago when her life had begun to resemble a wild ocean, full of huge crashing waves and unpredictable tides, stronger than any she had ever known, pulling her towards something. And that something turned out to be Denise, the woman who had finally helped her come to her senses, leave her husband, and at long last come home to herself.

Sue broke into Joyce's thoughts. "Are you here alone?"

"Isn't everybody?" Joyce answered vaguely. Sue laughed. Is she flirting with me, Joyce wondered, tilting her bowl to catch the last drop of soup with her spoon. This is a meditation retreat, not a music festival, for God's sake. There are rules here, and one of them is no sex. Well, flirting isn't exactly sex, but it's the last thing I expected. Maybe she's just being nice to me, taking me under her wing because I'm new at this. Just because someone's being friendly to me doesn't mean that they want to sleep with me. Lots of incest survivors mistake friendliness for something else, Joyce reminded herself. I'm okay. She's just being nice.

Joyce shook her head as if to clear it. Well here it is already, the Big I, and I haven't even started meditating yet, The Big I was incest of course. It seemed like Joyce had been dealing with her incest memories forever, but in reality it had been only the past year and a half. Ironically she had begun to remember at the happiest time in her life—when she was falling head over heels in love with Denise. Rhea told her that happened a lot—just when you feel safe and se-cure—boom—your memories hit you like a ton of bricks. I wish Rhea was here now, Joyce thought, knowing she couldn't stare into her empty soup bowl forever. Rhea was in Joyce's support group for sur-vivors and she would have understood. But Rhea wasn't here and neither was Denise. Joyce was on her own.

She looked up from her bowl and caught Sue smiling at her with perfect teeth. "So which cell block did they put you in?"

"Down in the gym." Joyce smiled in spite of herself. Cell block was a good way to put it. The gym was in the cold and damp base-ment of the building. Makeshift rooms had been created with ply-wood partitions that didn't reach up to the ceiling, and curtains over each doorway. It was almost like sleeping in a dressing room, except there was no mirror of course. Each "room" had a bed, a few shelves and a lamp—sparse, but adequate. When Joyce had registered she was told that this retreat was particularly crowded, so latecomers had to be put in the gym. And of course Joyce had been late. In her usual ambivalent fashion she had waited until the very last possible mo-ment to make up her mind. These days she could barely decide what to put on in the morning or what to eat for breakfast, let alone whether or not she wanted to go on a meditation retreat and possibly unearth even more memories she didn't want to know about.

Sue interrupted her thoughts again. "I'm down in the gym too. Maybe we're neighbors."

"I doubt it. Boston is a long way from New York." Joyce looked down again. I don't like this woman, she thought, though she didn't know why. There doesn't have to be a reason, Joyce told herself. Trust your judgement. Then she thought, oh you're being ridicu-lous—what do you think the woman is going to do, jump you in the bathroom? Maybe it's your internalized homophobia. You think every lesbian in the world is preoccupied with sex. Oh God. Joyce's head was beginning to ache.

I wish Denise was here, she thought. She would know how to handle this situation. She'd just get up and say *See ya*—in a way that would let Sue know she meant just the opposite, that she wouldn't see her at all—and just walk away. But I can't do that. Joyce looked around at the hundred or so other meditators, or would be meditators like herself. She had tried to convince Denise to come with her, but Denise didn't go in for that "crunchy granola stuff" as she put it. Besides, Joyce didn't want to get too dependent on Denise. She'd had enough of that with her marriage. "And anyway," Denise had said, reading the brochure over Joyce's shoulder, "it says no sex, drugs, booze, talking or making eye contact after the first sitting. You think I could last one day, let alone two, without being able to look at you, let alone touch you? You gotta be out of your mind." Joyce smiled. Denise always knew just the right thing to say.

Unfortunately Sue thought Joyce was smiling at her, and thus encouraged, went on with their conversation. "So what do you do in Boston?" she asked.

"Well, right now I'm a secretary," Joyce said. She was embarrassed to admit that she'd let her husband support her all those years and now she felt like a teenager having an identity crisis.

"Hey, that's great. I knew we'd have a lot in common. I do freelance word processing. Not very creative, but it brings in the bucks and that's what counts. I mean, if you're going to live in New York City, you might as well enjoy yourself, right?"

Joyce shrugged her shoulders. "What part of the city do you live in?" she asked, not really caring, but being polite more out of habit than anything else. Maybe I'll take a walk after dinner, Joyce thought, not listening to Sue's answer. I need to clear this woman's voice out of my head before the silence begins. "What?" she said, realizing Sue had asked her a question she hadn't heard.

"I said New York's nothing like this. Is Boston?" Sue opened her hand and gestured toward the big picture window in front of them which framed a lush meadow lined with weeping willow trees. "Hey, you look like the back-to-nature type. Want to take a walk after dinner?"

This is really too much, Joyce thought, feeling mad and close to tears. "No, I think I'm going to lie down on my bed for a while."

"Sounds like a good idea. Save your back while you can." Sue picked up her tea cup with both hands and drank from it. When she put down the mug her glasses were all steamy. "Listen, I'm in cell number ten, in case you need someone to rub your shoulders. It can be pretty rough the first time around."

"Thanks." Joyce got up, pushed her chair in and picked up her bowl. All around her people were rising and carrying their dishes over to the sink, yet Joyce hesitated as if she was waiting to be dismissed. When no one gave her permission to leave, she turned and walked away quietly.

"Have a good retreat," Sue called after her. Joyce flinched as though she'd been caught doing something wrong, though she didn't know what.

She walked over to the sink, rinsed out her bowl, and brought it over to the shelf marked "yogis" that lined one wall of the dining room. Then she went down to the gym and stretched out on her bed. The interaction with Sue had left her feeling weird and slightly depressed, and it was good to be alone. After all, that's what she had come for, wasn't it? But Joyce didn't really feel like lying on her bed. It was chilly in the basement. She wanted to be outside.

Why am I lying here when I know I want to take a walk, she asked herself. Yeah, why are you? Joyce heard Denise's voice echo in her mind. She leaned up on her elbows and stared down her body, past her full belly and round thighs to the tips of her sock-encased toes. What if I take a walk and run into Sue? Then she'll know I didn't want to take a walk with her and her feelings will be hurt. Who cares, Denise would say. You only met the woman an hour ago.

"You're absolutely right," Joyce said out loud. "God, I'm such a wimp." Not like Denise. Denise was thirty-eight, had been a lesbian since high school, and no one, absolutely no one told Denise what to do. Whenever Joyce compared herself to Denise and came up short, she had to remind herself that no one had abused Denise, no one had taken away her power, no one had made her do things she didn't want to do and then made her feel guilty for doing them afterwards.

So what do you want to do, Joyce asked herself, lie here on your behind or take a walk? She stared up at the ceiling wishing the answer were written there. She never knew what she wanted to do. Whenever Denise asked her Joyce would reply, "I don't know. What do you want to do?" It drove Denise nuts, but how could Joyce explain that after a lifetime of putting everyone else's needs before hers—first her father and brother, then her husband, then her husband and two sons—that to even admit she had needs of her own was as terrifying and at the same time as exhilarating as...as...maybe as the first time Denise had kissed her. Well maybe not quite as exciting as that, but close.

Even now, two hundred miles from home among one hundred strangers, I'm more concerned with hurting someone's feelings—someone I don't even like, mind you, than with doing what I want to do. Well, you find yourself wherever you go, Denise had said before she kissed Joyce good-bye. For someone who didn't go in for this "crunchy granola stuff," Denise sure knew a lot.

So did Rhea, who had gotten her into this in the first place. Joyce had met her six months before when she'd joined a group for incest survivors. Joyce admired Rhea who had been working on her healing for four years now and had come a long way. Rhea hardly had nightmares anymore, and she rarely had flashbacks when she was being intimate with someone. She told Joyce that a big part of her healing process was meditating and that she was sure Joyce would get a lot out of it too.

"You'll love it," Rhea said when they went to Harvard Square to buy Joyce a meditation cushion. "You just sit still and watch your thoughts come and go. No phones to answer, no meals to cook. And afterwards, you feel like you just ran a tape cleaner through your mind."

"I don't know," Joyce said, poking a square red and yellow meditation cushion with her finger. "I'm not sure I want to know what's going on in my mind. What if I get really scared or pissed off? What if I freak out?"

"You just sit there." Rhea spoke in a soothing voice. "That's the beauty of it. You focus on whatever's scaring you or making you angry, and it teaches you something. It's a gift."

"What about the Big I?" Joyce asked, finally picking out a lavender cushion.

"What about it?"

"What if it comes up?"

"Listen, if you can live through that, you can sure live through two days of sitting still."

Joyce brought the cushion up to the cash register and picked up a pack of sandalwood incense to smell. "But Rhea," she was really fishing now. "Is it one of those groovy New Age places where all the men and the women sleep together?" Ever since she'd moved in with Denise, Joyce had vowed she'd never sleep under the same roof as a man again.

"Oh no," Rhea assured her. "The men and the women are on completely separate wings." Joyce had imagined a huge bird, like a pterodactyl, with gigantic wings spread across the sky. A cluster of women stood on one wing and on the other, a group of men. Still, Joyce had brought her teddy bear, Ethel, with her so she'd have something safe to sleep with. Denise had bought Ethel for Joyce for her forty-ninth birthday, horrified that anyone could live for almost half a century without a teddy bear.

Joyce studied Ethel's face and thought about Denise. She'd never met anyone like her before. So tough on the outside and so sweet underneath. She never could understand what Denise saw in her—a washed up ex-housewife with middle-age spread, typing her fingers to the bone for a barely adequate paycheck. Joyce shook Ethel's fat arm as if the teddy bear was scolding her. So much for the discussion on self-love her group had had last Thursday night. But how was she supposed to love herself when a person she loved, or was supposed to love at least, had done such awful things to her?

"God this is getting intense," Joyce said out loud. "Okay Ethel, you hold down the fort. I'm going for a walk. I've got to get some air." She tucked the bear into her sleeping bag, slipped on her Birkenstocks, climbed up the steps and walked through the hallway out the front door.

The meditation center was located on a beautiful country road lined with lush maple trees. Joyce took in a deep breath of country air and sighed with pleasure. It's so nice here, she thought, starting down the road. August in the city was unbearable. Once in a while she and Denise talked about moving to the country, but it was more fantasy than anything else. They were both city kids, and besides, Joyce knew she'd never survive without a take-out pizza joint within walking distance. Still, this is wonderful, she thought, as she stopped for a minute, trying to catch sight of a bird she heard singing. The bird's song was interrupted by a mosquito buzzing in her ear. Joyce slapped at the side of her head and then remembered another rule of the retreat: Do not kill any living thing. "Sorry." She shook her head as another mosquito bit her neck, then turned and started walking again. I better get back inside before I'm one big bite, she thought. Rhea didn't tell me to bring the Cutter's.

Just as the meditation center came into view she saw a figure approaching her, and knew instantly it was Sue. Shit, she thought, and right away felt guilty. I wonder if swearing is against the rules. It's not very spiritual. Well, then again they can't expect you to control your thoughts, can they? At least I didn't say it out loud. Pretty soon I won't be saying anything out loud. Not for two whole days.

As Joyce approached Sue, she made up her mind not to speak to her, or even to look at her. But her eyes, as if they had minds of their own, sought Sue's behind her aviator glasses.

"Hi. I knocked at your door but you weren't there, so I came to find you. It's time to sit."

Why are you so interested in me? Is it because I'm the only other lesbian here? Joyce said nothing as she continued to walk. As she walked up the steps to the meditation center Joyce got a funny feeling in her stomach. She knocked at my door...how did she know where they put me? Did she ask? Did she look in and see Ethel? Joyce felt her face grow hot. Don't be silly, she told herself. The woman's been meditating for ten years. She has to have some respect for privacy.

"Well, mum's the word from here on in," Sue said, opening the door for Joyce with a flourish. "Don't think any thoughts I wouldn't," she added as Joyce walked stiffly past her.

She walked into a coat room where a bunch of people were taking off their shoes. Joyce lined her sandals up against the wall and smiled. It looks like a Birkenstock factory, she thought walking through another room with a polished wooden floor. This was the walking meditation room. Joyce turned a corner and her feet felt carpeting beneath her. Now she was in the main meditation hall.

It was a huge room, three times longer than it was wide with big curtained windows running down the length of it. The floor was covered with neat rows of meditation cushions, some of which were occupied by people sitting with their legs crossed and their eyes closed. Here and there, someone knelt on a wooden bench placed behind their knees. Toward the back of the room, a few people sat on wooden folding chairs.

Joyce made her way to her lavender cushion which she had placed in the third row before dinner, following the instructions she'd received at registration: Pick a place and put your things on it. You will remain in that place for the entire retreat. Joyce sat down on her cushion and sighed with relief. The place to her right was occupied by a woman and the place to her left was empty. One of Joyce's biggest fears was that she'd get stuck next to some gross man who'd pick his nose or belch constantly or God knows what the entire time. She glanced to her right. Who knows, the woman next to her might even be a dyke. Hard to tell. Joyce took in her short blonde hair, red T-shirt, and jeans. Whoops, no eye contact, she reminded herself, even though the woman's eyes were closed. Joyce wasn't exactly sure what she should be doing. As if reading her mind, a woman who sat up front on a little platform facing everyone else, rang a small bell.

The room had been quiet to begin with, but after the bell rang the quiet seemed to shift, to deepen. The woman spoke: "We will now begin our sitting practice. Formal meditation instruction will be given tomorrow morning after breakfast. For now, begin by following your breath. As your thoughts come and go follow them but always come back to the breath gently and without judgement."

It sounded simple enough. Joyce closed her eyes as the woman sounded the bell once more. Simple, yes; easy, no. Joyce was amazed at how her mind wandered away from her breath and off to the most inane things—TV commercials, the theme song from the Flintstones, old Everly brothers' tunes. She also wondered what they were going to have for breakfast the next day, and what they were going to have for dinner. And if she should wear her white T-shirt and her blue pants tomorrow or her blue T-shirt and her white pants. And if she should bother putting on mascara, the one indulgence she still allowed herself, or if it would just make her eyes stick together.

God, I must be a pretty shallow person, Joyce thought, if this is what's floating around my mind. I wonder what everyone else is thinking about. Probably deep and profound thoughts about the meaning of life. Well, at least they're getting their money's worth. Joyce straightened out her legs and recrossed them, with her left leg on top this time. Now now Joycie, don't get sarcastic. You just got here. Something will happen. But Joyce was afraid of just the oppo-site—that nothing at all would happen, that underneath all the old songs and the TV commercials was a big fat hole full of nothing. I have nothing to offer Denise, Joyce thought. Nothing to offer the world. Just nothing.

Is that a self-loving attitude, Rhea's voice asked Joyce. She had asked her the same question last Thursday after Joyce had told the group she had stupidly botched up a job at work. "I can't concentrate at work. My mind's too full of garbage," she'd said, and this proved it. Well at least I'm not thinking about the Big I, Joyce thought, and instantly her brother's face flashed across her mind. Before Joyce had a chance to focus on her breath, she heard a tinkling noise.

Saved by the bell, she thought, opening her eyes. People all around her were uncrossing their legs, cracking their backs, stretch-ing their necks from side to side. At the front of the meditation hall, the woman who had sounded the bell began to speak. "Tomorrow's first sitting is at six-fifteen. There will be a wake up bell at five-forty-five. We will sit until breakfast and afterwards there will be formal meditation instruction. The hall will be open all night for anyone who wishes to continue to practice." She then placed her hands together, palms facing each other in the middle of her chest and bowed. All the students bowed back.

Meditate all night? What a bunch of lunatics. I'm going to bed. Joyce stood up and followed the other students out of the hall. She picked up her shoes and went quietly down to the gym, where she got undressed and crawled into her sleeping bag.

The wake up bell was a soft tinkle, gliding across the surface of Joyce's mind, like the scent of honeysuckle carried by a soft breeze teasing her nostrils. Joyce slowly opened up her eyes. What a differ-ent feeling than the electronic beep of the alarm clock, that always made Joyce feel like she was waking up in the middle of an EKG. At home she could barely open her eyes at eight, but today, at five-forty-five, for some reason she was wide awake.

She got dressed and went upstairs to the woman's bathroom. A line of women were waiting to use the sinks with soap, towel and toothbrush in hand. It was bizarre not to speak to anyone. Joyce stared at people's backs and at the floor, remembering not to look anyone in the eye. She washed her face and brushed her teeth, put her toiletry bag away in the basement and came back upstairs to enter the meditation hall. No breakfast was fine with Joyce; she never had anything but coffee in the morning anyway. Except on weekends, when she and Denise would sleep late, lounge around in bed, make love and then around eleven or twelve, have a long luxurious brunch of french toast or pancakes or bagels with cream cheese.

Joyce's stomach growled, and she put her hands over it, embarrassed. No one said anything of course, because no one was talking. Everyone was briskly removing their shoes in the coatroom and then walking slowly through the walking meditation room into the sitting room. Joyce slowed her pace to match everyone else's. It was as if they were all walking in their sleep.

She made her way over to her cushion and sat down. The same woman who was on her right yesterday was there again today, legs crossed, back straight, eyes shut. The space to Joyce's left was still empty.

Joyce crossed her legs and looked at the woman sitting at the very front of the room facing the meditators. Obviously she was the teacher, even though she hadn't taught them anything yet. Joyce closed her eyes. A minute later she heard a bell sound, signalling that the morning meditation had begun. She looked up to see the teacher putting down a small bell by her side, and shutting her eyes. Joyce shut her eyes too.

She felt her belly rising and falling with each breath she took. She had no idea how long they would sit this morning—twenty minutes, forty minutes, an hour? What if her back gave out? True, she did sit at her typewriter eight hours a day, five days a week, except for her lunch break, when she sat at a table at a diner around the corner from her office, or outside on a park bench when it was sunny. All I do is sit, Joyce thought, and I had to come all this way and pay all this money just to sit some more? She smiled at the absurdity of it, and then her smile widened into a giggle. She opened her eyes quickly, but no one seemed to have noticed, or if they did notice they didn't care. Good, Joyce thought, seeing that even the teacher hadn't opened her eyes at the sound of Joyce's laugh. I'd hate to get thrown out of here before I even learn how to meditate.

She closed her eyes again. Somewhere behind her and to her right, a man cleared his throat. A little later, the sun shifted across the sky, and she could feel its warmth landing on her right shoulder. A few minutes after that, Joyce felt her left foot fall asleep. Keeping her eyes closed, she stretched it out in front of her and pounded her heel lightly against the floor, feeling pins and needles from her toes to her ankle.

Suddenly Joyce felt something warm on her skin and it wasn't the sun. Her eyes flew open to see a hand on her foot. She looked at the hand, the arm attached to the hand and the shoulder attached to the arm. Her gaze almost stopped there, because she dreaded seeing the face she knew she would see—that woman, Sue. Damn. Why doesn't she just leave me alone? Joyce wanted to say something, but she knew they were supposed to be silent, so she swallowed her words. Sue smiled, winked at her and continued to massage her foot. Joyce turned her gaze forward. Where the hell had she come from? She glanced out of the corner of her eye to her left again. Sue was sitting on a cushion next to her in the space that had been empty, and she hadn't even heard her plop herself down. Sue gave her foot one last squeeze and then took her hand away. Joyce quickly tucked her foot underneath her other leg and listened intently as Sue settled herself down on her cushion, shifting her weight, cracking her knuckles, clearing her throat. Joyce could practically feel the intrusion of Sue's body heat against her own skin, almost like their auras were touching.

Tears rose in Joyce's throat. Sue's breaking all the rules, Joyce thought. She felt like a child. Should I tell? Why doesn't anyone do anything? Why did she sit next to me? Joyce uncrossed her legs and recrossed them with her other foot on top. Maybe I should change my seat. But you're supposed to sit in the same spot all weekend.

And anyway, what's the big deal? She's not hurting me. She's just being nice.

But Joyce could feel sweat gathering in her armpits and her face growing hot. It was so quiet in the meditation hall she could practically hear Sue breathing right next to her, breathing in her ear. She squeezed her eyes shut, but she could still hear Sue breathing. Every time Sue exhaled, Joyce heard a slight whistle coming from her nostrils. If I have to listen to this for two whole days I'll go nuts, Joyce thought. *"Concentrate on what annoys you. It's a gift,"* Rhea had said. Some gift.

Joyce concentrated on Sue's breathing.. But no...wait...it sounded more like her husband breathing, breathing next to her all those years, holding her tightly in the night, until she felt she could hardly breathe herself. Joyce's chest rose and fell sharply as she followed the images in her mind. No, it wasn't her husband at all, but her brother holding her body down and breathing in her ear, "Don't tell. Don't tell or I'll kill you." Joyce's eyes filled with tears. I don't want to think about this now, she thought, squeezing her eyes more tightly together as if that would make the image go away. I've talked about it in therapy for over a year, I've talked about it in the group, I've talked about it with Denise—enough is enough already.

But try as she might Joyce couldn't get the picture out of her mind. She had squeezed her eyes shut thirty-nine years ago when her brother had explored her body, had touched her in places she herself had never known about before. And then he had laughed at her, calling her a chickenshit because she wouldn't touch him down there. And then he had made her.... Joyce shuddered, as waves of nausea rose up from her belly, and a vile taste formed in her mouth.

It isn't true, she thought, even though she knew it was. At first she hadn't believed it had happened, and then she had denied it for a while, hoping that if she pretended it hadn't happened it would go away. But her nightmares and her memories had continued worming their way into her life.

Joyce opened her eyes. Everything was still quiet, without movement or sound. Sue was still next to her, the teacher was still up front, her meditation cushion was still beneath her. You're safe here, she told herself as she looked around. One thing Rhea had suggested

she do when she was having a flashback was ground herself in the
here and now. I am at the meditation center, Joyce thought to herself. My brother is in New Mexico. He cannot touch me here. I am
safe.

But Joyce wasn't safe from the contents of her own mind. A
steady stream of tears fell from her eyes as she remembered what
her brother had done to her. How at first he'd laughed at her because she wouldn't touch him and then later, laughed at her because
she would. She'd learned early what would shut him up the fastest,
what would please him so she could get away, but at what price? She
had been too afraid to say no to him. Now whenever she saw a *Just
Say No* bumper sticker, she'd think *yeah, right Nancy*. Once in her
group, as an exercise, they had paired off and taken turns yelling
NO! to each other. Joyce had felt strong then, even though she had
never been able to say no to her brother.

She'd never dared tell anyone, because who would believe her instead of her brother? Her mother had died when Joyce was seven.
Her father went to work every day and every night he hid behind the
newspaper, falling asleep on the couch at eight. Joyce had married at
seventeen, just to get out of the house and away from her brother,
but things weren't that much different with her husband. He'd
laughed at her too, and made her do things she didn't want to do,
but Joyce had known by then, had always known, that there was no
use fighting. She had just stayed quiet, hoping that would make
things a little easier. Lots of times it did. Like today. She hadn't had
to say anything to Sue, and she had stopped rubbing Joyce's foot. It
was no big deal. And Joyce hadn't had to break any of the rules.

Joyce sniffled, wondering what to do with her dripping nose. To
her right, someone else was crying too. Joyce squeezed her eyes
tightly together, wishing everything would just go away—everything
in her head and everything in the meditation hall. She wished she
was home with Denise, lying in bed, feeling Denise's smooth back
pressed up against her breasts and belly, as they lay curled together
like the two s's at the end of a kiss. The memory of Denise soothed
Joyce, for she was used to pretending she was somewhere other
than where she was.

When her brother used to make her lie down on the army blanket in the basement after school before their father came home, Joyce had closed her eyes and imagined she was up in heaven with her mother, who sat her on her lap and rocked her in a big rocking chair perched on a cloud. She'd lay Joyce's head back against her breast and smooth her hair away from her forehead. In the fantasy, Joyce's mother looked like a cross between Donna Reed and Doris Day, for she really didn't remember what her mother looked like.

What she did remember though, was a silly little song her mother use to sing to her: *a girl named Joyce with a beautiful voice, drove around town in a pink Rolls Royce.* Her mother had sung to her and rocked her when Joyce was very, very little, before her mother got sick, and before she had died.

I want my mommy, Joyce thought, crying in earnest now, but still without a sound. Tears and mucus streamed down her face. My mommy. Joyce felt a hand on her shoulder and once more her eyes flew open. "No," she yelled, flinging Sue's hand away. She looked around wildly, wondering whose voice was so shrill, then heard it again. "No...no."

This is ridiculous, Joyce thought. Why am I losing control? She's just being nice.

"Shh...," Sue whispered, leaning closer. "I was only trying to...."

"No!" Joyce screamed again, saying no to that reasoning voice inside her head as well as to Sue's unwanted attention. I don't care if she means no harm. I'm sure my brother *meant* no harm either. She's bothering me. Joyce stood up self-consciously, wondering what to do. Wouldn't anybody say anything? Everyone was still sitting on their cushions with their eyes closed, off in their own worlds. Everyone except Joyce of course, and Sue who was staring at her. What if someone was really hurting me? Didn't anybody care? They all had their dammed eyes closed because they didn't want to see, just like her father.

Joyce looked at the meditation teacher. She was the only one whose eyes were open, the only one who had seen. But her eyes had no answers in them, they were just waiting to see what Joyce would do. There was no anger in her eyes, no disapproval, only kindness. Joyce felt her own eyes filling with tears again, and quickly got up and walked out of the room.

She slowed her pace once in the hallway, and made her way back down to her room. She kept expecting someone to follow her, but no one did. She walked into her room and curled up with Ethel, covering herself with her sleeping bag, for suddenly she felt cold, very cold, a cold coming from inside herself. Would Sue come looking for her? Would her brother? She kept crying as her body rocked itself to the chant she heard her mother singing in her mind—*a girl named Joyce with a beautiful voice, drove around town in a pink Rolls Royce.*

Joyce wiped her nose with the corner of the sheet. What should she do now? She had no idea what time it was, and if everyone else was still sitting or eating breakfast or what.

"Maybe we should go home, Ethel," Joyce said to her teddy bear, no longer caring that she was breaking the rules by speaking in a voice that sounded loud in the empty room. What if Sue comes down to find me? She said she knocked on my door. She knows where I am. Joyce's body began to shake. The basement was damp, not unlike the basement where her brother had....

"No," she said again loudly. If she touches me again, I'll kill her. I'll break both her kneecaps like Denise taught me from her self-defense class. It only takes seven pounds of pressure.

My God, Joyce wondered, what's wrong with me? The woman barely touched me. She only wanted to comfort me. Joyce felt a little calmer.

Then the rage welled up inside her again. I don't care. She had no right to touch me. Ever. Tears cascaded from her eyes as she understood...*and he had no right to touch me. It wasn't my fault. I am not bad.* She had heard those words before, but heard them only in her head not in her heart.

Joyce wiped her eyes with Ethel's right ear. I hate my brother. I hate that woman. Then she felt as if anger were oozing out of her like air from a balloon, leaving her deflated and depressed. Maybe it was a mistake to come here. Maybe I'll just go. All she had to pack were a pair of pants, a couple of T-shirts, a sweater, Ethel and her sleeping bag. I could be out of here in five minutes flat and no one would know. No one but Sue of course.

Joyce sat up and hugged Ethel to her chest. No, she said to herself, I am not giving that woman the satisfaction of ruining this retreat for me. My brother ruined enough of my life. I am not missing this retreat because of some woman I don't even know. I came here for me.

Joyce stood up resolved to go back upstairs and sit herself down on the lavender cushion she had spent thirty-five bucks on. I'm not a little kid anymore, she reminded herself. I can say no. I can leave if I want to. She climbed the steps slowly, imagining Denise on her left and Rhea on her right. They would be proud of me, she thought. I'll imagine them sitting on either side of me to protect me.

When she got to the top of the stairs, she stopped, feeling a presence near her. Was it Sue? No, this presence felt warm and gentle. Very faintly, Joyce could hear the familiar chant—a girl named Joyce with a beautiful voice, drove around town in a pink Rolls Royce. Joyce looked around. Of course her mother wasn't there to protect her. Joyce was alone. She knew all at once that Rhea and Denise could love her as much as they wanted, but they couldn't protect her either. She had to learn to protect herself.

Before Joyce entered the meditation hall she thought, I'll change my seat. That will solve the problem. Inside everyone was still sitting quietly with their eyes closed. She looked at the teacher but again her eyes held nothing but kindness. Joyce moved toward her cushion, determined to pick it up and move it to the back of the room, as far away from Sue as possible. When she got to the third row, she stopped in her tracks because Sue was gone. Gone. The place to Joyce's left was empty once more. Her whole body relaxed as she sat down, the smile on her lips threatening to explode into a gale of laughter. I'm going to be fine, Joyce thought. She felt like she had passed some sort of test. She knew she wasn't completely healed— that would take time—but she was definitely on her way. She sighed deeply and shut her eyes just as the bell sounded, signaling that the early morning meditation was over.

A True Story (Whether You Believe It or Not)

This is a true story, and it happened to me, Zoey B. Jackson on the twelfth of May, whether you believe it or not. And to tell you the truth, it's kinda hard for me to believe it myself. It's the sorta thing someone would make up to impress a girl they just met at a party or something. But believe me, I could never make this up. I could never even imagine such a thing happening and, least of all, happening to me. But it did, sure as I'm standing here telling about it.

Well, there I was, in the Famous Deli (which isn't famous for much except maybe its slow service) waiting for Larry, the kid behind the counter to make me two BLT's on rye. I was just standing there minding my own business, studying the different cheeses in the deli case wondering how they make one cheese taste different from the next and why do they bother? I mean cheese is cheese as far as I can tell. Cheddar, Muenster, Monterey Jack do they use different kinds of cows for different kinds of cheeses or what?

I guess my mind was a little fuzzy, sort of like a TV that's outa focus. I had just spent two hours trying to get a cat down out of a tree, and I wasn't in the greatest mood of my entire life. When I joined the fire department two years ago, cats stuck up in trees wasn't exactly what I had in mind. I wanted to be a fireman ever since I was a little girl, only my mama said I couldn't—little girls don't grow up to be firemen. Or policemen or businessmen or garbagemen or any other kind of men at all.

But I didn't care what my mama said. I usta dream about riding in a fire truck with the lights flashing and the sirens screaming, wearing a big red hat and racing through town with a black and white dog wagging its tail on the back. I got a piggy bank shaped like a fire truck for my birthday once, and I used to sleep with the thing. Still have it too.

So when I turned forty, two years ago, I decided to come work for the FD as a present to myself. I didn't want no fame or glory or anything, but I did have visions of myself on the front page of the Tri-Town Tribune all dirty and sweaty, having worked all night putting out a fire and saving a couple of lives. I was in the paper actually, but not for any heroic deeds or nothing, but because of my size. I don't know whether it's something to be proud about or something to be ashamed about, but I'm the smallest person in the history of the whole state to ever join the fire department and only the second woman. Probably the first lesbian too, but you know they didn't put that in the paper. I'm just about five feet tall when I ain't slouching, and I weigh about a hundred pounds soaking wet, but it's all solid muscle. I can whip that hose around like nobody's business when I have to.

But that night I didn't have to do nothing fancy. I mean whose idea was it to call the fire department to get a cat down out of a tree anyway? People watch too many cartoons, that's what I think. When we got there (we meaning me and Al) old Mrs. Lawrence was standing under that tree crying and carrying on like it was her husband or one of her kids up there instead of her stupid, old cat Matilda. She had Matilda's dish out there full of food, and all her favorite toys—a whiffle ball, a sock full of catnip and a tangle of yarn, and she was practically on her knees begging that animal to please, *please* come on down. Mrs. Lawrence was promising her all sorts of things; she'd feed Matilda fresh fish and sour cream every day, and she'd let her sleep in bed with her and she wouldn't yell anymore when Matilda sharpened her claws on the living room furniture, if only Matilda would *get down*.

I guess old Matilda had been up there for most of the day yowling and by this time it was ten at night and the neighbors were trying to get some sleep. Half of them were out there in their PJ's in Mrs. Lawrence's yard trying to figure out what to do. It was probably the most exciting thing that had happened in that part of town in about ten years.

So me and Al made a big show of getting the ladder out and climbing up there and getting Matilda down. Ornery thing she was, too—sunk her claws deep into that branch, fluffed out her tail 'til it was fat as a coon's, and hissed at Al fiercer than a rattlesnake. He finally grabbed her, getting his face scratched in the process, tucked her under his arm and climbed down the ladder with everybody cheering except poor Mrs. Lawrence, who couldn't even bring herself to look.

Once Matilda was safe in Mrs. Lawrence's arms, everyone went back home to bed, and me and Al got into the fire truck to come back to the fire station and make out a report. We stopped at the deli first though, for something to eat like we usually do. For some reason, most food tastes better at midnight than it does in the middle of the day, you know what I mean? We usually get sandwiches, sometimes coffee and a piece of pie. Al likes strawberry; I go for lemon meringue or banana cream.

So Al was sitting in the truck outside waiting, and I was standing by the counter inside waiting, and I was beginning to think Larry was standing behind the counter waiting, too, for the bacon to be delivered maybe or for the pig to grow old enough to be slaughtered or something, it was taking so goddamn long. But then in walked this woman and all of a sudden I didn't care if those sandwiches didn't get made 'til half past next July.

She sure was pretty. More than pretty. Beautiful. Gorgeous. A real looker. Awesome, like the kids on Mrs. Lawrence's block would say. I knew she was a stranger around here 'cause I know every woman in this town—those who do, those who don't and those who might. This one would, I was sure of it.

She was wearing jeans that fit her just right—tight enough to give a good idea of what was under 'em, but loose enough to keep you guessing just a little bit. She had on this red shirt that was cut straight across the shoulders so that her collar bones were peeking out a little bit. And I could just see the edge of her bra strap which was black and lacy. She had on these little red shoes that damn near broke my heart and a mess of silver bracelets on her right arm that made a heck of a noise sliding down her wrist and all crashing into each other when she reached into her purse for her wallet. There must of been fifty of 'em or more. Her pocketbook was red too, and so were her nails, and so was her lipstick. Not too red though—not cheap red or flashy red. There's red and there's red, you know what I mean, and this red looked real good. She had silver hoops in her ears, to match her bracelets maybe, and she was a big woman, which suited me fine. I like my women big, you know, like those old painters like Renoir usta paint. None of this Twiggy stuff for me. I like a woman you can hold onto. A woman you're not afraid you're gonna break if you squeeze too tight. A woman with a little meat on her bones.

Well, I took all of this in in about two seconds flat, and then I looked away 'cause I didn't want her to think I was being impolite or nothing. I know my manners. My mama taught me it's real rude to stare, but I just couldn't help it, and before I knew it I found myself looking at her again. Mind your manners, I said to my eyeballs, but they just wouldn't. I watched her unzip this little blue change purse thingy she had and take out two quarters for a soda, and then, before I could say boo, she was looking right at me with her deep brown eyes the color of a Hershey's Special Dark, which happens to be my favorite candy bar. She smiled at me slow, a real sexy smile like she knew she was looking good and I knew she was looking good, and she knew that I knew that she was looking good, and that made her look even better.

"Hey, Zoey, here's your chow."

Wouldn't you know it? Just when things were starting to get interesting, Larry got my order done. I took my sandwiches, paid for 'em and would've tipped my hat, but I'd left it out in the truck with Al. I just kinda nodded my head at her, or made some such gesture that was meant to be gallant but probably looked foolish. I walked past her, catching a whiff of perfume that almost made me dizzy, and left the deli with another vision to add to my fantasy life which is about the most exciting action there is around here for an old bulldyke like me. I dunno why I stay in this town giving all the PTA ladies something to gossip about. I could tell them a thing or two myself, but that's another story.

Well, we weren't back in the fire house for more than ten minutes when the phone rings. I let Al get it, since my mouth was full of sandwich and he had downed his in about three seconds flat.

"It's for you," Al said and I don't know who was more surprised, him or me. I never get calls at work. We're not supposed to tie up the phone in case there's a fire or another cat stuck up in a goddamn tree or something, and, anyway, I keep my personal life, what little there's left of it, pretty much of a secret, though it's crystal clear I'm as queer as a three-dollar bill even if I don't wear purple on Thursdays. I think it was the first phone call I got in the whole two years I'd worked there. I wiped the mayo off my chin with the back of my sleeve, took the phone and spoke in my most official sounding voice.

"Hello?"

"Hello. Is this Zoey?"

I knew it was her. I couldn't believe it, yet I wasn't surprised. A little startled, a little shook up, even shocked maybe, but not surprised. She sounded like she looked. Good. Sassy. Sure of herself. And hot.

"Yeah, this is me." God, what a dumb thing to say.

"My name is Natalie, and I was just in the deli a little while ago. I don't know if you noticed me or not," (she had to be kidding) "but I noticed you and I was wondering if you'd like to go out and have a cup of coffee with me sometime?"

How about right this second, I wanted to say, but I didn't. Get a grip, Zoey, old girl, I said to myself. Don't rush into anything now.

"Uh, sure, yeah, that'd be great," I said, sounding about thirteen years old.

"How about tomorrow then, around four?"

"Sure," I said, "you know where Freddy's is?" Freddy's is the only place in town that sells a decent cup of coffee and doesn't have a million high school kids throwing spit balls at each other in the middle of the afternoon. It's a little out of town, not sleazy or anything—it's not far from my place, as a matter of fact, but not smack dab in the middle of town either. I explained to her how to get there and then there wasn't much left to say.

"See you tomorrow, Sugar," she said, and I swear I could feel her tongue licking the inside of my ear right through that telephone.

I hardly slept at all that night, I tell you. I was more than a little curious and more than a lot flattered, and hell, I figured that any woman with that much sass deserved at least an hour of my time and hopefully more. I wondered where she had come from and what she was doing out there by herself all spruced up like that in the middle of the night. But to tell you the truth, I didn't really care. I was just glad she was where she was when she was, and that I was there too.

I tossed and turned, too full of BLT and lust to sleep, but I musta dozed off sometime 'cause the next thing I knew it was ten o'clock, and the sun was coming in through the windows, heating up my eyes like they was two eggs cooking on a grill. My bedroom is tiny—one wall is mostly all windows and the bed takes up almost the whole room. I don't mind though; in fact, I kinda like it like that. Feels sort of like a nest, though why I have a double bed at this point is beyond me. Ain't nobody been in it since Sally left over two years ago. Hard to believe it's been two years already. Time sure does fly, I guess. But it musta been, 'cause she left right before I turned forty, right before I signed up at the fire department. That's one of the reasons I did it. With Sally gone there was this empty space in my life, this aching in my belly I didn't know how to fill, and I just couldn't face all those awful lonely nights by myself. So now I sit in the firehouse two, sometimes three nights a week, playing poker with Al.

I sure didn't wanna be thinking about Sally this morning, so I got up, plugged in the coffee pot and went into the jane to splash some cold water on my face. "Looking good old girl," I said to myself in the mirror over the sink, which I noticed was speckled with old toothpaste. "Who says Zoey B. is over the hill, huh? Women are still beating down your door, old gal." I winked at my reflection—I am a pretty good winker if I do say so myself. I can also raise one eyebrow at a time; it's not as hard as it looks if you practice. I looked at myself and wondered what Natalie—God even her name was sexy—had seen last night standing in the deli that made her give me a call. Your basic brown eyes, two of 'em, natch, a straight nose, average lips, nothing special.

Maybe it was the uniform. Some girls really go for that sorta thing. Or maybe it was the grey hair at the temples, makes me look kinda distinguished. Some girls like older women. I wondered how old Natalie was and if she did this sort of thing often. Maybe her buddies, whoever they were, had put her up to it. Maybe a whole gang would be waiting at Freddy's to laugh their heads off at the old bulldyke that'd been taken in by the first pretty face that's shown up in this pint-sized town since 1959. Or worse, maybe there'd be some guys waiting with chains and billy clubs ready to kick ass. Like I said, it's no secret who I am and it's no secret that some folks in this town don't exactly like it either.

That was really hard on Sally, one of the reasons she left, I think. Nothing ugly's ever happened, but we were always thinking it might. Sally took herself to San Francisco where she says the streets are paved with queers and she can even hold hands with her new girl-friend all over town and nobody bats an eye. Not even the cops 'cause even most of the goddamn cops are queer themselves. That's something I'd sure like to see, I tell ya.

Well, I drank my coffee and messed around most of the day, cleaning up the house and doing chores. My place is small, just the bedroom, the kitchen, the living room and a small spare room where I keep all my junk—my tools and papers and stuff. Usta be Sally's room for painting—that's what she does is paint—watercolors most-ly. She even had a show of 'em in San Francisco, sent me a postcard all about it.

Well, at three o'clock I started getting nervous. First of all, what the heck was I gonna wear? Not that I had much choice. It was either jeans or jeans. Jeans with a ripped knee, jeans speckled with white paint, or jeans with two belt loops missing. I could wear my black chinos, but that'd look awful funny, me being so dressed up in the middle of the day. I put on the jeans with the belt loops missing and a white shirt I thought about ironing and my sneaks. By the time I'd finished fussing with my hair, which is only about two inches long and not all that much to fuss about, it was time to get my ass out the door. I sure didn't wanna be late—something told me Natalie wasn't the kinda woman who liked to be kept waiting.

It only took me ten minutes to walk to Freddy's. I got there at four o'clock on the nose and she wasn't there. Well, fine, I told my-self. I don't care. Ain't the first time Zoey B.'s been stood up, not the first time she's looked like an old fool. I sat myself down in a booth toward the back, ordered myself a cup of coffee and looked at my watch. Four-oh-four. Ah well, I thought, ripping open a packet of sugar and dumping it into my cup. I knew it was too good to be true. These things don't really happen. Not in real life anyway.

At exactly ten after four, the door to Freddy's swung, and I mean *swung,* open and in waltzed Natalie like she owned the whole god-damn place. She was looking so good I almost dove right straight into my coffee. I held onto that cup for dear life as she stuck her hands on her hips and looked around like she had all the time in the world. When she spotted me, a slow smile crept across her face that said, I knew you'd be waiting for me. I smiled too, thinking to myself, fool, of course she'd be late. She didn't just wanna meet me here. She wanted to make an *entrance.*

I watched Natalie walk across Freddy's slowly, giving me plenty of time to admire her as she weaved her butt in and out of tables and chairs on her way to where I was sitting. She was wearing this white, blousy kinda thing with a belt at her waist with these pink pants that had little black designs on 'em all over the place that reminded me of sorta slanty tic-tac-toe boards. She had on little pink shoes too, that knocked me out, round pink earrings that looked like buttons, and a shiny black purse. It's those little things that separate the femmes from the butches, you know. Sally taught me that. Accoutrements are everything, she usta say, and of course I had to ask her what the hell accoutrements were. They're just a fancy word for accessories, which is just a fancy word for earrings and pocketbooks and stuff. Sally was always throwing those fifty-dollar words around when she was angry at me, or angry at being stuck in this peanut-size town.

Anyway, I don't know anything about accoutrements. I have me an old leather wallet I stick in my back pocket, two pairs of sneakers, and earlobes as unpunctured as the day I was born. But Natalie, boy, I bet she has a jewelry box the size of Montana and a closet full of pretty little shoes that could just about break your heart She was wearing those same silver bracelets again that clattered down her arm in a fine racket practically every time she moved. It was like each one of them bracelets wanted to be the first to get down to her wrist and maybe win a prize. Her lipstick was one shade lighter than yes-terday, her smile one shade darker.

"Hi Honey, sorry I'm late," she said in a voice that let me know she wasn't sorry at all. "Have you been waiting long?"

All my life, I wanted to tell her, just to hear a woman like you call me honey. "Nah, just got here myself," I lied. Both of us knew I had been waiting and would have kept waiting forever, and then some, if

I'd had to.

She slid into the booth, put her purse beside her and leaned back against the seat looking at me

"Want some coffee?" I asked.

"I'll have tea," she said and leaned towards me with her elbows on the table as if deciding to have tea was some kinda intimate secret just the two of us was in on. Her blouse moved when she leaned forward, revealing the top of her cleavage and I almost forgot how to breathe.

"Hey Freddy, bring this lady a cup of tea," I hollered over my shoulder. Natalie smiled and settled back in the booth and her blouse settled back over her skin and her cleavage disappeared to wherever it is cleavages go when they're not out there in the open calling out to you practically by your own name.

Well, we kinda looked at each other again, with me grinning like a fool 'cause I just couldn't believe I was sitting there in Freddy's with this absolute doll who had come out of nowhere, and she smiling that I-know-what-you're-thinking smile and playing with one of her bracelets.

"So, uh, here we are," I said, always brilliant at making conversation.

"Yes," she said. Not yeah or yep or unh-huh, but *yes*. "Thanks for coming out with me."

"My pleasure," I said and I hoped she could tell I meant it. "I was sure flattered that you asked me."

Now she smiled a real smile and I could see her beautiful white teeth. She even blushed a little bit which only made her even prettier 'cause I saw that maybe she wasn't as sure of herself as she thought she was.

"I didn't know if you'd be glad or not. But when that boy behind the counter at the deli called your name, I knew it would be easy to find you. How many Zoeys could there be at the fire department of a town this size?" She waved her hand around like the whole town was sitting in Freddy's and that set her bracelets rushing back down toward her elbow this time, sounding like a million tiny little bells.

"I'll have to remember to thank Larry next time I see him," I said.

"Yes," she said again. It sounded almost like a hiss, like she had just run into the room and was a little outta breath when she said it. "I wanted to meet you."

"Why?" I asked.

"Because," she said, staring straight into my eyes, "I've always been interested in fires. Ever since I was a little girl."

"Really?" I couldn't believe it.

"Yes. And when I saw you in your uniform," she lowered her eyes and then lifted 'em again, "I knew I could ask you some questions about fires and maybe you'd have the answers." She leaned forward. "Now why, for example, do you sometimes fight fire with fire, and why is it sometimes better to soak the flames 'til everything for miles around is wet through and through? Then I've heard that some fires," she paused, like she was really thinking this out, "some fires burn even hotter when you try to put them out. And some fires can burn for days, weeks, months even, and there's just no stopping them." She started stroking my arm, which felt like it was on fire itself, and her fingertips were soft as feathers. "I thought maybe you could explain," she went on, "why some fires are just warm enough, some burn so hot they destroy you, some go out in a minute, some need to be stoked to keep them going, and some will just burn and burn on their own forever."

"Let's go," I said.

We stood up and I threw two bills down on the table. Freddy was just coming over with Natalie's tea, but we just walked right by him without saying a thing. We didn't say anything to each other either as we walked down the street. I just listened to Natalie's little heels clicking and my heart beating and thought about the fire burning deep inside my belly and wondering how in the world it could ever be put out. I never wanted anybody the way I wanted Natalie right that second and I didn't care if the whole town knew who she was and who I was and what I hoped we were just about to do. It was all I could do not to take her in my arms right there on the street. But, hell, this ain't San Francisco. The six blocks between my house and Freddy's seemed like five hundred miles.

Finally we got to my place, and my hands were shaking so bad I could barely get the key in the lock. There goes my suave bulldyke image, I thought, if I ever had one to begin with. I kept fiddling with that door for what seemed like forever 'til it finally gave way and we stumbled inside. Or rather I stumbled. I don't think Natalie's ever stumbled a day in her life. Natalie *entered* my place. She sauntered, sashayed, swished and swung those big beautiful hips from side to side, checking the place out like it was something special, like the Buckingham Palace. We were standing in the living room, and she had her back to me, looking at this painting of a sunset that Sally had done.

I didn't wanna tell her about Sally. I didn't want her to know I had ever been with another woman before or ever would be again. Nothing mattered but this moment. Nothing mattered but her. She filled up my house with all the longing I had ever known in my whole life, and I knew if I didn't have her that second I would burst and maybe even die. With my heart beating in my throat like a big bullfrog, I walked up behind her and cupped my hands under her gorgeous ass. She leaned back slightly, letting her weight settle into my palms, like she was sitting in 'em and I thought of that song for a minute, *He's got the whole world, in his hands.* But just for a minute 'cause Natalie turned her head and whispered into my neck, "How about showing me where you live, baby?"

I turned Natalie around and put my mouth down on hers for an answer. She was about the most kissable woman I ever met in my whole life. And even though I'm no Casanova or Don Juan or nothing, I've known a few women in my time. None of 'em kissed like Natalie kissed. Natalie sucked, nibbled, bit, chewed, licked, rubbed, stroked, caressed and damn near danced with those lips. And the things she did with her tongue I don't even have words for. I was dying, I tell you. My knees got all rubbery, and I thought they'd give out on me for sure. Finally she, not me, led us to the bedroom, like the tough femme that she was.

But once we got in there, she knew her place. She kicked off her shoes, slid all them damn bracelets off her arm, lay back on my bed and let me undo her buttons one by one, setting loose her glorious body an inch at a time. Her breasts were round and full as the moon, and her nipples were just made for sucking on. She pressed my head into her tits harder and harder 'til I damn near bit 'em off. I made love to her breasts for hours, weeks, years, it seemed, and that woman just couldn't get enough. Finally she took my hand and put it where it belonged. She was sopping wet, and if I didn't know better, I'd of thought she'd peed on herself.

I took off her pants and her pink lace panties gently, like she was a little baby, instead of the grown-up hot thing that she was. I slid four fingers into her easy, like a diver hitting the water in one clean smooth motion. She took me in all the way, and inside there it was soft as...soft as...hell, she gave a whole new meaning to the word soft. Soft and sweet and wet and wonderful. Oh I tell you she was all woman from those deep dark chocolate eyes down to the soles of her pretty little feet and I should know 'cause I explored every inch of her. I felt like a little kid in a candy store—my eyes just got bigger and bigger and I wanted *everything*. And each kiss I gave her, each touch, each lick, would make her catch her breath in the sweetest little gasp, like that was the first time anyone had ever touched her in that spot before. I tell you, some women are just made for loving, and Natalie was one of them, that's for sure.

Well, before I knew it it was dark outside with the windows all filled up with black and a little sliver of moon peeking in. I could barely see Natalie's face though I could feel it an inch away from mine. Maybe that's why I let what happen happen. It's almost like I didn't even know what was going on 'til we was in the middle of it, but before I knew anything, there I was, flat on my back with Natalie up above me, unbuttoning my shirt and sliding my jeans down.

Now I'm usually clear about who's the butch and who's the femme, and I like my women to just lay back and enjoy themselves while I give 'em what they want. That's how I always get my pleasure, from giving pleasure. That's the way it's always been and that's the way it's always gonna be and that's the way I like it. But Natalie had me under a spell, I tell ya. My whole body just wanted to leap right into her mouth—breasts, belly, legs, elbows, you name it. So when she finally reached for me down there, I didn't give her my usual, "No thanks, babe." I let her.

Listen, I sure don't want this getting around the PTA or even to my friends who are queer like me, 'cause it is a known fact, in certain circles anyway, that Zoey B. Jackson is a proper old-fashioned stone-bulldyke that doesn't flip for nobody. I ain't never been a rollover butch, but that night stands apart like it was a whole lifetime by itself, or a dream maybe, or a visit to another planet. No one I knew knew Natalie or ever would. My instincts told me that. And that I was safe with her. And that for some reason beyond what I could understand, I needed her to do to me what no one else had done, though more than a few had tried.

"Silky," she whispered, as her fingers stroked my cunt. "You're as soft as silk, see? This is what you feel like." And she took her panties, which turned out to be real silk, and rubbed 'em all over my body. I went wild, I tell you. Then she kissed my breasts, my belly, my thighs and finally my pussy, and when her tongue touched me down there I thought they'd have to pick me up off the floor in a million little pieces. I wondered why it had taken me forty-two years to lay myself down for a woman. I sure hoped all the women I ever made love to had felt that good. Just thinking about it got me even more excited, and before I knew what was happening, my whole body exploded like the fireworks they set off down by the high school on the Fourth of July and I was gasping and moaning and carrying on like a banshee.

I felt a little shy then but Natalie just laughed and came up to kiss me. I smelled myself on her face and tasted myself on her lips, and I tell you, that just got me going all over again. I'm usually a once-a-night girl—I don't need all that much to keep me satisfied, but that night I lost track of how many times I did it to Natalie, and she did it to me, and we did it to each other. Once Natalie even did it to herself. She slid her fingers into her cunt and then took 'em out and rubbed her juices all over herself, slow and easy, never taking her eyes away from mine for a second. Then she reached inside herself again and painted me too. Then she licked me clean, all over, 'til my legs swallowed up her face again.

What a night. I tell you we didn't even think about getting any sleep 'til about six A.M. when the windows were a pale pink and the birds were singing their wake-up song in the trees. I held Natalie tight and she lay her head against my chest and filled up my arms with all the sweetness in the whole world. I fell asleep with one of her legs braided in between mine and her soft breath tickling the base of my neck.

When I woke up hours later, the sun washing my face with heat, she was gone. Gone. I couldn't believe it. Lock, stock, and pocket-book, gone. I got up and paced around the house, fooling myself every two minutes. Oh she must be in the bathroom, I'd tell myself, and go looking. Or maybe she's in the kitchen making coffee. Nope. Maybe she's in the spare room looking at my stuff, spying on me. I wouldn't mind. But it was useless. She was gone. I climbed back into bed, forlorn as a big-pawed puppy whose owner just hollered at him to go home.

I stretched flat out on my back with my hands behind my head, thinking. I could still smell her, hell, I could practically still taste her in my mouth. I wanted her again so badly I almost touched myself. I don't want this going no further than you, me and the lamppost, but I even cried a little bit—just a tear or two leaking quietly out the corner of my eye. I buried my face in her pillow then, the pillow she slept on, that still smelled like her fancy perfume. And when I turned over and reached my hands up under my head again, I felt something cold, round and hard. One of Natalie's bracelets. She'd either forgotten it or left it under the pillow on purpose, for me.

I put it on and a second later took it right off. It looked silly, like an ankle bracelet on a dinosaur. I've never worn a bracelet or a ring or a necklace in my whole life. But when I got dressed later, I surprised myself and put it on again, just to keep her near me, you know. I pretended like we was going steady and I liked the feel of that bracelet sliding up and down my arm like a kid on a water slide. I wished I had given Natalie something and I probably would've if she'd stuck around a little longer. Or maybe what I had given her was enough.

So that's what happened to me, Zoey B. Jackson on the twelfth of May. It's a true story and here's the bracelet to prove it. Funny, I feel almost naked without it, wear it all the time now, case she comes back. Well, that's not really why. I guess I know Natalie ain't gonna pass through this town again, 'cept in my dreams maybe. Hell, who knows how long I'm gonna stay in this town anyway? Been thinking I might get myself to San Francisco one of these days, see what Sally's up to. Bet I could get myself a job there and wouldn't that be something, riding up and down those San Francisco hills in a big red firetruck? I ain't really a city person, but I don't know, these past few weeks this town's felt too small all of a sudden, like a sweater that got shrunk in the wash one day and don't fit right anymore. Al says there's something different about me too but he don't know what. Oh he noticed the bracelet right off—said it looked real fine, and was I gonna start putting out fires in high heels and skirts now? I musta blushed real red when he said that. If only he knew what I knew. And don't you dare tell him.

The Word Problem

"T.G.I.F.," Patty said, emphasizing the "F" by slamming the car door shut with her hip. "I thought this week would never end." But end it had, and here she was walking up the driveway towards a weekend of peace and quiet and Irene. What more could a girl want? Patty stepped into the hallway of her apartment building, and balancing her shoulder bag, the newspaper, her empty lunch pail, and an umbrella, she fumbled with her keys trying to find the little one that opened the mailbox. After all this time, it still amazed her that even though Irene got home from work half an hour before Patty did, Irene could let the mail sit in the box because Patty wanted to be the first one to sort through it. "No big deal, if it makes my girl happy," Irene would say. What a woman.

Patty gave the mail a quick once over: *Gay Community News*, *People Magazine*, something from the dentist, the phone bill, and a thick white envelope addressed to Patty in handwriting that looked vaguely familiar. Hmmm. Patty maneuvered her way through the hallway trying to disentangle the apartment key from all the others. Just as she was about to fit it into the lock, the door swung open.

"Hi Pattycakes." Irene stood back to let Patty enter the kitchen.

"Hi Reenie."

"Here, let me take all that." Irene removed the umbrella and the newspaper from Patty's arms. Patty hung her shoulder bag on a hook behind the door and planted her lunch pail on the counter before sinking into a kitchen chair.

"Mail call," she said, sorting the envelopes. "Patty Stein. Irene Rubin. Irene Rubin. Patty Stein." As she sang out their names, Patty made two piles on the table.

"Wait a minute, wait a minute." Irene left the sink where she was rinsing out the plastic container from Patty's lunch pail that still had bits of fruit salad clinging to its side. "First things first," she said, coming over to the round wooden table. "Where's my kiss, woman?"

"Your kiss? Oh my God, I left it in the car." Patty jumped up and headed for the door.

"Get over here, girl." Irene motioned with her arm and tapped the toe of her high topped sneaker with mock impatience.

"La-dee-dum, dah-dee-dee." Patty s-l-o-w-l-y sauntered over to the kitchen table, swaying her hips from side to side until she was standing in front of Irene. "Well?"

"Well nothing." Irene put her arms around Patty, arched her backwards into a dip and planted a nice wet kiss on her mouth. "There," she said, straightening them both up.

"One more," Patty said, kissing Irene again. "Think we're getting sloppy?"

"Well," Irene kissed the crease between Patty's eyebrows, "I guess anyone would slip up once in a while after nine years."

"Nine and a half."

"Nine years, nine months and," Irene hesitated for only a split second, "fifteen days, to be exact." She looked over Patty's shoulder. "Anything interesting over there?"

"Not much. There's *People*, and.... "

"People," Irene sang out, "People who read People," she picked up the magazine and started waltzing across the floor with it, "are the luckiest people in the world."

"Gee, I didn't know Barbra Streisand was coming over for dinner," Patty said, opening the envelope from the dentist. It was time to get her teeth cleaned again, not too exciting. The phone bill could wait, GCN made good morning reading with her hazelnut coffee. That left the thick white envelope with that familiar handwriting, addressed to Miss Patricia Stein. Patty had an uneasy feeling about this envelope, but curiosity got the better of her, so she tore it open, using the wooden letter opener Irene had gotten her last year for *Chanukah*. Inside the envelope was another envelope that said simply, *Miss Patricia Stein*. And inside that was a card that read:

Mr. and Mrs. Murray Silverman
request the honor of your presence
at the marriage of their daughter
Meryl Beth
to
Michael Stein
on the 17th of June, 1990.

"Oh my God." Patty's jaw dropped as she studied the rest of
the invitation: a map to the synagogue, an RSVP card and envelope,
directions to the bride's parents' house for coffee and cake the night
before the wedding. "The kid's getting married," she mumbled to
herself. "I can't believe it. Ree-Ree," she said a little louder.

"Hmmm?" A muffled reply came out from behind the cover of
People. "Listen to this, Patters. A woman who's one hundred and
nine years old, can you imagine, has this quilt exhibition in DC and
she didn't even start quilting until she was ninety. She says it's never
too late to try something new. Look at this picture. She doesn't look
a day over eighty-five." Irene held the magazine out to Patty, but let it
drop when she saw the look on Patty's face. "What is it, sweetheart?"

"My brother's getting married."

"No shit. Let's see." Irene came back to the table and picked
up the invitation. "Fancy-shmancy," she said, running her fingers
over the raised letters. "We going?"

"I don't know."

"Oh c'mon," Irene said, checking out the synagogue directions.
"It'll be fun. I'll wear my tux with the lavender cummerbund and bow
tie, and you can wear that backless black dress you bought in P-town.
You always *kvetch* that you have nowhere to wear it. We'll do the
hora and the alleycat...." Already Irene was dancing around the kitch-
en, singing, "*Hava, nagila hava....*"

"I should have known this was trouble," Patty moaned, staring
at the outside envelope. "This is my mother's handwriting." She held
her head in both hands. "If I would have used my brain a little, I
wouldn't have opened it on a Friday night and wrecked my whole
weekend."

"Why so glum, chum?" Irene did a few grapevine steps across the kitchen floor, sat down next to Patty and took one of her hands. "Anyway, how could you have known it was from your mother? It's not like she writes to you everyday."

"I know."

"Hey, c'mon, this is a cause for celebration," Irene said, toasting the air with an imaginary glass. "*Mazel tov, l'chiam* and all that."

"Irene," Patty said, shaking her head. "We can't go. We're talking about my family, not yours, remember?"

"I know, but maybe this would earn you a few brownie points, you know?"

"Not if I show up with you wearing a tux...."

"So all right, I'll wear a dress. It's a wedding, Patty. No one's gonna make a scene."

"Irene," Patty repeated, holding up the RSVP. "See this card?"

"Yeah. So?"

"So read my lips: 'Miss Patricia Stein will/will not attend.' Notice it does not say Miss Patricia Stein and Miss Irene Rubin, let alone Ms. Patricia Stein and Ms. Irene Rubin. It doesn't even say Miss Patricia Stein and guest. Do you catch my drift?"

"Oh," Irene nodded slowly. "In other words, I'm not invited."

"In other words, I'm not going."

"Patty, you have to go. It's your brother's wedding."

"I'm not going!" Patty flung the RSVP card down and started pacing around the kitchen. "God damn it! I can't believe it. Can you fucking believe it, Reenie? How long have we been together? Almost ten years. *Ten years* for God's sake, and she still pretends you don't exist. She completely ignores you. Completely." Patty stopped where she was, flung up her hands and stared at Irene.

"You're repeating yourself darling," Irene said, but when Patty didn't laugh, Irene softened her voice. "C'mere, Pat-Pat." Irene patted her lap and Patty sat on it, resting her head on Irene's shoulder. Irene stroked Patty's long black hair. "Maybe it's a mistake," she said softly.

"Mistake my ass."

"I couldn't mistake your ass in a million years." Irene pinched Patty's *tuchus* and Patty laughed. "You sure it's from your mother?"

"Of course it's from my mother."

"Maybe the bride's mother wrote out the invitations."

"My mother would still have to give her the guest list." Patty leaned forward and rested her elbows on the table. "God forbid my mother should tell Mrs., Mrs...." she reached for the invitation, "Mrs. Murray Silverman that her daughter has a lover."

"Maybe she did," Irene said, tracing circles on Patty's back with the flat of her hand.

"Are you kidding?" Patty spoke to the invitation. "She'd choke on the word."

"Maybe she said significant other."

Patty laughed and turned to face Irene again. "Maybe she said girlfriend?"

"Companion?"

"Main squeeze?"

"Partner?"

"Spouse?"

"Mate?"

They laughed, having gone through this list themselves many times before, wondering how to solve "the word problem" as they called it. They'd decided lover sounded like all they did was have sex; significant other sounded like everyone else in their life was insignificant; companion sounded like one of them was ill; partner sounded too business-like; main squeeze sounded too sleazy; spouse sounded just too plain weird; and mate sounded too primitive.

"If she said anything," Patty said, leaning back against Irene again, "she probably said roommate."

"Maybe," Irene said, thinking aloud. "Maybe she said my daughter has a roommate and Mrs. Silverman said 'that's nice, but there's just too many people, we can't invite everyone.' Maybe she tried Patty."

"Why are you defending my mother?" Patty leaped off Irene's lap and started pacing again. "I'm sure she tells everyone, if she mentions me at all, that I'm a thirty-eight year old spinster." Patty folded her arms and leaned her butt against the counter. "Hell, they're probably coming up with a whole list of eligible nice Jewish men to introduce me to at this shindig. I'm thirty-eight years old. I don't need this." Patty let out a long breath, crossed the kitchen and stood behind Irene's chair. "I'm sorry, baby. I didn't mean to yell at you." Patty kissed the top of Irene's head and started massaging her temples.

"I know, Pats. It's okay." Irene leaned her head back against Patty's soft belly. "So what are you going to do?"

"I don't know. Not go I guess"

"Not go? But he's your only brother."

"So?" Patty stopped making little circles with her fingers across Irene's forehead. "I haven't talked to him in over a year anyway. And if he doesn't respect my relationship, why should I respect his?"

"To show you're more mature."

"Mature manure." Patty sat down at the table again. "Oh God. Here I was on a Friday night in a good mood, all ready to relax and be with my girl, and now I feel like shit."

"Maybe a little food will perk you up." Irene got up and opened the oven door. "Ta-dah!"

"Wow." Patty looked at the baked stuffed chicken sitting in a flat pan. "I thought I smelled something. How'd you whip that up so fast?"

"They let me out early for good behavior." Irene shut the oven door and opened the refrigerator. "Here's a little something for my girl." She turned toward Patty with a long stemmed red rose.

"Ree-Ree, you're the greatest." Patty stood up and kissed Irene's cheek. "Thanks. How'd you know I'd need a little treat tonight?"

Irene shrugged. "Woman's intuition. Now how about putting that in a vase and setting the table, while I take care of this bird?"

"Okie-doke." Patty got her favorite glass vase out of the china closet, the one Irene had given her, filled with wild daisies on her birthday seven years ago. She filled it with water and set the table with the silverware that had belonged to her grandmother, and the off-white china plates that had belonged to Irene's great-aunt Selma.

"I'll go change," Patty called over her shoulder as she headed for the bedroom. But instead of changing she flopped down on their big double bed and stared up at the ceiling, where she had pasted glow-in-the-dark stars last year in a pattern that said, PATTY LOVES IRENE. The next night Irene had surprised her back with a similar message: IRENE LOVES PATTY. Patty focused on the tiny stars, barely visible in the daylight, and tried to count them. She was up to twenty-six when Irene's voice floated in from the kitchen.

"Supper, Patty. Come and get it."

"I'm coming." But still Patty didn't move herself off the bed, though she did shift onto her side and shut her eyes. "Just give me five minutes," she mumbled, as if five minutes could resolve the family crisis that had just arrived in the mail. She began rubbing the crease between her eyebrows, where her headache always started. Maybe she could ignore the whole thing. When her mother called, if her mother called, she could just play innocent. "Invitation? What invitation? It must have gotten lost in the mail." Maybe she could say she was busy. When was it—June? Maybe she could invent a conference or something, though she was really terrible at lying. "And you can't pull anything over on my mother," Patty said out loud to no one. Why, she had even known the night Patty had lost her virginity.

She'd slept over her best friend Miriam's house, as she had many times before, but this time had been different. This time, during their make-out sessions, while Miriam was pretending to be the boy (after all they had to practice, just in case one of them was ever asked out) they had gone "all the way." When Mrs. Finklestein dropped her off at home the next morning, Patty had walked in quietly, as usual, and joined her parents at the kitchen table where they were eating bagels and reading the *New York Times*—her mother doing the crossword puzzle in pen, and her father scanning the sports section. As Patty was slathering half an onion bagel with cream cheese, her mother had looked up and asked, "Have a nice time?" Patty nodded and her mother studied her. "You look beautiful today Patty," she had said. "I mean you always look beautiful, but you have a special glow about you today. I don't know what it is."

Patty knew what it was all right. She tried not to blush, but as the brand new memory of Miriam Finklestein's fingers against her breasts and inside her vagina washed over her, she turned as red as the piece of *lox* she was smoothing onto her bagel. Patty's mother hadn't known that a girl had taught her about the birds and the bees, but she knew something was up. Patty had excused herself as soon as she could, and rushed upstairs to study her face in the bathroom mirror. She looked the same to herself, but somehow her mother knew.

When Patty had told her mother she was a lesbian, two years later with the safety cushion of being three hundred miles away at college between them, her mother didn't act surprised. "You'll grow out of it," she'd said cooly, and she hadn't spoken a word about it in the twenty years since.

"Patters?" Irene stood in the doorway, wiping her hands on a dish towel dotted with miniature ducks. "You okay?" She moved into the room. "C'mon, let's have supper and then we'll talk about it. Here." She open Patty's third drawer, pulled out her red sweat pants and her black sweatshirt with the word "P-town" scrawled across the chest, and tossed them on the bed.

"Okay." Patty sat up slowly and pulled off her sweater. Then she stood up and bent down to unlace her work boots. She stepped out of them, unbuckled her overalls and let them drop.

Irene lifted Patty's T-shirt over her head. "Nice outfit," she said, kissing Patty's bare shoulder.

"You like it? I got it on sale, thirty-eight years ago, a steal, believe me. It's held up pretty well, don't you think?" Patty turned sideways to study her naked reflection in the mirror on the wall behind the bed.

"Not bad." Irene came up behind her to run her hands up Patty's sides and around the front to cup her breasts. "Very nice design," she said, giving Patty's nipples a tweak.

"Hey!"

"Hey yourself." Irene kissed the back of Patty's neck. "C'mon gorgeous. Let's eat."

"I need a hug." Patty turned around and leaned against Irene. She let herself be held for a long peaceful moment and then sighed.

"You okay, Pattycakes?" Irene asked, stroking her hair.

"Yeah, I guess so." She leaned forward to get her sweatshirt from the bed. "It's just so frustrating. You think they don't affect you anymore, you know? I mean, I haven't seen them in years, I've spent thousands of dollars talking about them in therapy, and then one letter from my mother and I'm flat on my back, spacing out on the ceiling. I'm a failure."

"Hey." Irene handed Patty her sweat pants.

"What?"

"Do I look like the kind of woman who would live with a failure for eight years?"

Patty laughed. "You got a point there."

Irene took her hand and led her back into the kitchen. She had served them both, giving Patty both wings, her favorite part.

"You even did my potato for me, you sweet thing," Patty said, picking up her fork. They ate mostly in silence, the comfortable silence that comes with being together for so many years. They were both usually tired on Friday nights and after supper, anyone dropping in on "the old farts" as they called themselves, would most likely find Irene sprawled on the couch engrossed in a mystery novel (currently she was working her way through a used copy of *Murder in the Collective*) and Patty curled up beside her, knitting a sweater, sorting through old photos to put in an album, or working on some other such project. Irene didn't understand how Patty, who was a potter, could relax by doing something with her hands after throwing pots all day, and Patty couldn't understand how Irene, who was a typesetter, could possibly find it soothing to look at even more words after her forty hour a week job.

And so they stayed, with Patty perhaps getting up to make some tea, or Irene maybe wandering into the kitchen for a piece of fruit, until ten, when they would go to bed, make love and then fall asleep. It was comforting, if not exciting; soothing, if not exhilarating. Both Irene and Patty were too tired to make love during the week, so Friday night had become their regular time to "do it." Especially, as Patty pointed out, since they were both pretty much cultural Jews, as opposed to religious, the least they could do was follow the tradition that said it was a blessing to make love on the *Shabbas*. And Irene of course had agreed.

So this Friday night wasn't all that different from any other Friday night, except that afterwards Patty, who usually fell asleep in two seconds flat, was still wide awake at eleven-forty-five. She tossed and turned, first lying flat on her back, then curled on her side, then on her stomach with her arms under her head. Finally Irene snapped on the light.

"What's the matter, Patty?"

"I can't sleep."

"This much I know. Why can't you sleep?"

"I don't know."

"Yes you do." Irene leaned up on her elbow and looked down at Patty with one eyebrow raised. "So *nu?*"

"*Nu* shmu."

"That's funny. Did you just say *nu* shmu?" Irene asked.

"Yes I did."

"Hmm. The only other person I ever knew who said *nu* shmu was a girl named Patty."

"Patty Stein?"

"I think that was her name."

"Not Patty Stein, the beautiful potter."

"As a matter of fact, yes."

Patty leaned up on her elbows. "I remember her. What ever happened to her?"

"Well, she couldn't sleep one night and she was driving me crazy, so I ate her up." Irene leaned over and started nibbling Patty's belly.

"Hey."

"Yum-yum." Irene made some chewing noises.

"You are so weird," Patty said, shaking her head. "It's a good thing you met me...."

"Because you're as weird as I am." Irene pretended to swallow and then used the sheet to delicately wipe her mouth. "Delicious. Now why can't you sleep?"

Patty sighed. "Because of all this wedding jazz."

"Oh yeah. We never did really talk about it, did we? I'm sorry."

"That's okay. It can wait until morning."

Irene shook her head. "Not if my girl can't sleep." She reached for the nightstand that held the telephone, a pad and a pen "Let's make a list. What are your options here?"

"To go or not to go, that is the question." Patty sat up too and made a grand sweeping gesture with her arm. "Whether 'tis nobler...."

"All right, all right, enough with the *schmaltz*."

"That's not *schmaltz*, that's Shakespeare." Patty dropped her arm. "That's all I know anyway." She swiveled her body so she could rest her head on Irene's lap. "Okay, options. One, not go."

"Two, go." Irene started writing.

"Make a sub-heading under number two," Patty said, nuzzling into Irene's soft belly. "A— go with Irene; B—go alone."

"Got it." Irene studied the list. "Anything else?"

"Hmm." Patty stroked her chin. "How about ignore the whole thing?"

"I think that would fall under number one, not go."

"Right. Okay, new category. No, wait, give me the pad." Patty reached for it, but Irene held it up over her head.

"No, I'm the secretary."

"You always get to be the secretary." Patty's voice was bordering on a serious whine.

"Well, you always get to be the boss."

"That's true. Well, in that case, Miss Rubin...."

"That's Ms. as in the magazine."

"All right, Ms. Rubin, please start a new list."

Irene tore out list number one, crumpled it and tossed it over her shoulder. "All right," Patty continued. "Number one, don't go. Under that put A—send back RSVP; B—don't send back RSVP." Patty waited until Irene had finished writing. "Number two, go. A—with Irene; B—alone."

"What else?" Irene asked.

"I don't know, Ms. Rubin. What else is there?"

"That." Irene lowered the pad and pointed with her pen to the night table.

Patty's eyes followed the pen. "What?"

"That," Irene repeated, still pointing. "You see that kind of rectangular shaped white box over there, that has little buttons with numbers on them and a long cord attached to one end? Here, ever use one of these?" Irene leaned over to grab the phone, but before she could even say Ma Bell, Patty was shaking her head.

"I'm not calling my mother," she said flatly.

"Why not, Pats?"

Patty shook her head again "What would I say to her?"

Irene shrugged. "What do you usually say to her?"

"Happy birthday or happy mother's day." Patty said dryly. "You know that's the only time I ever call her."

"Well...."

"Well what?" Patty sat up and leaned her elbows on her knees. "She's not like your mother, Irene. You know that. My mother has three subjects to comment on—food, the weather and who's gotten married recently."

"Still, you could call her." Irene traced the length of Patty's arm with her finger.

"Why do I have to be the one to call her? She never calls me. I didn't even know Michael was engaged for God's sake."

Irene sighed softly. Whenever Patty talked about her family, it was best to tread lightly.

Patty went on. "They blame me for being alienated from them. 'You never call us,' my mother says. Would she call me if she had to pretend my father was her roommate? Would she call me if I asked her nothing about her life? And then it's all my fault. She'll get mad at me for ruining Michael's wedding by even bringing this up. She doesn't even know she's completely insulted me. Insulted us." Patty's voice had become shrill even to her own ears. In a softer tone she mumbled, "I just can't win."

"What?" Irene took Patty's hand.

Patty sat up and looked into Irene's eyes. "I just can't win, Reenie. If I don't go, they'll be pissed; if I go with you, they'll be pissed; and if I go alone, I'll be pissed. Maybe I'll kill myself."

"Patty! Don't even joke like that."

"Well I can't help it. They make me so depressed."

"Maybe you should call your mother," Irene suggested again. "You always say you want a better relationship with her."

Patty shrugged. "You call her."

"Okay, I will." Irene reached for the phone again.

"Hey." Patty was on top of her in a flash. "Don't you dare."

"Why not?"

"Well for one thing, it's after midnight. And for another thing...." Patty's voice trailed off. "What would you say?"

"I'd say...," Irene made a fist and held it up by the side of her face. "Hello Mrs. Stein? This is Irene Rubin. I'm just calling to tell you that even after nine and a half years, your daughter is still the best fuck in town."

"Irene Rubin!" Patty shrieked, but her voice sounded pleased.

"How's that for shock effect?"

"That would do it all right." Patty kissed Irene on the nose. "But seriously now...."

"Seriously, someone in this bed should call her." Irene raised her eyebrows at Patty.

Patty rolled off Irene. "Let's sleep on it, okay?"

"Okay, cookie." Irene fluffed up her pillow and lay down on it. "I love you Patty."

"I love you Irene." Patty curled into Irene's back and Irene clicked off the light.

The next morning after a breakfast of blueberry pancakes and hazelnut coffee, Irene cleared the table and planted the telephone on Patty's place mat. "Go on, reach out and touch someone," she said, nudging Patty gently.

Patty reached up and softly squeezed Irene's breast. "How's that?"

"Nice, but that's not what I meant."

"Do I have to?" Patty looked up at Irene, who nodded firmly. "What'll you give me?"

Irene thought. "How old are we this morning?"

"Three."

"Hmm. How about a lollipop?"

"Yucky." Patty stuck out her tongue.

"A cookie?"

"No."

"I'll be your best friend."

Patty shook her head. "You are my best friend, silly."

"I know." Irene picked at a blob of maple syrup stuck to the table. "How about we go back to bed for the rest of the day?"

"Couldn't we do that anyway?" Patty asked hopefully.

"No baby." Irene sat down next to Patty. "C'mon. I'll sit right here and hold your hand."

"Okay." Patty picked up the phone and put it down. "Wait a minute, Irene, maybe you should call."

"Patty."

"No listen." Patty stroked the receiver as if it were Irene's arm. "One thing about my mother—she's cold, she's distant, she may even be heartless, but she's not rude. Especially to strangers. If you point out that she's made a faux pas in the etiquette department, you just may get through to her."

"I don't know, Patty."

"C'mon Irene. I can't be more alienated from her that I am now. What have we got to lose?" Patty slid the phone toward Irene.

"I'm only doing this because I love you." Irene picked up the phone and then put it down. "Wait a minute. What'll you give me?"

Patty shook her finger at Irene. "Why you little opportunist, you." Irene said nothing. "Well," Patty said, "how about I do the laundry for a month?"

"Wow, that's a little extreme."

"I knew you'd see it my way." Patty handed the receiver to Irene. "No, wait. I'll go into the bedroom and dial, and then I'll yell for you to pick up." She marched out of the room before Irene had a chance to change her mind, flopped down on the bed and dialed her parents' number. "Okay," Patty yelled, thinking to herself, what am I crazy, as she heard Irene pick up the phone.

After three rings, Mrs. Stein picked up the phone and Patty stopped breathing.

"Hello?"

"Hello, is Mrs. Stein there?" Irene asked.

"This is she."

That's my mother, Patty thought, Ms. Grammatically Correct.

"Hello Mrs. Stein, this is Irene Rubin, your daughter's...." Irene hesitated for a split second, a mistake that Mrs. Stein took advantage of.

"Oh yes, you're Patty's roommate, aren't you?" Mrs. Stein said, solving the word problem herself, "How nice of you to call."

Shit, Patty thought. She makes Bette Davis sound as sweet as Glinda, the good witch of the north. Patty could feel the blueberry pancakes in the pit of her stomach begin to curdle.

Irene bravely continued. "I'm calling because we received Michael's wedding invitation, and I wanted to tell you we're both really looking forward to the wedding."

There. It was done. Patty watched her life pass before her eyes—the first lopsided pot she had made in fifth grade, rolling the clay into snakes and then coiling them around each other; her high school graduation where her grandparents had been so proud; her first summer away from home on a dude ranch in Colorado.... Mrs. Stein's voice cut through Patty's thoughts in a tone cold enough to freeze fire. "Is my daughter there please?"

"Just a moment." Irene put the receiver down and called loudly. "Patty, phone."

Oh shit...Couldn't she have told her I was out? Or that I had died or something? Patty felt herself sinking into a familiar despair and sighed before she spoke. "Hello?"

"Patricia?"

"Who's this?"

"This is your mother."

Oh, my father's roommate, Patty thought, but of course she said nothing.

"I'm calling about Michael's wedding. Now, the ushers are all wearing white jackets and black pants with very light blue shirts, and the bridesmaids are all wearing light blue gowns as well, sort of a sky blue really. Mrs. Silverman and I are wearing dark blue, not really navy, that would be too dark, but more like a royal blue. So I was hoping darling, that you would think along those lines, so you would fit in with everyone."

Fit in, Patty thought. She's got to be kidding.

"Maybe you could come down a few days early and we could go shopping," Mrs. Stein continued. "Everyone's dying to meet you. As a matter of fact, Meryl has a cousin about your age, an engineer, I'm sure you'll like him. Now Patty, don't say anything until you meet him. We thought you could sit next to him at the reception."

"Ma." Patty had pretty much checked out into la-la land as her mother was speaking, trying to fathom the fact that Mrs. Stein hadn't yet mentioned Irene in this whole conversation. Patty swallowed hard. "Ma, I'm not coming."

"What? Oh Patty, don't be ridiculous. Is it the money? Your father and I have already discussed it and we're perfectly happy to pay your airfare."

"Ma, I'm thirty-eight years old. It's not the money."

"I know how old you are Patricia. As a matter of fact, I was there the day you were born."

Patty thought she heard Irene, who was still listening on the kitchen extension gasp, or maybe stifle a laugh. "Listen Ma. I'm not coming because you didn't invite Irene."

"Irene? Is that the girl you live with? Are you still living together? That's nice dear, I'm sure it helps with your expenses, but we couldn't possibly invite her. There were so many people and weddings cost a fortune these days, I'm sure you can understand that." Mrs. Stein gave a little laugh. "Your cousin Alex didn't ask us to invite his roommate at Dartmouth and after all Patty, as you just pointed out to me, you are thirty-eight years old, not nineteen. Don't you think you're getting just a little too old to have a roommate?"

Patty sighed. What was the use? Her mother would never change because obviously she didn't want to change. Maybe Irene was right. Maybe she should go, and earn a few family brownie points. She'd buy a nice blue dress and sit with Meryl's cousin the engineer and make everybody happy. Everyone except herself. "All right Ma, I'll go."

"Thank you darling. Now call the airport and tell us when you'll be coming. Tell them to send the bill to your father."

"All right." Well at least I won't have to lose a week's salary on the plane ticket. Patty's voice was dull. "Goodbye Ma."

"Goodbye, sweetheart."

Patty hung up the phone and stayed put. All of a sudden she felt sleepy. She lay her head down on the night table next to the phone and shut her eyes. Even the thought of moving her head onto the pillow was exhausting.

"Patty," Irene called from the kitchen. "Come in here." Patty dragged herself into the kitchen and flopped into a chair. "What happened?" Irene asked.

"Nothing. You heard." Patty said, rubbing her eyes. "Can we take a nap now?"

"No." Irene's voice was stern and Patty sat up, surprised. "What's wrong, Irene? I'm going, okay, isn't that what you want?"

"I changed my mind." Now it was Irene's turn to stomp around the kitchen "She treats you like shit, Patty. As long as you play along and pretend you're who she wants you to be, everything's fine."

"So this is news? I've been telling you this for years."

"But I never heard it before." Irene stopped pacing "I should have listened in on a conversation between you and your mother years ago. I don't know, it was just different to actually hear it." Irene shook her head. "You're not going."

"I'm not?"

"No." Irene sat down at the table next to Patty. "Listen love, I'm not going to let you shut yourself off so you can go down there pretending to be a single straight girl, just to make your mother happy. We're a team. If you go, I go."

"You think?" Patty was beginning to come out of her stupor.

"Yes."

"So what now?"

"Call her back."

"Now? Can't I wait until tomorrow?"

Irene shook her head. "No."

Patty reached for the phone. "Wait a minute. Maybe I should just go."

Irene sighed. "You're right. I shouldn't tell you what to do."

Patty looked at the phone. "I guess I should call the airport then."

Irene looked at the phone too. "I guess you should."

Patty picked up the phone, then slammed it down. "I can't do it Irene. I can't kill myself to make her happy."

"That's my girl." Irene raised Patty's hand to her lips and kissed it. "You should probably call now though, before you lose your nerve."

"You're right." Patty reached for the phone. "Wait, what'll you give me?"

Irene laughed. "Why you little oppportunist, you."

"What goes around, comes around," Patty said, making a circle in the air with her finger.

"All right, I'll do the laundry for a month too."

"Yay!" Patty jumped up and kissed Irene. Then she sat down and dialed.

"Hello."

"Hi Ma, it's Patty."

"Hello darling. Did you arrange your flight?"

Patty gripped Irene's hand. "I changed my mind Ma. I'm not coming."

Mrs. Stein sighed. "Patricia, we've been through all this already."

"Listen, Ma." Patty took a deep breath and spoke very fast. "I am not coming unless Irene is invited too. Irene is not my roommate. She is the woman I share my life with and I expect you to give my relationship the same respect you give Michael's. If Irene was a man, there'd be no question about it, even if we'd only been together for five minutes. Ma, Irene and I have been together for more than nine years." Patty paused to catch her breath. "Ma," she said in a gentler voice, "I know it's hard, but you've got to accept the fact that I am a lesbian."

"Don't you dare use that word with me."

"Lesbian, lesbian, lesbian."

"Patricia, I'm warning you...."

"Warning me what?" All of a sudden, Patty's rage, which had been brewing for years, finally boiled over. "Warning me that you'll send me to bed without any supper? Warning me that you won't pay for my art classes?" Patty could hardly believe her ears. "That won't work anymore, Ma. I'm not your little girl. I'm a grown woman. I make my own choices."

"Patricia really. This is all so unnecessary."

"You're right, Ma. It is." Patty paused and Irene inched her chair closer. "I'm sorry I yelled at you."

"I accept your apology."

"But I'm not coming unless Irene is invited too."

"Patricia, I really am surprised at you. Weren't you the one who was always telling me I should be more independent from your father? And now you can't travel a few hundred miles by yourself for a weekend? That's not like you."

Patty laughed She had to admit it was a nice try. "It's not the same thing, Ma."

"I don't see the difference."

"Of course not." Patty shook her head. "Listen, Ma. You wouldn't go to a wedding that Dad wasn't invited to, would you?"

"Oh Patricia, don't be ridiculous."

"Why is that any more ridiculous than Irene not being invited?"

"It's not the same thing." Mrs. Stein's voice had just a touch of irony in it. "Patricia darling, you've got to accept the world as it is. If you're going to make your own *choices,* as you put it, you're going to have to pay the price."

"So it's all my fault," Patty said slowly. "You're not going to take any responsibility."

"I can't assume responsibility for your *choices.*"

I should never have used that word, Patty thought.

"What do you want from me, Patty? This isn't easy for me either you know. What am I supposed to tell Meryl's family?"

My heart really bleeds for you, Patty thought. "Tell them the truth, Ma. Tell them 'Patricia's not coming because she's a lesbian and her lover wasn't invited.'"

Irene raised her eyebrows at Patty. "Two L words in one sentence," she whispered. "I'm proud of you."

Mrs. Stein, however, was not impressed. "Patricia, what do you want from me?" she repeated.

Good question. Patty thought for a minute. "I'll tell you what I want, Ma," she said quietly. "I want you to say, 'Of course Irene is invited to the wedding. I don't even care what you wear. I want you to come because you're my daughter and I love you and I'm proud of you.'" Patty's voice broke, but she pushed herself to go on. "I want you to say you're sorry you haven't visited me in ten years and that you'd love to come see the pots I make and meet my friends. I want you to say you're interested in me. I want you to say you love me." Patty's cheeks were wet with tears.

"Patricia dear, I can't spend my whole morning on the phone with you. I've got to pick up your father's suit and get to the bank before twelve. Why don't you call me later when you're not so upset, all right, darling?" Mrs. Stein's voice was cheerful again.

"Ma," Patty sniffed. "Maybe we should ask Michael what he thinks. After all, it's his wedding."

"Patricia." Mrs. Stein's cheerfulness vanished. "You are not going to bother your brother with this nonsense."

"This nonsense happens to be my life."

"That's just like you Patricia, to think of no one but yourself, even on your brother's wedding day."

"Right. I'm the bad one. You ignore my entire life and I get blamed for it."

"Patricia, there really is no point in discussing this further."

"That's the first thing we've agreed on this whole conversation."

"Really, Patty, you're giving me a terrible headache."

Patty didn't respond.

"Patricia?"

"Good-bye, Ma." Patty hung up the phone and stared at Irene. "*Nu?*"

"*Nu* shmu. Come here honey." Irene stood up and took Patty by the hand into the bedroom. They sat down on the bed and before they could get under the covers, Patty was crying again.

"That's right. Let it out. Let it all out." Irene lay down and held Patty tight, stroking her back as her tears fell.

"I hate her," Patty wailed into Irene's chest. "She isn't proud of me. She doesn't even love me." Patty's whole body shook with her sobs.

"I love you. I'm proud of you," Irene said, stroking Patty's hair away from her wet cheeks.

"I know," Patty said, wiping her nose on her sleeve. "But I want someone in my family to be proud of me."

Irene pushed Patty back gently, so she could look into her eyes. "Patty, I am someone in your family."

"I know," Patty said again, "but I mean someone from my family-family."

"Patty." Irene kept her gaze steady. "Who do you consider family—someone you talk to twice a year, or someone who wakes up with you every morning and goes to sleep with you every night and shares the bills with you and laughs with you and cries with you and loves every inch of you from your *punim* to your *pupik*?"

Patty smiled. "You're the greatest, Irene." She kissed her cheek. "I wish we could really be related. Maybe you could adopt me."

"Your mother would have to agree to that."

"I don't think that would be a problem." Patty chuckled and then her chin quivered. "Reenie, why does my choice have to have such a big price tag?"

Irene shook her head and caressed Patty's cheek. "No, Patty-Patty. Your mother's choice has the price tag."

"I don't get it."

"Patty, your mother is choosing not to accept that you're a dyke. The price she's paying is that she doesn't get to have you in her life."

"I never thought of it like that," Patty said, wiping her eyes with the back of Irene's hand.

"That's why you're going to marry me," Irene said, clasping Patty's hand between both her own. "You need someone like me around to think of these things."

Patty's eyes grew wide. "Are you serious, Reenie?"

"Of course I'm serious. I don't go around proposing to just anyone, you know."

"I hope not."

"Besides, I'm sick of you being sad that you don't have a family. So we'll make it official. We were gonna have a party for our tenth anniversary anyway, remember? So let's really do it up big."

"We're getting married," Patty said to herself, as though testing the words. "What about the rabbi?"

"Wait a minute, wait a minute. First things first. You haven't said yes yet." Irene sat up and motioned for Patty to do the same. "Patty, will you marry me?"

"Yes Irene, I will marry you."

"Hooray!" Irene threw her arms around Patty. "We're getting married!" She squeezed her tight and then kissed her.

"We're getting married," Patty repeated, a little dazed. "What'll I wear?"

Irene laughed. "You sound like your mother."

"Well it is important." Patty said with a pout.

"Hey, no pouting. We just got engaged."

"When should we do it?"

"Well, let's see." Irene thought for a minute. "Hey, I got it." She snapped her fingers.

"What?"

"Let's do it the same day as your brother. Our anniversary is June fourteenth. The seventeenth must be a Sunday. Wouldn't that be ironic?"

"Reenie, that's only two and a half months away. We can't get it together that fast."

"Sure we can. Don't you want to be a June bride?"

"Yeah but....."

"But, but, but." Irene reached behind Patty and patted her *tuchus*. "Don't you know a dyke in that rabbinical school in Philly?"

"Yeah, Shosha Weinberg. But what if she can't come then?"

"We'll call her up and then we'll arrange the date."

"Get the pad. We have to make a list." Patty reached for the night table. "We have to find a space, make a guest list, a food list, get clothes...." As she spoke, Patty made notes on the pad. "We'll need a DJ, and we'll have to plan the ceremony...."

"What'll we do about our names?" Irene asked, as Patty scribbled madly.

"What do you mean?"

"Well should we be the Stein-Rubins or the Rubin-Steins?"

"Oh Rubinstein," Patty said, writing it down. "Like Helena."

"Whose Helena?"

"The queen of cosmetics. Maybe we should invite her too."

Irene frowned. "I don't think so. Hey, wait a minute." She stopped Patty's pen. "This solves the word problem."

"How?"

"You're not my main squeeze anymore."

"I'm not?" Patty's lower lip curled.

"Nope. You're not my girlfriend or my significant other or my lover or my partner or my spouse or my mate. You're my fiancé and soon you'll be my wife."

"Wife," Patty said, writing down the word. "I like it." She smiled up at Irene and brushed a tear from her eye. "Reenie, how can I be so happy and so sad at the same time?"

"Well, that's the way it goes kid. My Great Aunt Selma used to say, 'In every tear a laugh, in every laugh a tear.' I just feel like such a jerk because it took me this long to ask you. I'm sorry you had to be in so much pain."

Patty shrugged. "If that's what it took, that's what it took." She smiled again. "Hey, now at least I have one thing to thank my mother for. Maybe it's a blessing." She kissed Irene's cheek and then went back to her pad and pen. "Now, we'll need to get a list of caterers together and find one that won't feel weird about a lesbian wedding. Then we'll have to see about...."

"Wait a second." Irene stopped Patty's pen again. "Speaking of blessings... we agreed to stay in bed all afternoon, right?"

"Right."

"And what would two people who just got engaged do in bed to celebrate?"

"Let's see." Patty studied Irene's face. "Make lists?"

"Guess again."

"Well," Patty's lips curved into a smile. "Perform their wifely duties?"

"I think so," Irene said, brushing the nape of Patty's neck and unbuttoning the top button of her pajamas.

"Umm. My pleasure," Patty said, laying back on the pillow.

"No, my pleasure."

"No, mine."

"Mine."

"Let's take turns."

And they did, for the rest of the glorious afternoon.

Yiddish and Hebrew Glossary

Chanukah (Hebrew)—Festival of Lights, lasting eight days, commemorating the Maccabees' victory over the Syrians and the dedication of the temple at Jerusalem.

Hava nagila (Hebrew) — Let us rejoice (also a song)

hora (Hebrew) — circle dance

keppie — head (derivitive of kop)

kinder — children

kvetch — complain

l'chiam — to life (a toast)

lox — smoked salmon

maideleh — young girl

mamela — an endearment (literally "little mother")

mazel tov — congratulations

mine — my

momser — bastard

nu — so, well now

oy — an expression of fear, surprise, sorrow, exhaustion, joy

oy gevalt— the same as oy, only more so

punim — face

pupik — belly button

putz — putter

schmaltz — excessive sentimentality (literally rendered chicken fat)

schmuck — a nasty jerk

seder (Hebrew) — the traditional Passover meal (literally order)

Shabbas (Hebrew) — the Jewish Sabbath

tochter, tochterla — daughter

tuchus, tushy — buttocks

vey iss mir — woe is me

photo by Sue Tyler

Lesléa Newman was born in Brooklyn, N.Y. and now lives in Western Massachusetts with the woman she loves and their two cats (of course). At the tender age of thirty-four she has seven books under her belt (when she wears one) and she has also been the proud recipient of a Massachusetts Artists Fellowship. Currently she is hard at work on a new novel. When she is not writing or teaching writing, Lesléa...ah, but that's a secret.

Other Titles Available
Mystery/Adventure by Sarah Dreher

Stoner McTavish ($7.95) ISBN-0-934678-06-5 The original Stoner McTavish mystery introduces psychic Aunt Hermione, practical partner Marylou, and Stoner herself, in the Grand Tetons rescuing dream lover Gwen.

Gray Magic ($8.95) ISBN-0-934678-11-1 Stoner's friend Stell falls ill with a mysterious disease and Stoner finds herself an unwitting combatant in the great struggle between the Hopi Spirits of good and evil.

Something Shady ($8.95) ISBN-0-934678-07-3 Stoner travels to the coast of Maine with her lover Gwen to rescue a missing nurse and risks becoming an inmate in a suspicious rest home.

Captive in Time ($9.95) ISBN 0-934678-22-7 Stoner finds herself in a small dusty town—in 1871. There are mysterious fires and a young woman is being blamed— and Stoner can't find a phone to call home.

Adventure/Romance

MARI by Jeriann Hilderley ($8.95) ISBN 0-934678-23-5 Mari, an Argentinian political activist, meets New York musician, Judith. They fall in love—and struggle with the differences between their cultures and their lives.

Dark Horse by Frances Lucas ($8.95) ISBN-0-934678--21-9 Fed up with corruption in local politics, lesbian Sidney Garrett runs for mayor and meets Joan.

As The Road Curves by Elizabeth Dean ($8.95)ISBN-0-934678-17-0 Ramsey had it all; a great job at a prestigious lesbian magazine and the reputation of never having to sleep alone. Now she takes off on an adventure of a lifetime.

All Out by Judith Alguire ($8.95) ISBN-0-934678-16-2 Winning a gold medal at the Olympics is Kay Strachan's all-consuming goal—until a budding romance with a policewoman threatens her ability to go all out for the gold.

Look Under the Hawthorn by Ellen Frye ($7.95) A stonedyke from the mountains of Vermont, Edie Cafferty, off on a search for her long lost daughter meets Anabelle, an unpredictable jazz pianist looking for her birth mother.

Runway at Eland Springs by ReBecca Béguin ($7.95) When bush pilot Anna finds herself in conflict over flying supplies for a game hunter, she turns to Jilu, the woman running a safari camp at Eland Springs, for love and support.

Promise of the Rose Stone by Claudia McKay ($7.95) ISBN-0-934678-09-x Mountain warrior Isa is banished to the women's compound in the living satellite, Olyeve, where she and her lover, Cleothe, plan an escape.

Humor

Cut Outs and Cut Ups A Fun'n Games Book for Lesbians by Elizabeth Dean, Linda Wells, and Andrea Curran ($8.95) ISBN-0-934678-20-0 Games, puzzles, astrology —an activity book for lesbians with hours of enjoyment.

Found Goddesses:Asphalta to Viscera by Morgan Grey & Julia Penelope ($7.95) ISBN-0-934678-18-9 *Found Goddesses is wonderful! All of it's funny, some inspired. I've had more fun reading it than any book in the last two years.*—Joanna Russ

Morgan Calabresé; The Movie N. Leigh Dunlap ($5.95) ISBN 0-934678-14-5 Wonderfully funny comic strips. Politics, relationships, life's changes, and softball as seen through the eyes of lesbian Morgan Calabresé.

Short Fiction/Plays

The Names of the Moons of Mars Short Fiction by Patricia Roth Schwartz ($8.95) ISBN-0-934678-19-7 In these stories the author writes humorously as well as poignantly about our lives as women and as lesbians.

Lesbian Stages Sarah Dreher($8.95) ISBN-0-934678-15-4 *Sarah Dreher's play scripts are good yarns firmly centered in a Lesbian perspective with specific, complex, often contradictory (just like real people) characters.*—Kate McDermott

Order from—New Victoria Publishers, P.O. Box 27, Norwich, VT. 05055